20.79

**W9-ALZ-901**

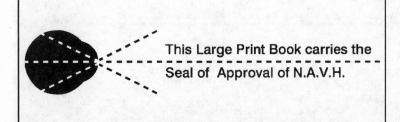

This Large Print Book carries the
Seal of Approval of N.A.V.H.

# THE UNEXPECTED WALTZ

# THE UNEXPECTED WALTZ

## KIM WRIGHT

**THORNDIKE PRESS**
*A part of Gale, Cengage Learning*

GALE
CENGAGE Learning·

Farmington Hills, Mich • San Francisco • New York • Waterville, Maine
Meriden, Conn • Mason, Ohio • Chicago

GALE
CENGAGE Learning®

**LIBRARY OF CONGRESS CATALOGING-IN-PUBLICATION DATA**

Wright, Kim, 1955–
  The unexpected waltz / by Kim Wright. — Large print edition.
    pages ; cm. — (Thorndike Press large print women's fiction)
  ISBN 978-1-4104-7118-5 (hardcover) — ISBN 1-4104-7118-7 (hardcover)
  1. Widows—Fiction. 2. Rich people—Fiction. 3. Life change events—Fiction. 4. Friendship—Fiction. 5. Ballroom dancing—Fiction. 6. Large type books. I. Title.
  PS3623.R5545U54 2014b
  813'.6—dc23                                    2014017215

Published in 2014 by arrangement with Gallery Books, a division of Simon & Schuster, Inc.

Printed in the United States of America
1 2 3 4 5 6 7 18 17 16 15 14

*To my teacher and friend,*
*Max Maleshko*

# CHAPTER ONE

I was born the year Disneyland opened, the year Elvis sang "Heartbreak Hotel" and McDonald's raised their golden arches, the year James Dean died. My first car was a powder-blue Mustang with white bucket seats and the summer before I turned sixteen, Elyse and I used to drive it up and down the road between our houses with the 8-track blaring. Elyse would prop her long, tan legs against the dashboard and click through the songs with her toe. Our favorite band was the Rolling Stones, promising us over and over that time was on our side.

I believed them. When I was young, I thought the future stretched out before me like some long, shimmering road, and that the girls would always stay pretty and the boys would just plain stay. I was a member of the luckiest generation to ever have been born in the luckiest land on earth.

So it was a bit of a shock to wake up on a

perfectly average August morning and find my husband dead in the bed beside me.

"Nothing has to change."

Is he kidding? Everything's changed. I'm a fifty-two-year-old widow, which is the last thing on God's green earth I ever expected to be . . . No, wait a minute. Rich is the last thing I ever expected to be, and evidently I'm that too.

A year has passed since Mark died, and I'm sitting in a conference room listening to his lawyer tell me that we really must settle the estate. Apparently there is a socially acceptable number of days that a widow can spend lying in bed watching HGTV and eating takeout, and I have just passed that limit.

The lawyer's face is grave, not with the professional solemnity the occasion demands, but with a more personal kind of regret. This man played golf with Mark. He's been to our house for dinner. He has, on many occasions, poured me a glass of wine or pulled out my chair. I don't know the other attorneys gathered around the table, but I assume the sheer number of them is evidence of the size of the estate. It has taken a long time to make financial peace with Mark's sons in California and

Japan, to set up educational trusts for the grandchildren he rarely saw, to wait out probate, to honor his commitments to various charities and schools. But now everyone has been paid up and paid off and the lawyer extends his palm to me. For a strange moment I think he's expecting me to tip him, but then I see he's trying to shake my hand. He's what . . . seventy? Seventy-five? Somewhere near Mark's age and thus well past the point when most men retire. Maybe he's upset because this all cuts too close to home. The big house, the German car, the heart attack, the fifty-page will, and, finally, the younger, blonder second wife sitting here before him, fidgeting like crazy in her black knit St. John suit.

"How much is left?" I say, and I know it's the wrong question. It sounds vulgar, grasping, as if I really did marry an older man for the money just like everyone at the country club said I did. I'm fouling up everything. I didn't realize so many people would be here or that they would seat me at the head of this long, scary table.

"I think we all can agree that the important thing is not to touch the principal," the lawyer says. "But we can close out the estate account and easily create enough cash flow . . ."

That isn't what I asked him. I look away and my eye catches another attorney, a bespectacled young woman in a business suit, whose hair is pulled back in a bun. She reminds me of those secretaries in old sit-coms who stand up from behind their desks, unclip their hair, fling off their glasses, and suddenly become beautiful. Her expression is appropriately serious, but nothing about her disguise fools me. She's one of those women who try to hide their femininity, but that trick never works for long. Suppressing sex is like holding a beach ball under the surface of the water — the harder you push it down, the harder it will eventually spring back up.

This young lawyer sees me watching and she winks, or at least I think she does, but that's too creepy, that she would look down this long line of men and wink, so I probably imagined it. I imagine lots of things. I see stuff no one else seems to see, and besides, coming here always rattles me. I never feel like I'm dressed right. I met Mark when we both worked at a bank, but I doubt that anyone around this table would believe I used to be a junior VP of finance. When I'm faced with these legal papers, I become math impaired, unable to divide or subtract in my head. The female attorney is staring at a document on the table, biting her pale lip. She didn't wink at me. I must be losing my mind.

"Actually," I say, in my most cheerful and reasonable voice, "I'm asking how much there is in total."

"Without touching the principal and without acquiring even the slightest risk, we can deposit eleven thousand a month into your checking account," the lawyer says. On the one hand, my mind reels because it's a staggering amount of money for someone who owns her house and car outright, for a woman whose favorite food is pizza, and whose idea of a vacation is visiting her best friend from high school and sleeping on the couch. But on the other hand, he's saying that even from the grave Mark has put me on an allowance. A very generous allowance, but an allowance nonetheless.

"You won't have to leave Mark's house," the lawyer says, and then quickly corrects himself. "What I mean is, you won't have to leave your home." He was actually closer to the truth the first time — Mark was living in that huge empty house when I married him and all I really did was decorate it. Hang some curtains and paint some walls, cram some rosebushes into the ground. Everyone always saw my husband as strong and powerful, but another image zooms back to me now, the first time he took me over to see the house. Mark looked as shy as a little boy as we stood in the foyer, which was so empty that it echoed, and he said to me "What do you think of this big old box? Do you think you can fill it with something, like music or color or flowers . . . or a life?"

His little misstatement seems to have rattled the lawyer. He clears his throat and adjusts his glasses before continuing, glancing down at the stack of papers as if he doesn't know damn well what they say. "Yes, the house is yours," he repeats, "and there's no need to get a job, of course." And here a slight titter of laughter runs around the table at the very suggestion of something so ridiculous as Kelly Wilder Madison filling out a W-4 form. "Mark arranged for the continuation of his contributions to the charities he supported so you'll still be —"

"Invited to serve on their boards," I finish for him. "Welcome at the teas and galas and auctions."

"Of course," he says. "The only thing you really need to know is that —"

"I get it," I tell him. I stand up, my head still swimming, and the lawyers all rise at once, like a congregation getting ready to sing. "I understand what you're saying.

Nothing has to change."

I want things to change.

I know I'm lucky. I know that a cash flow of eleven thousand a month is what my daddy used to call a high-class problem. But I've lived for too long in a world where everything is controlled and monitored and predictable. I know the number of steps leading into every medical building in Charlotte, North Carolina. I've parked in the handicapped spaces, run in and gotten wheelchairs and run back, and counted out pills and become a master of low-sodium cuisine. And I've made tablescapes — endless tablescapes, which are like centerpieces, only bigger. They run down the full length of the table and their purpose is to give the meal a theme. Tablescapes cost a frigging fortune and they take forever to do, but they're my specialty, the task that's delegated to me at every charity dinner. Sand dollars and blue glass in the summer, gourds and leaves in the fall, holly and crystal in the winter, and tulips wedged into overturned moss baskets in the spring.

I know none of that sounds very original. In fact, I know it's downright ordinary and that meals don't need to have themes. But years ago I did a tablescape that everyone liked, and in the world of charitable causes, if you do something right one time, they expect you to duplicate it, with the smallest possible variations, for the rest of your life. After a while, I actually started to dream about tablescapes . . . but that's not the point. The point is that I've spent the last twenty years of my life pretending to be a whole lot more conservative and stupider and nicer than I really am.

"You deserve a younger man," Mark said to me once, but he said it in bed so he probably was talking about sex. When he had the first heart attack and his doctors told him to be careful, we knew what they meant. That night I scooted over beside him and laid my head on his chest and told him that this was all I wanted. He made a sad little grunt of disbelief, but it was true. I've always liked cuddling better than sex, and besides, when I married him I knew what I was signing up for. I wanted a safe place and Mark gave me one.

According to this tableful of lawyers, he's still giving me one.

On the way out, I ask the receptionist if they validate parking, a question that seems to amuse her. She takes my ticket, but I know she's thinking that the widow of Mark Madison doesn't have to worry about two

14

dollars an hour for parking. The widow of Mark Madison could spend the whole day driving in and out of parking decks all over town, just for the hell of it. She thinks I'm silly, or maybe even tight and mean, one of those women with millions of dollars in the bank who dock the maid for being fifteen minutes late, but she stamps my ticket and as I turn to go I see the young female attorney again. She is standing in the doorway of her office. I smile and she nods slowly. Like she's congratulating me for something, but I can't imagine what.

When I get in the car there's a call on my cell from hospice. I tell myself I'll wait until I'm out of the deck and reception is better before I return it, which is a stall. I know why they're calling. They've found me someone new.

My last client — hospice calls them clients for some reason, as if we were styling their hair or remodeling their kitchens — was a man named Mr. Duggan who didn't seem to have a single memory beyond his Louisiana boyhood. I used to come in every day to just sit at his bedside and listen to him talk. "You're good at watching people die," one of the nurses said, and when I flinched, she quickly added, "What I mean is, you have a lot of patience."

Strange thoughts preoccupy people near the end. They don't regret mistakes, or at least the ones I meet don't. Maybe those who have maimed or molested or raped lie on their deathbeds filled with remorse, but most people have lived polite little lives and they tend to think more about what they didn't do. The chance that slipped by, the door they were afraid to enter, the lover they let walk away. Mr. Duggan in particular talked a lot about pirates. I'm pretty sure he'd never been a pirate — he was small and neatly groomed and well insured. He may have been remembering a dream or a movie, an old Halloween costume, or a game he played back in the bayou. Because that's another thing about the dying: they circle all the way back to the beginning. I've heard them calling their siblings and childhood playmates, their voices breathless, as if they were running hard across an open field. Wait for me, they mumble. I'm right behind you, I'm right here.

"He has no idea what's happening to him," Mr. Duggan's daughter used to say to me, her voice dripping with relief. "He doesn't even know who he is anymore." I'd nod because she needed me to nod, but inside I disagreed. I always had the funny feeling that this man was having the most lucid moments of his life. Later, after his daughter was gone, I used to go back into his room and lean over his bed. "Where are you now?" I'd ask him. "Tell me everything you see."

Because this is what I have agreed to do: I have agreed to make tablescapes and to be the one who sits and waits once a situation has been declared truly hopeless. The doctors don't stop by much anymore when the patient is CTD, as they say in the shorthand of oncology. Circling the drain. The nurses only come in for the pain meds and the families hover in the doorways, assuring one another that it's over long before it really is. It mostly falls to us, to the volunteers, to be the final witnesses. "What does the shoreline look like?" I'd whisper to Mr. Duggan. "Are you off the coast of Africa? Or is it more like Jamaica? Maybe China?"

CTD. The phrase is funny and cruel and accurate. Because I've always imagined our lives to be funnel shaped. They grow narrow as we age and we all begin to swirl faster and faster until the concept of a day or an hour or a year no longer has any meaning. Maybe there's even some sort of gentle sucking motion that pulls us down with the last breath and we pass from one world to the next just as easily as water goes through a tube. I hope so. I hope it was like that for Mr. Duggan. I wasn't there when he died, but if you take all that stuff people say about Jesus and Buddha and Muhammad and set it aside, I've noticed it's usually the pirates who go easiest when their time finally comes.

They haven't given me a new client since Mark died. That's hospice policy. After a volunteer loses someone in her own family they switch her to fund-raising or clerical work for a year. Thanks to Mark's friends, most of whom have way more time and money than they know what to do with, I've been good at bringing in cash. I thought they might leave me in fund-raising indefinitely, but just last week when I was in the office, the client coordinator called out to me as I was walking past her door. She asked me how I was doing and I said fine, that it had been almost a year. She'd frowned and said, "A year? Already?"

So that's why they're calling, to give me a new client. I drop the phone back into my purse. Why didn't I insist that the lawyer tell me how much money I have? I'm a grown woman and I have a right to know, but I let him cow me just like I always do. If Elyse had been there, she would have grabbed him by the lapel and said, "Bottom-line it for us," but Elyse is living in Arizona now, throwing pots and drumming and chanting by the light of the moon with a circle of crazy women, and besides, I can't rely on her forever. I'll run by the library, I decide, and then I'll stop at the grocery and pick up something for dinner. And tonight I'll get my bottle of wine, go into Mark's office, and write the law firm an e-mail. For the subject line I'll type "Bottom-Line It for Me."

# CHAPTER TWO

And that's how it all started, at the lawyer's office, with my being told I'm some variation of rich. Or maybe the story really begins an hour later, in the grocery store, at the moment when I stole the apple. Because I'm not naturally a thief. In fact, that apple is the only thing I've ever taken in my whole life that wasn't mine.

Okay, maybe the second.

The shopping area closest to my house is a place with fountains, gazebos, and park benches called the Village at Canterbury Commons. I used to be sarcastic about the name, but now I've faced the fact that I'm paying good money to be near all this simulated charm, and besides, the center has everything I need. A ridiculously upscale grocery, a Starbucks, a Walgreens, a ball-room dance studio, a day spa, a branch of the library, and the holy trinity of takeout:

Chinese, Mexican, and Italian.

The grocery is almost aggressively dark and cool inside, and it's designed to emulate a medieval hill town on market day. There are slate tiles beneath my feet and rough wooden beams over my head and there are trees, live trees, clustered in the corners. The aisles are deliberately crooked, to make them seem all the more like winding streets, with nooks and random alleyways, as if you're lost somewhere in Italy. The stock boys look like waiters in their black double-breasted tunics and they whisk by with sample trays bearing jams and cheeses and dark chocolate dusted with kosher salt. I've come here often in the last year, despite the expense, because they make up so many individual salads and put them in the coolers. It's an easy place to shop for one.

In the seafood grotto they've piped in the sound of crashing waves. They're overdoing it, trying too hard, the way people always do when they're faking. I select a single piece of tuna, which the man behind the counter wraps in brown paper and ties with a string. It's like an old-fashioned gift, the kind of tuna Julie Andrews would sing about. I have my quinoa salad and my bottle of pinot gris and all I need now is a piece of fruit for dessert. The produce section holds the true masterpieces of the store — strange fruits with strange names. Jujube. Mamey sapote. Rambutan. Horned melons. They tumble artfully across burlap sacks, reminding you that they're fresh off a dock somewhere, and the displays are carefully lighted, with the shadows planned to fall a particular way, to tempt the eye in a certain direction.

Despite the bounty — or maybe because of it — I'm not a good shopper. I buy the same stuff over and over, because otherwise I become paralyzed with possibility. Take this pyramid of artichokes, with their leaves curled around each other, all green and purple and plump, arranged in perfect symmetry, protecting the edible heart. I could reach for one. I could carry it back to my kitchen, but when I got there I wouldn't know how to cook it. I've seen them roasted on a grill but I've never understood exactly what that entails. I suppose I could put it in a pot and steam it, but how long does that take and if you overcook it, don't you risk turning everything brown and mushy? Besides, at some point in the process you must take scissors and snip off all the thorns and I'm not sure how to do that either, and then there are these key limes which are as small as olives and an ugly yellow color. I know this means they're the good ones, the real key limes and not the engineered clones, but how many of them would it take to make a pie?

The phone in my purse vibrates and I look down. Hospice again. I'll have to call them back, but maybe not today, when all I want is to go home. The library books in my tote bag were each chosen because the blurbs on the back promised happy endings. No kidnapped children or exploding car bombs or emerging family secrets. And at the last minute I threw in a Jane Austen — sweet Jane Austen, who never fails to fix it all by the last page, who marries off her heroines to the only men in England who value a woman's character over family fortune, the only men in the world who have ever valued intellect over beauty. I'll go home and read and eat my tuna and drink my wine and deal with hospice tomorrow.

There's a little girl sitting in the buggy beside me, kicking her chubby legs. She's holding a pink and gold fruit in her hands like a ball. A guava, I think it must be, or is it a papaya? I grab something from the near- est stand. My hand comes back with an apple, but an apple is good enough, and I feel suddenly exhausted, suddenly teary, and I'm relieved when the phone stops ring- ing. I can't face death right now. I can't even face a guava.

I pay and leave, loaded down with the books, the wine, and the groceries. The surprising weight of a single woman's Friday night. It's hot out here on the street, way too hot for the black suit I'm wearing, but it was the only thing I owned that seemed appropriate for the lawyer's office. Another wave of dizziness rises up in me. I never ate lunch, and there's no telling what, if anything, I had for breakfast. I stop for a moment to shift the bags and take a bite of the apple, and it suddenly hits me that I didn't pay for it. That I held this apple, this sad little apple, the whole time the checkout kid was scanning my groceries. How distracted must I be to not notice I had something in my hand even while I was sliding my credit card and approving the amount? Why didn't the checker say something? I've never shoplifted in my whole life and I've turned to go back and pay when, from the dark recesses of my purse, my damn phone vibrates again, sending a jolt into my side like a cattle prod. I'm looking down and digging for it as I push open the door with my hip. Just when my hand finds the phone, it stops vibrating, and I look up.

I'm inside a large, bright room.

The walls are covered in mirrors and for a

minute I see nothing but images of my own body, reflected back at me from every angle. The floor is wide and blank, like an ocean. There's a rack in the corner crammed full of spangled dresses, a big oaken bar with stools, a sagging couch, and an enormous blinking sound system, the components awkwardly linked together with a visible snarl of cables and cords. Music is on. Sinatra.

This isn't the grocery. I've managed to stumble into the dance studio beside the grocery. Canterbury Ballroom, I think they call the place, and I notice it, in a peripheral sort of way, when I go into the grocery every day. The studio has trophies in the window, like the kind they give children for soccer and karate, along with a group of framed pictures. Women in thick fake eyelashes with their hair slicked back, smiling these maniacal smiles as they wrap their arms around spray-tanned men in open shirts. I've always wondered how such a tacky place ended up in such a pricey part of town.

"Hello there," a voice says, and a girl stands up from behind a desk. Her hair is one of those colors never seen in nature, somewhere between red and purple and brown, and the style is very severe, a china bowl cut with long bangs. "Did you come in about the free introductory lesson?"

"I don't know why I'm here," I say, and the girl nods patiently, as if something about me has already made that all too clear. As I step deeper into the room, I can see that two people are in the corner, dancing — or at least sort of dancing. An old woman is being steered in circles by a much younger man in a black T-shirt and black pants. He carefully matches his steps to hers, moving slowly, slightly off the beat. Two of a kind, Sinatra sings. Two of a kind.

"I'm Quinn," the girl says, extending a hand. Her fingernails are short but the polish is the exact same color as her hair.

"I'm Kelly Madison. No . . . no. I mean I'm Kelly Wilder." Apparently at some point in the course of this morning, I have decided to take back my maiden name.

Quinn nods again, as if she's used to greeting people who don't know their own names.

"This is embarrassing," I say, "but I accidentally stole an apple from the grocery next door" — and here I shift the bag again and hold out the apple to prove my point — "and I was trying to go back to pay when my phone rang and I looked down and I ended up here . . ." It sounds even stupider when I say it out loud.

26

And Quinn nods yet again, with that same annoying yoga-girl exaggerated calm. "So you don't want to dance?"

"Well, of course I do. Everyone wants to dance. I mean, someday I want to dance but right now I'm just trying to pay for my apple. Coming in here was an accident."

"You know," Quinn says, tilting her head, "I've never believed in accidents."

"Neither have I," I hear myself saying. And it's true. I believe in a lot of things, but accidents are not among them.

"So you're here for the free introductory lesson."

"Evidently."

Quinn turns and her hair moves as a perfect unit. "We have a few forms for you to fill out," she says, walking behind the desk.

Forms? I almost bolt. An introductory lesson sounds harmless enough, but filling out forms is a commitment. Sinatra has finished and the man is heading toward the music system. He brushes by me as I duck my head and rummage through my purse for an ink pen. It's impossible to write and hold the groceries, so I put them down on the couch and, after a moment, sit down myself. The form is pretty much what you'd expect — name, address, and contact info, including next of kin. In case the samba kills you, I guess.

And then a single question: Why do you want to dance?

I sink back into the couch and stare at myself in the mirrored wall. There are gold chains stretched across my chest, hooked to big gold buttons. My clothes are expensive, but the word "frumpy" also comes to mind, and it occurs to me that this suit is a uniform for a job I no longer have. And my face . . . it's like the air is slowly but steadily seeping out of me and I've started to pucker around the seams. Living among people twenty years older has given me a false sense of my own youth and now, surrounded by mirrors, I see exactly how much I've aged. That the hair I've always described as "ash blond" is actually streaked with gray.

"Our group class starts at seven," Quinn calls out. The room is so big and so empty that her voice echoes. "Feel free to stay if you want to. Today we're doing jive."

"I can't," I say. "I've got tuna."

"There's a refrigerator in the back."

"Oh. That's very kind of you. But I have a salad too."

"It's a big fridge."

The man in black has pressed some buttons and music swells up again, something with violins. I know the song but can't quite place it. I smile at Quinn and shake my head. I'm not the sort of woman who just wanders in off the street and puts her groceries into a strange refrigerator and starts to jive, and furthermore I don't know why I want to dance but I suspect it has something to do with the fact that I live alone in a five-thousand-square-foot house, I have eleven thousand dollars a month automatically deposited into my checking account, and I have absolutely nothing to do all day. I struggle to my feet — the couch is not only lumpy but low — and carry my bags and the form to Quinn's desk.

"That last question is a stumper," I say, but Quinn merely looks up from her computer screen and asks if I can come in at four o'clock next Thursday afternoon for a lesson with someone named Nik.

"No *c*," she says.

"Nik with no *c*," I repeat.

"Short for Nikoli. He's Russian." She shrugs. "Both of our male instructors are. Oh, and one more thing. When you come for your lesson, wear the highest heels you have. Preferably ones with slick bottoms."

I am already halfway out the door when I turn and look back doubtfully. I'd assumed I'd wear running shoes and workout clothes.

This is exercise, isn't it? Something like Zumba class at the Y?

"Heels," Quinn says again, plopping a heavily tattooed leg onto the desk in a single fluid movement. Her shoes are at least three inches high and the bottoms are covered with suede. The straps cross in front and buckle behind the ankle. Very sexy in a Betty Boop kind of way.

"I don't have any shoes like that," I say. "Nothing remotely like that." What does this girl take me for? If I had shoes like that I wouldn't need to come here in the first place. A woman who owned shoes like that would be leading a conga line down a gangplank somewhere in the tropics. She'd have a loud, outrageous laugh and a thousand lovers, and I get a sudden faint glimmer of why I might want to dance. But I push the thought down like a beach ball and say, "The only heels I have are something I bought to wear to somebody's wedding."

"Wedding shoes are better than nothing," Quinn says. "But the higher the heels, the better you'll move. No really, I swear. It's like you have to deliberately get yourself off balance before you can learn how to balance. I know it doesn't make any sense, but trust me."

For some reason I do trust her, but I still

30

stand, halfway in and halfway out the door. It would be easy to say forget it and walk away, but my eyes drift once more to the couple in the corner. What dance is this — the foxtrot? A waltz? Or just an elaborate sort of shuffle he's made up to accommodate a woman clearly old enough to be his grandmother?

Yet . . . there's a heartbreaking kindness in the way he dances with her. He deliberately reins himself in, downplaying his youth and strength, and he turns her gently, again and again, as if he is showing her off to an imaginary crowd. She is barely moving but he has managed to make her come alive. Everything about the woman is absurd. There are smears of turquoise on her eyelids and even from this distance I can tell that she dipped a shaky finger into a pot and slashed the color on like war paint. Her hair, most likely a wig, seems a little off center, as if she is Carol Burnett pretending to be one of her old movie stars. Some grande dame unaware that time has passed her by.

But this man is completely focused on this woman. He sees her. Most men do not look at aging women. I know this because in the last five years I have begun to fade from the eyes of men. And yet this particular man, young and strong as he is, sees this particular woman. He swirls and bows and pivots around her, honoring the space she occupies. And when she finally turns back toward me, I can see that she is radiant with joy.

One of my feet is inside the studio, on the glossy floor of the ballroom, and the other is on the sidewalk. It would be as easy to go one way as another. I have Jane Austen and pinot gris and a single piece of tuna inside a sack and if I'm sure of anything, it's that I don't ever want a man to touch me again. I doubt I have to worry about it. That part of my life is probably over, and yet I can't seem to look away from the couple in the corner. The woman's face is happy. And mine, I know even without looking, is not.

It would be easy to say forget it and hurry home.

I should say forget it and hurry home.

But instead, for some reason I will never understand, I lean back toward Quinn and ask, "Exactly where'd you get those shoes?"

"I really fell down the rabbit hole today," I tell Elyse. It's just after nine. I've grilled the tuna, covered it with salsa straight from the jar, and emptied the salad onto a plate. I started on the wine two hours ago, and I'm a little floaty as I wedge the telephone under my chin and carry everything to the table.

"Like how?" Elyse's voice through the phone is indistinct. She's either out on her patio, where reception isn't good, or her mouth is full, or both.

"For starters, I went to the law office and they told me I'm rich."

"Well, that's swell, but we already sort of knew that, didn't we?" She pauses for a moment and swallows. "How rich?"

"They wouldn't tell me."

"Wouldn't tell you? Why not? Is it set up like a trust fund?"

"I guess. They deposit eleven thousand a month in my checking account. I'm not supposed to worry about anything."

"Jesus. You didn't ask them the principal amount? I mean, is it yours to do what you want to with, or does the estate control —"

"I don't know. And I don't want to talk about that part right now." I feel a little tickle of shame. After dinner I really do need to send that lawyer an e-mail demanding he give me the total. I stab a lettuce leaf and shake it until most of the dressing flies off. "Because that's not even the weird part of the day. After I left the law office I went to the grocery and somehow, I don't know how, I ended up in the dance studio beside it and I signed up to take a lesson. So get out your calendar and circle the date in red. This is the day Kelly Wilder officially lost her mind."

"You're going back to Wilder?"

"The point is, I signed up to take a dance lesson."

"What's weird about that? You always liked dancing."

"This isn't club-style dancing. It's ballroom, the sequins and spray-tan shit that comes on public access late at night."

"Ballroom's hot," Elyse says. "Everybody's doing it."

"Exactly. I'm a cliché. And then, as if the lessons weren't bad enough, I furthermore agreed to buy special shoes to do it in. They have really high heels and straps that wrap around your ankle and the soles are suede, and you can't even wear them on the pavement, you have to carry them around in a little silk bag. Why would they make shoes you can't walk in?"

"Probably so you can slide your foot."

"What?"

"Suede soles would make it easier to slide your foot. Dancing is a sport, so you need a sport-specific shoe."

"I hate it when you're logical." I take a gulp of the wine. "But I haven't told you the strangest part of all yet," I say. "All the lawyers were moving in unison, like zombies, and I got the feeling that one of the female lawyers was winking at me. Then when I was in the produce aisle at the grocery I got all flipped out about what kind of fruit to buy. There were so many choices and they were all so beautiful and there was a little girl holding a guava and for some reason the whole thing made me feel like crying and I ended up with an apple."

Elyse is silent. She waits.

"They have a thousand kinds of fruit," I say. "Glamorous exotic stuff, and I choose this scuffed-up little red apple like you can get at the BI-LO. And then — you're going to love this part — I accidentally fucking steal it. I mean I hold it in my hand all the way through the checkout line and by the time I realize what I've done, I'm out on the street. You know me, what a nerd I am. I turn around to go back and pay and I accidentally wind up in a ballroom studio instead and then before you know it I'm agreeing to get suede-bottomed shoes and let some Russian who's probably sprayed orange lead me around the dance floor for a million dollars an hour. I've become that woman, Elyse. You know — the old pathetic kind who pays men to fuss over them."

"Maybe the apple was enchanted."

I laugh, despite myself.

"Well, you have to admit the whole thing's pretty Disney-fied," she says. "There's a mysterious fortune, a number that cannot be uttered aloud. A stranger winks at you. You take a bite of an apple and boom, you're pulled into the ballroom against your will. And now you've got to find some magic shoes that the minute you put them on will make you start to dance."

"They're just a pair of fuck-me heels. Nobody said they were magic."

"Personally, I blame Cinderella," Elyse breezes on, and across two thousand miles I hear her fork clank against her plate. "Or maybe Dorothy from *The Wizard of Oz.* Between those two, there isn't a woman alive in America today who doesn't think her whole life would be transformed if she could just find the right pair of shoes."

"What'd you make tonight?"

"Tuna too," she says, laughing softly.

Elyse and I like eating together. North Carolina and Arizona are in different time zones but I eat late and she eats early, so it isn't an issue. I always sit in the chair that faces the setting sun and sometimes I wonder if she sits facing east. She knows I need these little rituals, that I'm not yet accustomed to having dinner alone and maybe

36

never will be. I imagine her out on her adobe patio, her hair tied in a loose knot at the back of her neck, squinting like a French film star. Living out west agrees with her. She seems taller since she moved there, rangy like a cowgirl, with a kind of elegant messiness. Elyse doesn't bother with Botox or Spanx or highlights to hide the gray. She doesn't need to. For Elyse, pretty would be a step down.

"I'm cracking up," I say, surprising myself. For the second time today I feel like crying, but then again, I often cry when I drink.

"Oh, Kelly, you're not cracking up. You're trying to act like it was an ordinary day, but it wasn't. Settling the estate means the last link to Mark is broken, so of course you're rattled. The dancing is a great idea. You can't stay all boxed in and bunched up forever."

"I know, I know. It's been a whole year."

She hesitates. "It's been a lot longer than a year."

I sit up straight. It feels like she's slapped me.

"Mark wasn't so bad," I say. "It's not like he could help getting sick."

"I didn't mean Mark," she says. There's static on the line. She must have walked off the patio. She must be standing in the sand

37

among the cacti, looking up at the mountains. "Are we ever going to talk about Daniel and what happened way back then? How he broke you?"

For almost forty years, Elyse has been my witness. The sister I never had. The sister I never particularly wanted. The only person in my life who knows about not only Mark and Daniel but the man before that and the one before that. Whenever I left a job or a boyfriend or moved into a new apartment, she was right there, but I guess I counted on her to have the same selective amnesia I had. Because when you're young and going straight from one mistake to another, you want your friends to remember only the things you want them to remember. You want them to say, "Yes, he's the first. The first one who really matters. All those other times were just for practice. Here, in this moment, is where your real life begins."

Elyse has never been especially good at this. Her memory's a damn bear trap and it's never let go of Daniel. How like her to bring him up now, on this day when I'm already half-drunk and half-upset.

"I didn't realize I was broken," I say. "Or at least I didn't realize that's how you saw me."

"I don't. You know I don't. Okay . . . no

talk of Daniel. At least not yet. But have you ever noticed how when you lose one thing, your mind kind of circles back to everything else you ever lost? You break up with a guy and boom, it's like all the guys you ever broke up with suddenly pull in your driveway and get out of the same car. Or you walk into a funeral home and you remember every other time you've ever been there and the next thing you know, five funerals are going down at once. You start crying and you don't even know why, and people say 'What's wrong?' and you say 'Nothing,' but you still keep crying. So I'm just saying that losing Mark might be like losing Daniel all over again."

"I have no idea what you're talking about," I say, although of course I do. Elyse likes to point out obvious things in a really surprised tone of voice, like she's single-handedly broken some great new philosophical ground. It's one of the things about her that is simultaneously annoying and endearing.

I carry my plate over to the rubber dish rack in the sink. It was hard to find this dish rack. Apparently they don't sell many of them anymore — I had to go to Walmart and Target and then Sears. But I never seem to dirty enough dishes to bother running the dishwasher. I use the same coffee mug, wineglass, plate, and three utensils over and over, washing them, letting them dry in the rack, and then picking them back up again for the next meal. It's ludicrous. A kitchen this size really belongs on the set of a Food Network show. Or it should at least be in the home of a woman who does more than open a prepackaged salad and put a piece of tuna on the grill. My bed looks like it's hardly been slept in. Just one corner turned back, and I carry the newspaper to the recycling bin the moment I finish the su-doku. Everything stays creepily clean because even though I barely leave an imprint, I feel too guilty to fire the maid. It's like I think any minute the real owners of this house will be home and I'm going to have to get out fast.

"I didn't mean to upset you," Elyse says.

"You didn't," I say. "But that dance studio . . . it was so tacky, Elyse. All silver and blue and sparkly and over-the-top. It was like you took everything that's me and created the opposite. I think I've gone and done something stupid."

"Well, thank God," Elyse says. "It's about time."

# CHAPTER THREE

There's a photograph of me and Elyse in my kitchen, above the desk where I stack my cookbooks, and after she and I say good night, I pour another glass of wine and wander over to look at it. It's from our college years, the summer we spent in Europe.

Our parents had bought us Eurail passes, the good kind with unlimited travel, and it didn't take either of us long to figure out we hated the youth hostels with their hairy shower drains and Czech girls trying to steal our jeans. It was much better to sleep on the trains, so the nights when we couldn't afford a hotel room we would just go down to the station around ten and climb on the first one that stopped. We were good at flirting with the conductors, and if the cars weren't full, they sometimes upgraded us to a sleeper compartment. There were many mornings that summer that we would awaken with no idea where we were. Elyse would push aside the blinds and wait for the depot sign to appear. That's how we went to Seville and Dresden, to Bern and Antwerp.

It's how we went to Florence too, and I pick up the picture that shows me and Elyse, standing in the Accademia, where they keep Michelangelo's *David*. Elyse had been insistent that if fate had taken us to Florence, we may as well see him. She was an art major and had a somewhat old-fashioned idea of a European tour. She dragged me through an untold number of cathedrals and galleries and she repeatedly referred to an out-of-date, torn-up Fodor's guidebook.

The euro had not yet been invented, and we changed countries frequently, so the currency was always an issue. The side zipper pocket of my backpack held kronor and francs and guilders and pence, a jangling mass of European money that I would hand to shopkeepers to sort out and just hope that they were honest. The line to see *David* was long, so we decided to buy the special pass that lets you go in with small groups. This privilege cost something like a million lira, but who knew how much that was? It seemed like a gelato was a million lira, and so was a bottle of wine or a flight to London.

But paying extra did mean we were shunted toward a much shorter line that wrapped around a little gift kiosk while the rest of the tourists glared. I wanted to rent headsets but Elyse said no, we didn't need them, that I would understand everything if I just took a deep inhalation and let the art come inside me. It was August and by this point Elyse and I were really getting on each other's nerves. I was tired of her lectures about observing and absorbing, and perfectly willing to pay a million more lira for some nice calm English voice to tell me what the hell I was looking at.

"You'll understand as much as you let yourself understand," Elyse said, and I'd given her the finger while pretending to scratch my cheek. She was so sure, even then, that she would become an artist, which I guess she has, even though it's hard to reconcile her hand-thrown Hopi pots with the grandeur of *David*. "My queer little bowls," she calls them, stressing her southern accent on the word "queer," but there's pride in her voice too, the pride of someone who has never once wavered, who has always known precisely what she wants out of life.

My dreams were vaguer, and thus easier to ignore. I told people I planned to go into business, and fervently hoped that they didn't ask me what kind. Because I really had no idea what I meant by that statement, only that I knew I wanted to earn my own money. It was a strange ambition to have in the seventies, especially for a girl. Everyone else was about drugs, sex, and music; money was just something that we simultaneously disdained and counted on our parents to provide. But Elyse would laugh and ask whether someday, when she was a starving artist and I was a captain of industry, would I open up my big brass gates and let her in? And then she would add, "Thank God one of us is practical."

That day in the Accademia in Florence, I let Elyse talk me out of the headsets, just as I've let her talk me in and out of things our whole lives, and they finally admitted about ten of us past the velvet rope. As we entered the gallery, we all turned in unison to face down the hall toward the sunny rotunda where *David* was standing. He looked exactly how I expected him to look, only better. For a second I almost got what she'd been talking about.

"He glows," I said to Elyse, and she smiled.

"Yes," she said. "Some of them do."

The place was packed and, special group

pass or not, we were going to have to work our way down slowly to the rotunda. At least there was plenty to look at and sometime in the middle of that European summer I had started to notice that what's on the way to the famous stuff is often more interesting than whatever it was you originally thought you should see. The hall was lined with a series of statues called *The Prisoners,* big, heavy blocks of marble with wild half-carved men. They were thick-limbed and powerful but trapped within the blocks, their bodies writhing as they struggled to break free.

"I wonder if the sculptor meant to leave them that way," Elyse said.

"We'd know if we'd gotten the headsets."

She consulted her guidebook. "'The Prisoners,'" she read. "'Sometimes called *The Slaves.* Michelangelo started this series when he was fifty-nine and worked on them until he was seventy.'" She snapped the book shut. "Shit, that's eleven years. They must be as finished as he wanted them to be."

The last slave on the left bothered me the most. His arms were flexed in an obvious struggle to pull his head free from the marble. "It's like the statues are making themselves," Elyse said solemnly. The night

45

before, as we'd traveled from Rome to Florence, she'd read to me how Michelangelo claimed he didn't create *David* — that he'd found him sleeping in the marble, completely intact. That he'd simply picked up his chisel and carved away everything that wasn't *David*. It's a sweet thought, I guess, that some perfect man is already out there waiting and all we have to do is find him and brush off the dust, but Elyse had snorted when she finished reading and said, "Bullshit."

I looked at the dates on the brochure they'd handed us along with our tickets. Michelangelo finished *David* when he was a young man himself, not even thirty, and *The Prisoners* had come much later in his life. It was odd, I thought, that in the beginning he was looking for pure beauty already formed and in the end he was willing to let the art fight its own way out of the stone. The headsets probably would have explained it all.

The crowd loosened up a bit as we passed through the gallery and got closer to the rotunda where *David* was waiting. We walked around the base of the statue a few times and then sat down on a bench. I haven't been to Italy since, but I doubt you can walk right up to *David* now. They probably have ropes and Plexiglas and high-tech security. But on that summer day, Elyse and I just sat there, shockingly close, looking up at the veins in his arms, the rippled muscles across his shoulders. You could see his ribs and the slight indentation around his sternum, and the toes of his left foot were unfinished.

"He's subtle," Elyse said. "What makes him human is that he's not too smooth."

"I know," I said. "In fact, the closer you get, the wonkier he seems. When you really stare at him, his hands are too big and his feet are too big. His whole head is too big."

"He looked perfectly proportional from the end of the hall," Elyse said, rubbing the back of her neck. "Of course, art changes depending on where you're standing." So we stood up and walked out of the dome, linked arms, and began to approach *David* from different angles. There are paintings and statuary all around him in the Accademia. Wonderful things, I'm sure, and priceless, but none of the tourists seemed to look at any of them. *David* was the star.

Elyse and I walked toward him from the north and east and south and west and finally ended up back on the same bench where we had started.

47

"The man on the pedestal," Elyse said softly.

"He's afraid of something," I said.

Elyse shook her head. "Not afraid, just wary. He's looking at Goliath."

"His penis is kind of small," I said. "Considering the rest of him."

"Well," Elyse said slowly. "It's not like it's erect, is it?" We sat in silence, contemplating this. We were young then, and pretty. I'm not sure either of us had ever seen a penis that wasn't erect.

"Even so," she finally said. "You're right, it doesn't look promising. And there's something weird about his pubic hair."

"Way too perfect. Like it's been brushed and styled with a blow-dryer." We got the giggles and they rang through the dome.

"I like *The Prisoners* better," I said.

"Yeah," said Elyse. "Me too."

"But you were right," I admitted. "We really didn't need the headsets."

As we were leaving, Elyse asked someone to take our picture. Just a quick snapshot with one of our cheap cameras. At some point through the years I had it blown up and framed, and it's my all-time favorite photograph of us, which is why I keep it here in the kitchen, even though it's faded to gold and gone a little fuzzy. It's the im-

age of two girls caught at the end of something, although of course we didn't know
that at the time. Elyse had handed the
camera to some cute young guy in the
crowd. An American student, like us, just
one more boy who'd be going home at the
end of the summer, just one more boy
wandering through Paris and Amsterdam
and Rome. When we asked if he spoke
English, he'd dropped his headset down his
neck and said, "A little bit. I'm from Pitts-
burgh." Everyone laughed and of course
we'd decided the next logical step was to
find a café and a cheap bottle of wine. When
he lifted the camera to his face, he told us
to say "Parmesan."

Kind of funny. At least he was trying.
Elyse and I exchanged one of our glances.
Mine, I thought to her. This one is mine.

In the picture Elyse and I are standing in
the bright dome of the Accademia. We're
both wearing jeans and T-shirts. Our back-
packs lie at our feet. Elyse must have just
released her hair from its braid, because it's
expanded around her head like a low halo,
and I've pushed my sunglasses back and am
smiling broadly, so broadly that my eyes
have squinted down to nothing. You can't
see much of David at all, there's the irony,
but Daniel's shadow falls between us on the

floor. He is crouched and bent with his arms all akimbo and his shadow looks like the passing of some great bird, an albatross or an eagle. It was the summer just before we both turned twenty. Before life began to chip away at us like a sculptor into marble, reducing us from endless unformed possibility into the women we would ultimately become.

# CHAPTER FOUR

"Her name's Carolina," the client coordinator says. "And get this. Her sisters are named Virginia and Georgia."

In a split second this woman's whole life flashes before my eyes — a montage of stray dogs and trailer parks and high school equivalency tests. "Well," I say, "it's easier when there are siblings still alive."

The coordinator glances at me. "She's only thirty-four."

"Jesus. Breast?"

She nods and we both instinctively let our hands flutter across our own chests, in a gesture that's part prayer and part self-exam. Breast cancer is usually one of the luckier ones — it involves a part of the body you can live without and is statistically quite survivable, if caught early. But they don't always catch it early, especially in women who don't go to the doctor unless they're sick. Women who wait until they can feel the lump through their shirt before they make an appointment.

"Kids?"

"Twelve and fifteen."

"Husband?"

"Not in this jurisdiction."

"I'm not sure I want this one, Teresa."

"No one does." She hands me the folder. "Just go meet her. Give it a chance. She's very . . . plucky."

For the first time in a year I walk down the hallway that leads to the patients' rooms. I started volunteering here after Mark had his first heart attack and we moved to the gated community. He would have preferred I go on the board of the symphony or head a gala for the art museum. Something elegant and clean, but the doctor had told me that the walls of his heart were as thin as tissue paper and I'd headed straight to hospice that very afternoon. It was pure superstition. A search for some sort of talisman. Maybe I thought that if I faced death head-on every day, then it could never sneak up on me.

I didn't even try to explain this to Mark. He was angry all the time by then and he took my choice of hospice as a major rebellion, some attempt to humiliate him at the club with what he called my Jesus complex.

He didn't like the fact that I spent my afternoons cutting old people's toenails and driving their spouses to Kmart, or the time I came home smelling of some poor woman's post-chemo vomit. "Why are you wasting your time?" he'd ask me. "Anyone can wash hair and pick up pizza. You should be doing something that matters."

When I walk into the Dogwood Room — we name them after flowers — Carolina is propped against a wall of pillows with the TV remote in one hand and the bed control in the other. A lumpy red afghan is stretched across her knees and her hair is thin but neatly tucked behind her ears. Her expression is a little expectant, as if she were sitting in a plane on a runway.

I introduce myself and she gives me a big crooked smile and says, "I just love this place."

Not the most typical reaction to finding yourself in hospice, but maybe this was what Teresa meant when she called Carolina plucky. Because the woman doesn't seem that sick and certainly not confused. In fact, considering the age of her kids and her general condition, I'm surprised she elected to come in as early as she did, but she seems to be treating the place like a hotel. This may be the first time in her life she's had a bed, a TV, and a toilet all to herself.

I start toward the chair but she pats the bed with surprising vigor, so I sit down beside her. Or, more accurately, I lie down beside her, because the minute my butt hits the sloping mattress I roll flat on my back, looking up at the clouds painted on the ceiling.

"Tell me all about yourself," she says.

I've never had a client ask me anything about my own life. I sneak a peek to my left. Carolina is also staring intently at the clouds, like they might start moving.

"It's more important that I understand what you need me to do," I say. Apparently I've just agreed to be her volunteer. "I know you have kids. Do they need help with homework? Groceries brought in? Rides to soccer practice and things like that?"

She shakes her head. "My sister, Virginia, never had her own and she came straight-away and I've lived in the same development and worked at the same salon for seventeen years. There's people fussing over those boys left and right. You don't have to worry about any of that."

"So what do you need?"

"I want you to talk to me. When you get sick, people stop talking to you. I mean, really talking. They just keep telling you to

54

try and get some rest now." She folds her arms across her chest. "I want to be entertained."

"I can do that," I say. I'm not really surprised by her bluntness. Death's just one more foreign country and people begin to speak a different language the closer they get to the border. Sweet old ladies start to curse. Cynics start to pray. And people like this woman, who I bet never asked anybody for anything her whole life long, suddenly come up with a whole list of demands.

"We can talk about whatever you want," I tell her. "And I can bring movies, if you like them, and whatever food you crave. The stuff that comes out of the kitchen here is nutritious but it isn't very tasty."

"I want sugar and salt and fat," she says. "I don't know why they'd bother trying to be nutritious now. That just seems mean."

"Their intentions are good," I say, although privately I agree with her. Some people don't have the stomach for working with the actual clients. Soft volunteers, Teresa calls them, and they have odd little ideas about what dying people need. They paint clouds on blue ceilings and show up with grandma gifts like hand-knit afghans and salt-water taffy. And they insist on paying twenty percent of the whole annual budget for a dietician to plan meals full of calcium and roughage and antioxidants, even though at this stage in the game you could probably make a better argument for spending the money on tequila.

"I'll bring you whatever you want," I say. "I've got plenty of experience sneaking ice cream and barbecue past the guards."

"What kind of movies do you watch?"

"Old ones," I say.

"Like *Pretty Woman*?"

"No, really old ones, from the thirties and forties and fifties. Have you ever heard of Bette Davis?" She shakes her head. "Joan Crawford? Katharine Hepburn? I know you know Marilyn Monroe."

She brightens. "I want Marilyn Monroe and a Meat Lover's Supreme. Thin crust. Can we do that?"

"Sure."

"And you still have to tell me something about yourself. You've probably got a whole file on me and I don't know anything about you. Like . . . are you married?"

"My husband died a year ago."

"Did you love him?"

I force myself to an upright position and look back at her. "Of course I loved him. What kind of question is that?"

She folds her arms behind her head.

"Okay, we'll start with something easier. What are you going to do this afternoon when you leave here?"

"I'm going to let a Russian man teach me how to dance."

"You're jerking me."

"Am not. Just this very morning I spent a hundred and ten dollars on a pair of high-heel dance shoes."

She looks at me and we both burst out laughing. Her bangs fall forward and she pushes them back again and I think that yeah, you can tell she worked in a beauty salon because although her hair is thin, she's trying hard to keep it neat. This woman cares what she looks like. The chemo probably broke what was left of her heart.

"See?" I say. "You think you have me pegged but I'm full of surprises."

"I never said I had you pegged," she says, and when she grins I see that she's chewing gum, the kind they give you to help with the nausea. She's slumped farther down in the bed and her breathing is a little labored. Our conversation has both revved her up and worn her out and I make a mental note to remember this, that she's sicker than she seems. Without thinking, I reach toward her and she grabs my hand. It's an awkward sideways grip, but we do a little shake thing with it, like we're agreeing on something. Working out some sort of deal, the details of which will be determined later.

"Are you scared?" I ask her.

She tilts her head and looks up at the clouds. "Not yet," she says.

I wasn't sure what to wear to my first dance lesson. It's the continual conundrum of fashion — you want to look like you tried, but not too much. I remember the old woman I saw in the studio and how, even with her slow and unsteady movement, her dress swayed around her legs. All that furling and unfurling — it was almost as if the dress were a living thing and she was merely riding along within it.

So after digging around in my closet, I find a Lycra dress with a full skirt that I bought to wear on my last and only trip to Europe with Mark, because the salesgirl promised it would pack well. It's teal blue, an awkward color — awkward because it is a color at all and I normally wear beige or black or gray. It always makes me feel like a stewardess on some airline that went bankrupt in the seventies, but when I turn side to side the dress swishes. It makes what I imagine to be the sound of dance. I pull my hair back too, but loosely, not in an ostentatious ballerina bun, which might indicate that I think I'm better than I am, but in a hairstyle I stole from Elyse, a sort of sloppy French twist.

Even with all the fussing, I still arrive at three-thirty for my four o'clock lesson, carrying my new dancing shoes in their little blue sack. Quinn's not at her desk, but is instead with a student. Surprising. I wouldn't have guessed she was a teacher as well as a receptionist. I walk to the back of the room, uncomfortably aware of how loud my sandals sound on the polished wooden floor, and sit down on the couch. The studio is a different place without music.

Quinn and the man are not dancing but are rather standing in front of the mirrored wall, frowning at their reflections, holding hands. At first they seem utterly immobile, but then I see that they're each slowly extending the right foot, tilted with the toe in the air and the heel grazing the floor, and then slowly pulling it back. Quinn does this easily; when her foot slides forward, her body stays relaxed and erect and the knee of her standing leg flexes. She has good range in her step. She must be naturally limber, or maybe the ability to slide your heel like that is more a matter of balance.

The man is a whole other story. He's tall,

with a ruddy face, and something about him is familiar — where could I have seen him? The country club? Some fund-raiser? He's handsome, I realize, with a belated jolt. What's wrong with me that I see a man and it takes me a full five minutes before I figure out whether or not he's good-looking? If this were a movie, he'd be cast as a duke or an earl, perhaps even a king. There's something haughty in his expression, something aristocratic. Something that implies he rides horses and jumps over fences, followed by packs of yelping dogs. But his face is frozen in concentration and when he pushes out his heel, it doesn't slide smoothly, like Quinn's, but rather sticks and then jerks forward as if there are bumps in the dance floor that only he can feel. Worse, when his leg is fully extended, he leans his torso backward to compensate, which makes him look like a vaudeville comedian, someone who is about to stride onstage with a cane and straw hat. It doesn't make sense. He looks like the lord of the manor but he dances like a clown, and he must know this, so why is he dancing at all?

I bend down to put on my shoes. The woman at the store had talked me through the process, the crisscrossing of the straps, the buckle that rests in the indentation of my heel. I get them on without much trouble, but when I stand, the straps shift a little. Perhaps they should be tighter. The woman said that if they hurt when you're sitting, that means they'll fit perfectly when you're standing, so if you're in pain, that's a good sign. Because hey, we can't have our foot sliding around, can we? Do we want our foot rocking back and forth in our shoes while we're dancing, do we want our toes slipping out from under us while we're trying to grip the floor? I'd shaken my head vigorously, like a schoolgirl sucking up to the teacher. No, we certainly don't want that. But the shoes are a full size smaller than what I usually wear and this alarms me too. The woman had given me one of those little shriveled-up nylon socks to make it easier, and she knelt down to help me turn my foot and insinuate it into the shoe. "A perfect fit," she'd said.

I refasten the straps, yanking until they hurt, and stand up again. The heels are higher than any I've ever worn and as I push off the couch, I feel like I'm unfolding. I've never been this tall. I take a tentative step. The suede soles will take some getting used to. Elyse was right, they're designed to slide smoothly, but still . . . I look at the ruddy-faced man again and wonder if men's dance shoes work the same as women's, if they also have suede bottoms and fit too tight. The man's tongue is sticking out of the corner of his mouth, like that of a child learning to write. Back and forth he jerks his heel, with Quinn standing beside him, leaning in and saying something softly. Telling him that it would be easier to slide his right heel forward if he bent his left knee a little more — at least that's what I assume Quinn might be saying, since that's what I'd like to tell him.

Is this a dance lesson? Is this what I can expect? The woman I saw the first day had been glowing with joy, but this man's misery is palpable. Of course that woman had been terribly old and probably past the point of improvement, and Quinn is clearly trying to teach this man something. They've been sliding their heels back and forth now for ten minutes and while it doesn't look like he's getting any better at it, Quinn must think he's capable of more, for why else would she be standing so patiently, speaking so quietly, and holding him steady with the grip of just one hand?

I put my palm on the wall beside the couch and flex my left knee, pushing my right foot forward just a couple of inches and raising my toe.

It isn't that hard. Well, I did lean back just a little and I was touching the wall. You probably just have to hold your core really tight, that's the trick. It's probably more about the muscles in your abdomen than the muscles in your leg. The man and Quinn aren't aware of me at all. They're utterly intent, and I slide my foot a bit farther this time, almost on the verge of taking a step. Okay, that's a little tougher, but by squeezing my whole pelvis and exhaling like in yoga I manage to stay upright. Am I ready to let go of the wall?

"Is called heel lead."

The man who has come up behind me is maybe three inches shorter than I am, at least when I'm wearing these heels, and almost laughably muscular. His eyes are dark, deep-set, and quizzical, and his black shoulder-length hair flips up at the ends, like a girl's. He has the same intimidatingly good posture and strange formality that I noticed the first day, in the man who'd danced with the old lady. It must be a particularly Russian type of bearing.

"I'm Kelly," I say. "I guess you're Nik."

He cocks his head. "Is not as easy as it looks, this heel lead. This is where we start?"

"What? No, no we don't need to start there."

63

"You are practicing —"

"No, I'm not practicing. I mean I guess I was, but only because I was watching them and this . . . this is the first dance lesson I've ever really seen and like this is the first step I've ever really . . . I mean, you're the boss, you're the teacher. We can start wherever you say, but I don't particularly want to start with something so . . . Actually, I need music. I think I'd be more, you know, relaxed if we had music." I'm aware we are almost whispering, that he is standing unnervingly close to me, yet the silence of the room makes every word sound too loud and still I can't seem to shut up. I let go of the wall and lurch. He's thirty years younger than I am. I was not prepared for this.

He nods but does not smile automatically, like an American might do. He's not going to laugh or say something to break the tension. If an American man stood this close or spoke this softly it would mean something, and it probably means something here too, but something I don't yet understand. Nik smells of cigarette smoke and breath mints and another scent I can't identify. He's entirely too young, maybe, now that I stop to really look at him, not even twenty-five. I wish I'd known how short he was before I bought these damn shoes.

He extends a hand to me and I grab it and try to shake it before I realize he's inviting me to dance. So my right hand is in his right. I've had so many clumsy handshakes lately. I seem to be shaking hands all over town, agreeing to any number of deals I don't understand. But even though we are awkwardly linked, the boy doesn't release his grip. He just backs onto the dance floor, pulling me along, and his palm is soft but very dry, almost as if he has dusted it with powder, as if he were a pool player or a gymnast, someone who must not let go, no matter what. He's a child, possibly on steroids, and his hair is very strange. The gel in it must be the third thing I smell, or maybe it's whatever he's rubbed on his palms.

"We could start with cha-cha," he says.

He takes me to the corner, far away from Quinn and the lord of the manor, which I appreciate. He has me stand behind him while he goes through a sequence of moves that I am supposed to watch and then emulate. It's simple enough — a side step, a rock forward, then back, and a stuttering little three-step to the side, which I suppose is the cha-cha-cha part. His steps are small,

I notice, which lets him move in a fast and controlled, almost mechanical manner. I watch once and then join in and he seems surprised.

"I used to be a cheerleader," I say. "I know how to pick up routines."

This information does not appear to enlighten him. I guess they don't have a lot of cheerleaders in Russia. "Very good," he says. "We add hips."

We add hips.

He turns, frowns. "Very good again. Do not jerk hips. Foot movements are sharp, but hips roll through. Smooth and gentle."

A little trickier. I try the sequence and he stops me.

"Hips sway and feet are sharp," he says. "But top of body relaxed. Shoulders stay level. You are duck. This means —"

"I know," I say. "Active on the bottom and serene on the top."

"Serene?" he says slowly. "Just a minute." And he goes over to the desk and pulls out an iPhone. I spell the world "serene" for him and he types it in. He doesn't ask for the definition so I guess he got it from the context.

"I will have more English," he says with a shrug, as he flips on the stereo and walks back toward me. "You learn fast, so now we dance with music."

"Thank you," I say.

"Thank you what?"

"For saying that I learn fast."

He looks puzzled. "No need to say this," he says. "I speak the truth."

Okay, I think, so that's a hint. He's not going to flatter me and, in fact, he'll probably get offended if he thinks I'm trying to flatter him. All we're doing today is gauging my level of raw talent — a pure assessment, and thus no reflection of his abilities. But soon Nik will begin to see me as the product of his teaching and then I suspect that my progress — or lack of it — will matter very much. He's got pride. He's the sort of man who wants to know what people mean when they use a word like "serene."

"Latin hold," he says, stepping toward me, "is loose. Relaxed like hips." He drapes my left arm over his right so that my hand comes to rest on his shoulder, almost at the base of his neck. He takes my right hand in his left so that we are standing close to each other. I have not been close to a man for a long time, and never like this. The muscles in his arms and shoulders. The faint smell of cigarettes, the dark and slightly slanted eyes, the dryness of his hand. I'm not sure where to look.

"This is what we most times do in lesson two," he tells me. "But I do not think you will be the one to step on my foot." Apparently his willingness to put on music and take me into hold is a sign that I'm having a good first lesson . . . or maybe anyone can do these steps immediately and he's only suggesting I'm advanced as part of his sales pitch. That's what Mark would say if he were here. I can hear his voice in my head, telling me that I'm gullible, which I suppose could be true, and yet I have the feeling that I really am doing well. How long has it been since I've tried something new, come someplace on my own without either Elyse or Mark to prop me up? I'd forgotten the simple joy of learning, the joy of mastering one thing and then moving on to something else. It's a pleasure we normally concede to the young.

But now Nik is frowning again. "Arm should not lie like dead squirrel in road," he says, tilting his head toward my left arm. "Even when in hold, lady must support her own weight. Keep shoulders back and arms to side. Not lean on man."

I jerk my arm back, strangely stung. "I wasn't leaning on you."

"A little."

I pull myself upright.

"Now," Nik says. "I step forward and you step back. Begin with right foot. In dance, lady is always right. Only in dance. In everything else, man is right."

He's teasing. Making a little joke. At least I think he is. It's impossible to tell by his expression.

But now that I'm self-conscious about my posture, it's harder to move. He counts me down and we start the pattern and I'm going through the steps okay, but I seem to have lost all sense of rhythm, like the dance has suddenly been sucked right out of me. This sort of thing happens to me a lot. I call it the Curse of Early Promise. I tend to do well at things in the beginning, when they don't matter, before I've had the chance to think too much or get nervous, and then at some point it all clinches down around me. I don't know whom I'm trying to please, exactly, or why it matters how well a fifty-two-year-old woman keeps her form during a cha-cha lesson in a dance studio in the suburbs of Charlotte, North Carolina, in the middle of the afternoon. And yet I'm trying with everything in me to hold my arms loose and shoulders back while simultaneously making fast, small steps and rolling my hips gently through. Firm yet serene. Sharp yet smooth. On my own feet and still completely responsive to his movements. Even though it seems impossible to be all these things at once.

"Exhale," he says.

I exhale.

We lose the beat for a minute. Find it again. I bang my knee against his.

"Maybe inhale too," he says. "Good idea to do both."

I stop and step back from him, dropping my arms. "I'm fucking it up, aren't I?" I say. "When I try to balance, I get tense and when I relax, I get all wobbly. But there's got to be some way to be both balanced and relaxed, isn't there? I know there is. I could do it when I was a kid. But I've forgotten how to work my body."

"What does it mean," he says, "to have balance?"

"It means like, I don't know, like your weight is distributed evenly so you don't —"

"No," he says. "I know definition. I am asking how you, Miss Kelly Wilder, will know it when it happens."

I shake my head and we stand for a moment, neither of us moving, while the cha-cha music throbs on in the background. Then he glances at the clock.

"Thirty minutes," he says.

It couldn't be. It seemed maybe five. I thought we were going to have another chance to dance. Because I really do think I can get it. I just need one more song.

But Nik is already walking toward the front desk.

"That was first lesson," he calls over his shoulder.

# CHAPTER FIVE

It doesn't take me long to drink the Kool-Aid.

After my free introductory lesson, Nik offers me three for $99, then three more for $165. And then, when they're over, the next offer is ten for $850. The math isn't hard, but I still do it in my head twice, just to make sure I haven't failed to understand. The price per lesson really has almost tripled.

Nik seems nervous as he slides the contract toward me across the desk, and I say yes so fast I think I startle him. How does he want it — check? Charge? When he hesitates, I offer to go to an ATM and bring him back cash. Later I will learn that he hesitated because it's standard to offer a free lesson with the ten-lesson deal and he didn't know what to do when I agreed immediately. I'm not just drinking the Kool-Aid, I'm guzzling it.

The next time the cleaning lady comes over I give her a task, probably her first since Mark died. She helps me push all the furniture out of the foyer and roll up the rug, exposing the smooth wooden floor. Then we carry down the full-length mirror from my closet and wedge it into the corner so that I have my own small version of the studio, right inside the front door of my house. Marita shows an admirable lack of curiosity during this whole operation, even though I've got on my dance heels, which are slipping and sliding on the stairs. I wear them all the time now, trying to break them in, to make them as unconscious as bedroom slippers or flip-flops, and I also wear the black Lycra practicewear I got at Target.

The foyer looks strange with all the furniture smashed into the living room and the floors so naked. Like I'm moving, or maybe like I was never here in the first place.

"To hell with feng shui," I tell Marita, who solemnly nods. "Anything that gets in the way of dance is bad karma."

But when I flip on the speaker system and the Gipsy Kings come roaring out, she smiles. She will not dance with me, firmly shaking her head as I try to pull her into my bad salsa, but she stands on the broad, curved staircase, watching as I sway, first

73

side to side and then forward and back.

The music is so loud that it takes a minute for me to realize the doorbell is ringing. I pull it open to find an ostentation of the neighborhood ladies clustered on the stoop. That's what Mark used to call them when they were all together, an ostentation of ladies, and I think he got the term from what they call a group of peacocks. But despite the fact he made fun of their super-charged Range Rovers and designer bags, he always urged me to go with these women whenever they called to invite me to some sort of shopping outlet or garden show or play. He wanted me to have friends in the community. It bugged him, I think, that this was always more his home than mine.

The ostentation walks the development every morning, a reasonably ambitious undertaking, for the yards in this neighbor-hood are so large and the homes so spread apart that one lap equals over two miles. They usually do it twice. Right after Mark died they stopped by often, but I rarely went with them, and at times did not even bother getting out of bed and coming downstairs to open the door. After a while they gave up, just as after a while they stopped bring-ing by their offerings of jams, cakes, and pastries. It's a southern thing, I guess, this compulsion to bake after someone dies. Ever since I was a child I've always associated the taste of sugar with grief.

"Hello," they chorus as I open the door.

It's the usual conversation. Come and walk the circle, they say. It will be good for you to get out. But the few times I pulled on my Nikes and went with them, it hadn't been good for me at all. They eat and then they walk to work off what they've just eaten, and then they go home and cook some more and while they walk they talk about who is sick or dying or cheating or drinking or not quite as well off as she seems. It's exhausting in ways that have nothing to do with four miles.

"I'm sorry," I say, even though it's nice of them to ring my doorbell after all this time. Nice of them to keep trying when I give them so little encouragement. "I know I need to walk, but today I'm moving furniture."

They look at me with collective doubt. I am in my dance heels and black practicewear and the Gipsy Kings are yodeling now.

"How are you doing?" one of them asks. It strikes me as a real question, sincerely meant, and deserving of a real answer.

"I think I'm doing better," I tell her.

"You look better," she says. "You look . . . tall."

"It's the shoes."

They back down the steps, their chatter fading with them. "Marita," I say as I close the door, for she is still standing on the staircase. "Do you think I really am doing better?"

"*Si,*" she says. *"Mucho mejor."*

That night, in Mark's study, I read about the instructors on the Canterbury Ballroom webpage and try to weave in what they say about themselves in their bios — the European competitions they've danced in, their schooling and stated ambitions — with the shards of information I've picked up during my lessons. Anatoly is the owner of the studio, the man I saw dancing the first day I went in, and he's been in the country the longest. He calls himself "the founder of the ballroom," a touchingly elevated term for a business that employs three people in a fifteen-hundred-square-foot storefront.

Anatoly is twenty-seven and Nik is twenty-four, but they both claim to have been dancing for more than twenty years, a fact that — if true — suggests a way of life I will never understand. The absence of a childhood, the sort of drive it would take to leave one world and start again in another, and how much this Canterbury Ballroom must matter to them, how many dreams it holds. They want to become Americans, they say. They want condos and cars. To drive to California with the top down, to send their children to Harvard. Their desires are unapologetic. They list them right there in their bios.

The forty-five minutes of my lesson time are holy, so we rarely stop to talk, but still, in the course of dancing, Nik and I have shared random pieces of our history. I know that he was eight when he was selected from his village school to go to the dance academy in Moscow. He knows that I was twelve when I hyperextended my knee at cheerleading camp. He misses his mother. I am a widow. He's allergic to peanuts and I like Ella Fitzgerald. He is in the United States on a student visa. That's the best way to get into this country, he says, and I start to ask him where he's studying, before it hits me. His schedule at the dance studio is brutal . . . thirteen lessons a day. He isn't studying anywhere.

As three weeks turn into four and one month into two, the studio continues to obsess me, like a new lover. Whenever I go to the grocery I park at the far side of the lot so I have an excuse to walk past and peek in the door, to try to figure out who's in there and what they're doing. Normally, I keep a daily to-do list, with everything carefully recorded, but I never write down the time of my dance lesson. I don't have to. Thursday at four o'clock is where my week begins and ends and at times I think it's strange . . . why I have taken to it so quickly, how dance has moved from something I always sort of meant to try to becoming my religion. I wonder if I'm nothing more than just one of those lonely women who flits from Korean cooking to basketweaving and then I stop myself. It's not the same. God knows, through the years I've decorated and redecorated, I've eaten and dashed to burn off what I've just eaten and then eaten again. I've pickled my vegetables and woven my baskets and that was nothing more than a way to escape from my mind and body, to fill my hours without emotion or thought, while this . . . even in just a few weeks, dance has pressed me back into my body, forced me to think and feel things I've avoided for years.

Nik knows all this. He knows I always get there early, so that I can sit on the couch and watch the other lessons. The student in his three o'clock slot is a petite woman named Pamela. He has used the words "yesterday" and "tomorrow" with her, so evidently she takes a lesson every day. She must be a whale, which is what they call the people who spend the most money, those who think nothing of dropping four thousand dollars on a ball gown or flying their instructor to Vegas for a weekend competition. Just one or two whales can keep a whole studio going, so they must be nurtured carefully. Everyone stops what they're doing when Pamela comes in. They greet her with enthusiasm, as if she has just returned from a long trip.

Pamela is a Silver level dancer, which is pretty high up on the competition ladder. First there is Newcomer, which I guess is what I am, and then most people dance Bronze, which has many subcategories: Pre-Bronze, Bronze I and II, Bronze Open, and Bronze Closed. It's incomprehensible to me, like levels of the military, and I never can keep straight who is supposed to salute to whom. But this woman is clearly far above me and I study her while I am pretending to check e-mail on my phone or fiddling with my shoes. Pamela looks like a little doll when she swirls.

Nik has watched me watching her, so I know it's only a matter of time until he starts pressuring me to take more lessons. And why not? I have the money and it's getting harder and harder to wait all week for Thursday to roll around. Besides, we started with Latin, the sexy stuff, but then after spying on Pamela I told him I wanted to try the more formal dances too, things like waltz and foxtrot. The studio is like a little Baskin-Robbins, so many colors and flavors. You get a taste of one on your plastic spoon and it's good, but then something else starts to look even better.

Today we're working on the foxtrot, which he says is both the easiest and hardest dance. The steps and timing are simple — slow and slow backward, then quick-quick to the side, a neat little L-shaped pattern across the floor. But to do it well is difficult, involving heel leads and toe releases that when placed together form a sort of gliding movement that makes it seem as if you're skating across ice. The Bronze and Silver students curse when they're practicing, so the beauty of an advanced foxtrot apparently comes at a high price. A minute to learn and a lifetime to master, I guess, like that board game Othello that Mark and I used to play, but I'm not to the point yet where I have to worry about technique. When I asked Nik if we could focus on foxtrot today, he said yes, that I should enjoy it while I can.

We're in the corner practicing underarm turns when Anatoly suddenly looks up from his desk and says, "What is the capital of Tallahassee?"

There's a moment of silence and then Quinn says, very gently, "Tallahassee is the capital of Florida." She's constantly helping Anatoly study for his citizenship exams and I guess Nik will try to qualify after that. It worries me. Nik seems so vulnerable, connected to no one, a twenty-four-year-old on a student visa that eventually has to run out. I know he's allergic to peanuts, but I don't know where he lives, or with whom, or how much of my weekly eighty-five dollars he gets to keep.

"You should do two lessons," Nik says. "Tuesday and Friday."

"Maybe," I say. I don't know why I'm stalling him when he and I both know I'll end up doing it. I wonder how many thousands of lessons you have to take before they teach you Silver steps.

He walks me through a few more turns and a twinkle, then we go over to the computer to pick out songs. I like this part, where we begin to put the movement to music, even though I make lots of mistakes.

Music seems different to me lately. I listen for the beat. I surf among stations while I drive, trying to figure out what you would dance to each song, whether it's a samba or a salsa or a tango. Foxtrot music is especially great, all the big-band stuff from the old MGM movies. Nik points at the screen, his fingertip hovering above "Fly Me to the Moon."

He's considering it because it's slow, I realize, an easy practice song, but I don't care. When I was growing up my dad loved that song. Our shaky old hi-fi was as big as my bunk bed and I can remember albums stacked up to drop, one at a time, onto the turntable. It was the era of the Rat Pack, and space exploration. Telescopes on the front lawns of suburban houses, Tang on the breakfast table, and our teachers pushing TVs into our elementary school classrooms so that we could watch the astronauts coming and going. We were so sure that someday we'd all have flying cars, robot maids, and rocket-ship vacations. Everyone was wrapped up in the race to the moon and it was the Russians we were racing against. I start to ask Nik what it was like over there, then I remember he's a kid. The space race was over before he was born.

He points at "Fly Me to the Moon." "You

like this?"

"Very much."

We walk back to the corner and he invites me into hold. "If you do not want two lessons, you should take group classes," he says. "Much more practice for not much more money."

"How many seats are in the Senate?" Anatoly calls out.

"A hundred," Quinn yells back. "Two per state."

"Hold the slow-slow," Nik says. "You are rushing."

"I don't know about group," I say. They just put the October schedule on the wall beside the bathroom. At fifteen dollars a class or a hundred dollars a month for unlimited classes, the group classes are a definite steal, so I suspect they're populated by people looking to stretch their dollar or maybe, even worse, people who are dancing to meet potential dates, who consider this whole thing a social outing. Since I take my lessons in the afternoons, I haven't encountered many of my fellow students, most of whom come in at night after work, and I'm terrified at the thought of dancing with another civilian. Nik makes it easy. He puts me where I need to be and I would imagine that all the students who take private lessons are similarly dependent upon their instructors.

"I need a few more private lessons before I take group," I tell Nik. "Look. I'm even screwing up a silly underarm turn."

"Slow down," he says. "You have four whole steps to make turn. Slow, slow, quick-quick. You are back to me too soon."

"I don't want to be late."

"You are early."

"Isn't that better?"

"No. In true dance when man leads and lady follows, she is just behind him in time. Not a whole beat, not a second, just a —"

"Millisecond?"

"Yes. So slow down. Is better that I wait on you than you wait on me."

"Well, all right," I say. "But I always like to get to places early."

"I know," he says, with a trace of a smile. "You are nerd."

I laugh. He may be the only person who's ever figured that out about me.

We try it again, and damn if I don't make a four-beat turn in three beats. I'm back so fast that I've pulled us off the count and he has to hold us still for a second before he makes the next move.

"What are you scared will happen," Nik says in my ear, "if man has to wait for you?"

The question startles me. I stop dancing entirely and look at him. "I don't know. I never had enough guts to find out. Maybe I'm afraid that if I take my time, that when I get back, you will have disappeared. Gotten bored and gone off to dance with some other girl."

Or died, I think, but I don't say that part.

He is still smiling. "Let me wait for you. Is my job. I promise you I will not disappear."

One more song, one more slow shuffle around the floor and then the clock says 3:47 and he walks me back over to the desk, the two of us holding hands, as we often do. "Explain to her," he says to Quinn, "how all students must take group class."

"Is Pamela going to take group?" I ask Quinn.

A beat of silence is the answer. Of course she won't.

"Will make us stronger studio," Nik says.

Quinn nods. "It's true. Anatoly is really pushing it because he thinks if we're going to start showing well at competitions, the whole studio needs more practice. I've even talked Steve into starting with the new cycle and believe me, that wasn't easy."

Steve is the guy I saw practicing the heel lead the day I came in for my introductory lesson. He's the studio's only male whale, and he seems completely wrapped up with Quinn. During their lessons they talk as much as they dance, always huddling into corners to confer about something, and I can't imagine him risking the public humiliation of group. When two pros dance together, they're golden. A pro and an amateur are okay. But when two people who don't know what they're doing attempt to dance together . . . it could get ugly real fast.

"He's a doctor, isn't he?" I ask.

"How many justices sit on the Supreme Court?" Anatoly asks.

"Nine," Quinn says, and then to me, "He's a plastic surgeon. Don't tell me you haven't seen his billboards."

"Oh God," I say. That's where I know him from. "He's Dr. Boob."

I don't know why it's taken me so long to figure this out. Steve's face has gazed down at me from billboards located at the most desirable intersections in town for years, along with the words NOT JUST BIGGER. BETTER. His picture is almost too perfect to be real: the slight pucker of concern between his eyebrows, the brushstrokes of white at his temples, the large and uniform teeth. There have been times I've looked up at him during red lights and wondered if they hired an actor to play the part. Like someone phoned Central Casting and said, "Send us a tall, good-looking doctor-type whom women will trust."

"He doesn't like it when people call him that," Quinn says quickly, and a little defensively. "He devotes three days a month to pro bono reconstruction for the uninsured survivors of breast cancer, you know." She says this rat-a-tat, clearly a prepared speech she's given many times before, and I nod, wondering at the strange alliance between a plastic surgeon and a woman as unorthodox as Quinn. She's the un-Barbie, with her cartoon skin and spiky hair and the little belly that hangs over the top of her yoga pants, and she's smarter than anyone might guess. I thought there were seven people on the Supreme Court.

"I'm sure he's a great doctor," I say. "Devoted to his work."

"So you come to group," Nik says, nodding vigorously, as if it's all been decided. "If Dr. Boob can do this thing, so can you."

"Now they've roped me into a group class five times a week," I tell Carolina. I've come by, as I often do, right after my lesson to show her my new steps. It is hard to demonstrate an underarm turn with no arm to turn under, but she sits up patiently in bed with the Taco Bell bag in her lap and watches me try. When I stop, she claps.

"What's wrong with group class?"

"Just the fact that there are other people there. You know those plastic surgery bill-boards that say NOT JUST BIGGER. BET-TER.? That guy will be there." I start to tell her he does free reconstruction but I'm not sure what the idea of new breasts might mean to a woman who's already in hospice. But once again today she looks great, like someone who might rally and make it out of here. It doesn't happen often but it does happen. She has plowed through her burritos and sweet iced tea.

"Why do guys like that even take lessons?" she asks. "He can't have any trouble meeting women."

"I don't know," I say, taking off my dance shoes and sitting down in the chair opposite the bed. "Everybody has their own reasons, I guess. I think people look to dance to give them whatever's lacking in their day-to-day lives. You know, they want to feel elegant or sexy or feminine or powerful or something that normal life doesn't offer. So they go into the studio and for forty-five minutes a week they get to tap into that fantasy part of their lives."

"Sounds like you need to do it more than once a week."

A strange little dig, but I let it slide. "Group class might make me worse. The civilian dancers . . . we're not very good. I've watched group a couple of times and the instructor shows everybody a step and then they line up all the men on one side of the room with the women facing them. You rotate through, until you've practiced it with everybody, but some of these guys . . . I swear you can practically smell the fear on them. They hold out their arms to the women and they're shaking, and it becomes this great big circle of nerves. Everybody gets worse and worse, even the ones who started out pretty good. You know what I mean? You'd think the good dancers would make the bad ones better, but it's more like the bad ones are making the good ones worse. Everybody sinks to the lowest common denominator."

"How's Dr. Boob?"

"He hasn't started group yet either. He might not. His instructor just thinks he needs the practice."

"So he's a snob like you."

I stick out my tongue at her.

"I think you should do it," she says.

"Practice is practice and they can't all stink. Tell you what. Go to one class and report back to me. It's an assignment. Tell me who the other people are and what they want. You like figuring people out."

"I do?"

"Yeah," she says, balling up the Taco Bell bag and throwing it toward the wastebasket. She misses and it bounces across the floor. "You like sitting in the corner pretending to be busy but the whole time you're just secretly trying to figure other people out."

The first day of October falls on a Monday so Quinn is teaching jive. This doesn't seem like an auspicious start. Jive — despite its all-American, Victory Garden, bebopping roots — is rumored to be technically difficult. Whenever I ask Nik to show me the steps he always says "Next time."

I decide that jive calls for a full skirt, a bright red top, a high ponytail. The schedule I've stuck on my refrigerator door says that tomorrow is tango and for that I have my long fringe black skirt and my hair, I think . . . it should be slicked back again, but this time, nothing that bounces. Maybe a low chignon. It's silly. I know it is. I'm on the verge of becoming my own tablescape. But I've done this all my life and I can't seem to stop. I know how to pick out clothes to create a certain effect — how to be sweet, and smart and sexy and sophisticated and pretty much anything the occasion demands. It's all about the costume, because people don't look hard and they don't look deep. Ninety-nine percent of the time they just treat you like your clothes.

But after I'm dressed, I have a moment of doubt. As I'm walking out of the bedroom I look back and think how easy it would be to just get in bed and close my eyes. No one is counting on me to be there. I told Nik I would come, but he didn't believe me. Wouldn't be surprised in the least if I bailed. It's nearly dark outside the window and in a few weeks, after the time change, seven o'clock will be darker still. And most of all, it makes me nervous to think about dancing with a group of strangers. Moving into the arms of men, rotating from one to the other, having to smile and tell them all my name.

For a minute I give in to the temptation. I lie down on the bed, with my ponytail jabbing so awkwardly into the back of my head that I roll to my side and curl up in a little ball. The TV remote is on the bedside table and the top drawer is crammed full of menus from every takeout place in town.

Nothing has to change. That's what the lawyer told me. I could lie here forever and the world would still go on.

Elyse has always said that there are small moments that knock your life one way or another, the way an unseen rock beneath the surface of water can nudge a canoe off its course. She claims it's the tiny stuff that makes or breaks a life — or a marriage — and the first time she told me this was on my wedding day, as she and I sat on this very same bed stuffing her squirming daughter Tory into a flower-girl dress. Elyse had been doing all the right things that morning, smiling and chattering and popping champagne corks and muttering over the dozens of small silk-covered buttons on the back of Tory's dress, but I don't think she expected much from my marriage. She wasn't sure it would be enough and that's when she said it, how it was the little things that could break you. The disappointment you brush off, the compromise that seemed worth it at the time, all the comments you let slide, even if they sting.

You've got to figure out which of these small moments matter, she said. Which ones look small but are really big. And when you find them, you have to dig in and fight. Because otherwise you wake up someday, almost as if from a dream, and find that you've drifted to a place you don't even recognize. You don't know how you got there and you don't know how to get back. She looked up at me, her eyes suspiciously bright, and said, "No kidding, Kelly, it just happens. All of a sudden you're bewildered by your own life."

I didn't want to believe her. She was starting to come out of her marriage just as I was going into mine, and our friendship has always been like this, a bit out of sync. Oh sure, we've had all the same experiences, but we seem to have had them at different times, like two women stuck in the same revolving door, and even though we're often exasperated by life's strange timing, I think we count on it too. It's the way we protect and rescue each other. Like when we were younger and we had that rule that only one of us could get drunk at a time. Somebody had to drive.

But I cut her off on the morning of my wedding, before she could get going on one of her full-blown speeches or, maybe worse, start to cry. Yes, her marriage may have been disappointing, but that was Elyse. She has always expected too much out of life — and way too much out of men. And thus it was her destiny to be constantly disappointed, and I told myself I wasn't like that. I had always been the practical one who knew how to make do and adapt. To admit that Elyse had a point would have been to admit that my marriage also might fail, that I too might end up alone.

I turn, look at the clock: 6:25. I still have plenty of time. And I know this is one of those small moments when things could as easily go one way as another. I could march downstairs, get in the car, drive to the studio, and face my fears, or I could pull this annoying clasp from my hair and go back to sleep once again. Drift just a little farther down the river of dreams.

I arrive at the studio at six-fifty and lurk around watching the others file in. Pamela enters and I'm surprised she's deigned to try group, but she goes off into a corner by herself and begins practicing arm movements in the mirror. And then I get swept up in rapid-fire chatter with a woman in a pink angora shell named Isabel who before I can tell her my name announces she's been married three times and has a crush on Nik. "My husband can't believe I'm spending the money," she whispers, "and I tell him it's for exercise, which of course doesn't make any sense because the Urban

Fitness place up the street is like twenty bucks a month. But I figure ballroom's cheap when you factor in the BFE."

"BFE?" I ask blankly, watching another clump of people come through the door. A slim black man in a newsboy cap, two women in jeans, one of them stunningly tall. A gaggle of teenagers.

"You know how when men go to call girls they can pay extra and get the GFE?" she says, bending so close to me I can smell her tropical shampoo. "That means if you like double the price or something you get the girlfriend experience. The whore will go to dinner with you and kiss you and pretend like she likes you. I figure when I get to dance with Nik on Wednesdays, he's my boyfriend experience."

I doubt Nik would appreciate the analogy. "So you take private lessons?"

"When I can," Isabel says, "but I have to put it all on plastic. Group's my regular fix. I mean, Quinn teaches most of them and the guy students suck, but sooner or later Wednesday's here and Nik puts his arm around me. Money well spent. And who knows? I might sell a kidney and compete at the Holiday Classic down in Hotlanta. You going?"

"God no," I say. I haven't heard anybody

call Atlanta "Hotlanta" in thirty years. "I just started." From across the room Nik gives me a little wave, like he's glad that I'm here.

A few others drift in. A chubby and prematurely bald man whom Isabel introduces as Harry, evidently another regular, and a pretty young girl named Valentina who greets Nik and Anatoly in Russian. "Bought and paid for on the Internet," Isabel whispers. "Her husband's about a hundred but she's real sweet." One of the women in jeans retreats to the back couch, where she pulls knitting out of a big sack, while the tall one leans down to put on her dance shoes. "Lesbians," Isabel whispers. "Jane's the one who dances and she takes most of her private lessons with big, bad Anatoly, who likes to whip his ladies around and make them submit, you know what I mean, to his throbbing, masculine will. The other one just sits there knitting and watching him work her over. Makes you wonder what happens when the two of them get home, doesn't it?" It's all I can do to keep from laughing, but I've got to admit, Isabel's an absolute gold mine of information. I should just bring her to Carolina's room tomorrow, sit her down on the bed, and pull her string.

"Okay, let's get started," Quinn says, walking to the center of the room, and the regulars fall into a line. I stand at the end. Quinn tells us a few things I already know about the jive — quick, sharp movements and lots of bounce — and then the door opens and Steve strides in. Maybe he planned it this way, making his big entrance after we're already lined up, but Quinn gives him the same sort of smile Nik gave me: Thanks for coming, for being a team player. She takes us through the jive basic — a three-step shuffle to the right, then the left, ending with a rock step. Everyone seems to know that much at least, so she quickly adds on a little turn that ends with the couple in a sweetheart pose, shoulder to shoulder with their arms around each other's back. It doesn't seem to be a terribly hard step, but it's cute and it does require the man and woman to be quite close when they rock back. She teaches us the women's part, which is almost always the showiest and most complicated, and we practice on our own while she walks the men through their steps.

Then she says, "Here's what the whole thing looks like with a partner."

Apparently the highlight of group class is when the instructor chooses a student to demonstrate. In theory, the student is pulled from the line at random but I don't think any of us are clueless enough to buy that. The instructor is going to choose a student who he or she thinks can demonstrate the sequence with ease; otherwise you risk destroying the confidence of the remaining pupils before they even begin. The logical thing for Quinn to do is choose Steve, who not only takes plenty of private lessons but takes them with her. But when she glances at him, he makes a great show of checking his phone, pulling it from his pocket and frowning as if he's just been informed of some breast-related emergency. She settles instead on the obviously eager Harry, who stumbles gracelessly through it, counting out loud the whole time.

"Do we need another demonstration?" she asks. We sure as hell do. She says, "Pamela, would you care to show us how it looks from the feminine point of view?" Nik comes over from behind his desk to demonstrate with Pamela, and they run the sequence flawlessly. Pamela gives us a dismissive little smile as she walks back to the mirror, and it occurs to me that she's chosen to demonstrate all the time. This is probably why she's hanging around the studio during the group class hour, for this brief moment in which it's clear she's the special one.

Now we're ready to try it together. Quinn puts on "Crazy Little Thing Called Love" but slows it down so much that it sounds like Freddie Mercury has gargled glue. Each man is paired with a woman and Quinn directs me toward the dapper black man, who says his name is Lucas. There are a couple of women left over, which I suspect is typical, and for this round they dance alone. I envy them. Lucas and I go into Latin position, my hand at the base of his neck, his hand low on my hip. Quinn counts us down.

We get through it surprisingly well. Surprising considering this is the first time I've danced with anyone other than Nik, and I feel a surge of adrenaline when Lucas and I manage to finish facing the right direction, each on the correct foot.

"Good," says Quinn. "Rotate."

We slip down a man and the ladies who were solo now dance with a partner. I'm alone through this cycle, which gives me the chance to sharpen up my timing a little and watch the others. The tall lesbian named Jane is very good, I notice, very precise. But she keeps her steps small and her body tightly reined in. Isabel, who's a foot shorter, covers more ground.

Quinn moves us down the line of men again, so I am now with Harry. I soon realize that his need to vocalize is not limited to the demonstrations. He stutters out the name of each step as he makes it, which would be fine except I have to remember that he's calling out the man's part, so when he says "left" I have to go right and when he says "back" I should step forward. It's a little disconcerting but we make it through. Rotate.

Surprisingly, it's fun. The clock already says seven thirty. In one corner Anatoly is with Wilhelmena, the old lady from the first day I came into the studio, and in the other corner Nik is with a woman I've never seen, who's dressed as if she's come straight from work. There are people sitting at the bar in the back, drinking wine and talking. The studio is a hive of activity after dark, I think, a little ashamed of myself for being so reluctant to come at night. Carolina's right. I'm a snob.

Quinn gives us a couple of tips about what we're supposed to be doing with our heads and hands, which of course gives everyone a bit more to think about, and then I rotate down to Steve and it all falls apart.

I don't have the words to sufficiently

describe the horror of dancing with this man. He is Jell-O. Soft in his arms, in his hips, in his whole frame. His hand on my back is so ineffectual that I quickly flash back to Mark, after the first heart attack, trying to have sex without getting too excited, the frightening feel of a frightened man in your arms. He does not turn me. I turn myself but he is slow in his own turn so we clang our shoulders together when we try to go into the sweetheart pose and I rock back before him, almost pulling him off his feet. He looks down his patrician nose at me.

"Don't rush it," he says. "You were early on the rock step."

Don't rush it? I'm flooded with rage. I was completely on the beat. He was slow. He wouldn't have gotten into the closing position at all if I hadn't practically yanked him there and then he tells me not to rush it?

"Just one more thing tonight," Quinn says. She's been dancing her way down the line, switching between taking the male and female roles, and her forehead has a slight glow of moisture. I'm suddenly conscious that I'm sweating too. She shows us how to roll out of the sweetheart pose and back into basic and then we try the whole thing a couple of more times. Luckily, I'm once again at the point in the cycle where I just dance by myself.

"Next time we'll crank up the tempo and start on open kicks," she says. "By the end of the month we'll have a nice little routine."

I'm humming as I go back over to my stuff and begin to unbuckle my shoes. "We all go down to Esmerelda's for the five-dollar margaritas after class," Isabel says. "Want to come?"

"Sure," I say. "Everybody?"

"Well, everybody except Lucas. He's a Southern Baptist preacher and they'd have his head on a platter if they even knew he came here to dance, much less drink. And the instructors don't come. Anatoly doesn't think they should fraternize with the students. You know, got to keep their distance and all that. But the rest of us, sure."

"I'm in," I say, and we all change shoes and step out into the night. I love this time of year, when you know fall is coming. Jane's lover has pushed her way out from the couch to join us and to my surprise Steve and Pamela are both tagging along too.

"What's your favorite dance?" I ask Harry, who's beside me.

"Tango," he says, and to prove it he does a big jerky promenade down the sidewalk in front of the grocery.

"Bye, Lucas," Isabel calls out, and the preacher waves before climbing into his sagging gray car. "He's a good person," she says. "I don't know what sort of God would try to make a man ashamed to dance."

Esmerelda's is the kind of strip-center Mexican where they have sombreros and silver-framed mirrors on the wall and the chips and salsa on the table before you halfway sit down. "How long did you say you've been dancing?" Isabel asks me, as we wait to be seated.

"Six weeks maybe. No, more like eight."

"So was it a shock when the price went up?"

I roll my eyes.

"Yeah," she says with a giggle, interpreting the eye roll exactly as I hoped she would. "Here's the thing. Ballroom is cocaine and Anatoly knows it. He gives it to you free at first, then fairly cheap, and once he knows they have you completely hooked, that's when the price begins to climb."

"If my husband were here, he'd say we're all paying good money just to be flattered."

Isabel snorts. Not a play snort but an actual honk, like she's blown her nose. "Flattered?" she says. "Maybe the whales are flattered. The rest of us are paying good

103

money — rent money, car payment money, or at least Time Warner Cable bill money — just so we can fail at something."

Before I can ask her what she means by that a voice at my shoulder says, "That's a gorgeous ring."

Pamela has come out of nowhere to stand on the other side of me and has apparently managed to appraise my diamond ring at a glance. I don't know why I didn't take it off before I came to class.

"It's a family heirloom," I blurt out. "My mother's."

Why did I go and say that? I'm a terrible liar. I never can manage to keep the details straight. Now I've got to remember to pretend my mother is dead. Isabel makes a little tsk-tsk sound of consolation but Pamela isn't fooled in the least, and why should she be? One trophy wife can spot another at a hundred paces.

The server gestures that she's finally pushed together enough two-tops to make a table for eight, and we all start to file toward the back of the restaurant.

"I'm grubby," I say. "Where's the bathroom?"

"You always have to wash your hands thoroughly after group," says Pamela. I'm not sure how she knows this, since apparently she's never done group. "The women scare the men so bad their hands sweat. Come on, I'll show you."

She leads me down a dark-paneled wall to the little ladies' room, where we take turns rinsing our palms over the bright yellow and blue ceramic sink.

"You dance with Nik, right?" she says, looking at her reflection in the mirror as she talks.

"Right," I say. She already knew this. "My lesson is right after yours on Thursday. He's great."

She cuts off the water with her elbow and wipes her hands. "Yeah, he is," she says. "But don't get too attached."

I pull down a paper towel. "Why would I get attached?"

"You're single, right?"

My mind flashes back to Isabel and her BFE. "Yeah, but come on. He's a baby. His bio says twenty-four. It's a little sick that we're even dancing with him, don't you think?"

She doesn't answer. Just uses her forearms to open the door without touching the knob, and we walk back to the table.

When we get there, only two open seats are left — on either side of Dr. Boob.

■ ■ ■ ■

"I may as well not have been there," I'm telling Elyse an hour later on the phone. "First he flirts with the Russian Internet bride and then some poor little mess in angora who's the studio gossip, and then he moves on to this Silver dancer who, get this, orders chicken tortilla soup without the chicken or the tortillas, and he finishes up by hitting on a pair of lesbians. And all he says to me all night is that I rushed the rock step."

"Do you even like this guy?"

"God, no. Can you imagine dating a plastic surgeon who specializes in breasts? It would be the lowest circle of hell."

"Then why does it matter?"

"It doesn't. I don't even know how we got off on this doctor guy when I was calling to tell you that I had a good time. I'm going back for tango tomorrow."

"We got off on him because every man you've ever met has automatically fallen in love with you at first sight and for some reason this guy didn't. Of course it bugs you."

I walk off the deck and toward the back lawn with the phone pressed to my ear. The soil in the garden is soft and loamy, causing my heels to sink in like little golf tees, and with the next step I stumble, making a noise loud enough that all the way from Arizona Elyse asks me what's wrong.

"Remember how we always used to say that when we got old we were going to move to Scotland?"

"Sure," says Elyse. "We were going to get a job as caddies and wear sensible tweeds and stomp around in the mist."

"How old did you think we'd be when we were wearing those sensible tweeds?"

"I don't know. Maybe seventy? Eighty?"

"Exactly. We had a plan for when we were young and we had a plan for when we were old, but we forgot to make a plan for all those years in between. So what's a woman supposed to do between the ages of fifty and seventy? There's at least twenty years in life when you're not young and you're not old and there's absolutely no plan."

"We've sailed into uncharted territory," Elyse says. Her voice is light, breathy, almost on the edge of a laugh. Maybe she's agreeing with me or maybe she's only pretending to agree with me to humor me out of my mood. I look down at the rosebushes. A few buds are still intact and I give one a yank. I think it's one of the Moonstones, white with a pink center, but it's hard to see colors in the darkness so it might be a First Kiss or a Mermaid. I should scavenge whatever blooms are left for Carolina. She'd probably like them. She likes everything.

I ordered the rosebushes from catalogs when we first moved here, more romanced by the sounds of the names than by any thought of how the colors would look together or what would thrive in this crumbly clay soil. I don't particularly like roses themselves, or even the way they smell, but I do love their names, which sound like small promises. The garden came together so well that they put our house on the cover of *Charlotte Fine Living* magazine with me pictured in the foreground, sitting on a white silk couch that the photographer and his assistant had carried off the back of a truck and placed in the middle of the flowers. "She chose her roses by their names" was the first line of the article, a statement that makes me sound dreamy and a little bit daft, but everyone agreed that the picture of me sitting on that white couch in a white dress, gazing into the center of a Moonstone, was proof that our garden — that our very marital existence — was a great success.

"Kelly?" Elyse's voice is flickering. I must

have walked too far from the house. "Did you say something? You're breaking up."

"When it comes to men, I'm over," I tell Elyse. "I'm like a garden at the end of a season."

"Some weird stuff has come out of your mouth lately but that's the craziest thing you've said yet. You're all about men and you always have been. More than anybody I know. That doesn't just end with the snap of a finger."

"But what happens if you're sexual and you don't have anybody to be sexual with? I'll be like that tree that falls in the forest and nobody's there to hear it so it doesn't make a sound."

"I always thought that tree made a sound."

"That's not the point."

"You're the one who brought it up."

"It was an illustration, Elyse. A metaphor. Men don't see me anymore and that bothers me, even if they're crappy men I never would have wanted in the first place. It's one thing to face the end of sex and it's a whole other thing to face the end of the possibility of sex. I think I need therapy. Or drugs. Do you know what I really need, in all seriousness? I need to meditate."

Elyse laughs. "You just need to get laid." Getting laid is Elyse's remedy for everything. If you told her you'd gone deaf in one ear or wrecked your car, she'd tell you that you just needed to get laid.

# CHAPTER SIX

Elyse and I met at cheerleading tryouts, the summer before ninth grade, and I liked her before I even knew her name. My childhood had been a series of lessons — piano and painting and horseback riding and finally gymnastics. I wasn't particularly good at any of them, but after three years on the balance beam I knew I could handle any namby-pamby routines that a small-town high school cheerleading squad would put together. I was rock solid on a front flip. Pretty good for a back one. And I didn't mind being on the top of the pyramid just as long as I had somebody strong below me. Just as long as I knew that the person designated to catch me when I fell out of formation would really be there.

Elyse was strong. Anyone could tell that at a glance. She's always seemed at home in her body, owning it in a way few young girls do. When I asked her "Can you catch me?"

she said "Ab-so-lute-ly," slowly extending all the syllables in that way that I would later learn meant that she was annoyed by the question. But I scrambled to the top of her shoulders and when that shaky moment came for me to release her hands and stand, it was like we'd been practicing together since birth. I dropped and she caught me, so effortlessly that the judges wanted to make sure it wasn't a fluke. They made us do it again, over and over, until it was time to break for lunch.

"If you ever want to drop, I'll catch you," I told her, even though I wasn't totally sure I could do it. It seemed like the right thing to offer, but she had just tossed back her hair and said, "I don't drop."

When the two weeks of tryouts ended, they not only picked me and Elyse for the varsity squad — making varsity was practically unheard-of for ninth graders — but they put us in the middle of the formation. We were together so much that the older girls called us "the little sisters." Come to think of it, maybe Elyse and I became such fast friends because we were both only children, an unusual condition for that place and time, but whenever the other girls would call us sisters, Elyse would just look at me and wrinkle her nose. Based on what we had observed from our friends who had siblings, we sure didn't want to be compared to sisters. We liked each other.

The first football game of the season was in August. We were sweltering in our woolen turtleneck sweaters with the big blue *B*s on the front, but as I stood there in the gravel outside the stadium, I knew I was incredibly lucky. High school was going to crack right open for me, crack like an egg. When we all lined up to make a tunnel, I stood opposite Elyse and we raised our arms and clasped hands. It was the traditional way our team took the field. The pep band would begin to play and the football players would duck and run beneath the tunnel of the cheerleaders' raised arms, and just as we were standing there waiting for the music to begin, one of the players looked at me and mouthed the words "pretty girl."

Pretty girl, I thought. That's why I'm here. I didn't make the squad because of my front flip, polished though it was. It was more important that I looked the part, and sometime during that last empty summer before high school I had figured out the formula: straight blond hair streaked even blonder through a combination of peroxide, lemon juice, and Sun-In, a swirl of Heaven Sent perfume, short skirts, long T-shirts, and little pots of Yardley makeup. This was what had really earned me my place in the tunnel.

But at the time it didn't matter why I was chosen, just as long as I was. As I turned toward Elyse and leaned my weight into hers, I tried to figure out what I was feeling and came up with the word "thrilled." My mother always described emotion in a collective sense: "We are delighted," she'd announce, or "This isn't exactly what we had hoped for, is it?" Elyse used to laugh and say, "Why does your mother use the royal 'We' — does she think she's Queen Victoria?" It may have sounded grandiose, but it actually, I eventually realized, was my mother's way of informing me that every event has a corresponding official emotion: joy for weddings, sorrow for funerals, modesty for compliments, fear for anything new. Whenever I would find myself in an unexpected situation I would unconsciously spin the Rolodex of adjectives in my mind, looking for the one she would deem the most appropriate. And if it's the first Friday night of the football season and you're wearing a varsity sweater and linking hands with your best friend as the football team runs through the tunnel of your arms and one of those players notices you — then what you're feeling is "thrilled." That must be it.

What other word could there possibly be?

The football player who'd mouthed the words "pretty girl" to me was named Kevin Pressley, and he eventually did ask me out. The best part was that he had an identical twin brother who decided it would be convenient if he liked Elyse, so we could all double. I still consider this the kinkiest thing I've ever done.

Friday nights were for games, so on Saturday the four of us would go to the drive-in, a broken-down sandpit of a place where they showed vintage films. That was where Elyse and I first learned to love old movies. We loved the fact that the women in them were so beautiful, tragic in ways that we would never be, loved the fact that the men all wore double-breasted suits and knew how to kiss, and smoke, and — come to think of it — dance. We sat with a couple in the front seat and a couple in the back and we would watch for a while and then — just when the plot was getting interesting — the guys would begin to do the things that guys do, and at some point, Elyse would make this noise. That's how I learned what kind of noise you're supposed to make. That you don't do it too soon and you don't do it too big and it's not a matter of thrashing around and screaming. I was clever enough to realize that I shouldn't sound exactly like her, so I came up with a response that was a little higher and breathier. Something that I think of as my Marilyn Monroe, in contrast to hers, which I have always suspected was more of an Elizabeth Taylor.

After the first few Saturday nights at the drive-in, we had the protocol figured out. I would make my noise first. It seemed selfish to have everyone waiting on me when Elyse was really the one setting the pace, and this is undoubtedly how the myth was born that I'm an easier come than she is. Because the boys, the poor boys, there was never even a hint or a suggestion that anyone was supposed to do anything for them and maybe that's why they were always jumping out of the car and running off to the snack bar. God knows where they really went or what they really did, but while they were gone, Elyse would climb over into the front seat and we would watch the end of the movie. I would catch her up on the story, since I'd never fully stopped watching, and she never asked how I knew these things, just as I never asked her how she knew all the mysterious things she seemed to know. We would slump against each other, lost in the glamour of the black-and-white story, and at some point she would say, "Do you think there's something wrong with me? I don't know why I'm such a slow come."

My silence on the subject was cruel. It would have derailed anyone other than Elyse, who was and is the most confident person I have ever known. "I don't know why I'm such a slow come," she would say, but she never said this with any particular regret and I suppose I should have learned something, even back then, from her cheerful selfishness and how it never seemed to bother the boys. Not Kevin nor Keith, or whichever one she was with. My memory is fuzzy on this point and besides, I've always suspected that sometimes they switched us, both because they liked doing that creepy twin thing and because of a natural desire to find a more equitable distribution of the workload. It seems unfair to think that week after week they could come into the same drive-in and find themselves cast into such different movies — one of them in an Italian Western, climbing over endless miles of sand and rock, without hope, without water, embroiled in an epic quest for Elyse's elusive orgasm, while the other one, by chance, got the science fiction that was my sexuality, got a woman who only required a couple of clicks to teleport her there.

All women have their secrets, I guess, and this is mine. Through the years that would follow, whenever I look down to see the heads or hands of men between my legs or put my palms on the sides of their hips and look up into their faces, with those awful pained expressions they always get, I feel guilty. I want to tell them not to bother to hold back. They're trying so hard and wasting so much time and it's not their fault, really, it's just something that failed to grow in me. A therapist once called it an inability to relax, but it's more, I think, a reluctance to be greedy, to ask someone who is already trying so hard to try even harder, to inform a man who is already waiting that he must wait a little more. To tell him, in effect, that it doesn't matter if his jaw is aching or his hand has gone numb or his lower back is beginning to spasm, that no, it doesn't matter at all, he must keep going anyway. In those moments it's so easy to . . .

I never say "fake it," not even in my own mind. "Fake" is a harsh word and it's the wrong word. It's just that in those moments it's easy to give him something — a couple of muttered references to religion, a twist of the hips, a moment of held breath followed by a relieved gasp. I'm careful not to overdo it. I think that's a mistake a lot of women make.

And it isn't that I don't like sex. There are parts of it I like very much. I like the beginning, when it's sweet. I like the sense of falling, of a decision being made so fast that it's almost like you're not making it. A decision being made so fast that the next day you can stand in the shower and think words like "inevitable" and "fate." I like it when I lie back and a man looks at me, really looks at me. Intently, as if he's trying to memorize something. It would be enough for me if it stopped right there. I know my breasts are good, and my shoulders, and my waist, and so I am confident to be like this. My hips I'm less sure about — there is a low-slung belt of flesh just below my navel that I have never managed to totally lose and so I leave that part covered as long as I can.

I'm quick to cover up when it's over too, and through the years I've created sarongs out of towels and men's shirts because that's the other part of sex I like — when it's over. The middle — it's okay, I guess, but I sometimes get lost in it, as if I'm flipping through the pages of a very long book.

A Russian novel maybe, with strange names and confusing jumps in time, and at a certain point all I really want is to know the end. Do they live? Does he love her? Will God stoop down and set it all right?

And there are times, in this confusing middle, when my thoughts go back to that drive-in and those Saturday nights, when Elyse would make her noises and I would listen, somehow knowing that with every moan and mumble, our paths were diverging. The noises she made were as ugly as truth. She was actually feeling something. She was being carried away to a place I couldn't follow, and lying there, with the trembling weight of Kevin Pressley beside me, I could see our whole future. Being real was going to make her life more dangerous. Pretending was going to keep me safe.

"Pretty girl," the boy in the helmet said, and from that point on, men have, one by one, written the story of my life.

# CHAPTER SEVEN

"I am the frame," Nik says. "Which makes you . . ."

I'm ready for this one. "The picture."

"Yes. So if we both do our job, then you are the one they see."

He gets me into the proper dance position in stages. "Bend knees," he says. "Incline hips forward, settle your pelvis over mine, then tilt . . . No. Not so far. Your back does not bend. Is optical illusion." I'm surprised he uses the terms "pelvis," "incline," and "optical illusion," but Nik knows a lot of English nouns and verbs. It's the adjectives and adverbs that give him trouble. I don't think that as a language Russian has so many. We practiced the waltz last lesson, so before he has to tell me, I remember to extend my arms, trying to keep my elbows high and level and my chin jutting toward the sky. This is the princess dance. The prettiest and the most masochistic.

"This is good?" he says.

He's incapable of understanding sarcasm, so I don't bother trying. "I'm miserable."

"Don't look to me," he says. "Not to other couples on the floor. Look to line where the floor becomes the ceiling."

The scary part is that I'm beginning to understand him when he talks like that. I stare at the seam where the wall meets the ceiling. He spins me once and I drop my chin. This is your natural impulse when you spin, to tuck your head in and tighten your arms to your body and try to make yourself aerodynamic.

He steps back. "What," he says, "is nature of this dance?"

He asks me this question almost every lesson, so I'm ready. The cha-cha is flirtatious. The tango is passionate. The rumba is sensual and the foxtrot is playful and the jive is energetic. We have discussed all this before.

"Rapturous," I say.

He frowns. "This means?"

"Happy."

"All dance is happy."

Completely not true, but the last ten weeks have taught me that there's no point in arguing with Nik. "Happy in a certain way," I say. "Like when you die and go to heaven. You know, happy like an angel."

He nods. "Is good word." He walks over to his desk, pulls out his iPhone. I spell "rapturous" to him and he types it in.

"Yes," he says, walking back to me. "Like angel, so raise your chin."

I'm trying very hard, but then we go into a series of turns and I lose my form. Why am I so unable to spin? All the other girls can. When I do turns in the cha-cha or the jive, I control my vertigo by looking straight at Nik, but you're not allowed to look at your partner in the waltz, and besides, it's not just a turn here and there. The waltz is a dance of endless circles and maybe this is really why it frightens me.

"I'm sorry," I say. "Shit, I'm so sorry."

He shakes his head. He hates it when I apologize. "Close your eyes."

Against all logic, it works. A little voluntary self-blinding does calm me down but the minute I find myself relaxing, my eyes startle open like that jerk thing you do when you're falling asleep. It scares me to lose my position in the room, to not be able to see where the other couples are, or how close Nik and I are coming to the wall.

"I'm sorry," I say. "It's just that I get dizzy."

"Because your head go back and forth like

123

dog in car."

I glance at the clock. Twenty-five minutes to go. Usually my lesson flies by, but today time is dragging. He walks back over to his desk. Opens a drawer and digs around for a minute, then returns with a scarf.

"Here," he says, handing it to me.

The scarf is silky, a swirl of blue and green, clearly a woman's. "What am I supposed to do with this?"

He sighs, hugely, as if he's regretting the day he first left Moscow. He pulls the scarf from my hands, folds it twice, and ties it around my eyes. The world goes soft and black. The knot in back is tight, tight enough that I can feel the pulse in the dome of my head. I'm too surprised to be angry or frightened.

"Where did you get this?"

"Lady left it. Now we waltz."

I lift my right hand and he pulls me gently toward him. Puts his arm around me, moves me into his side, and in that exact same instant my left hand descends in perfect position and comes to rest lightly on his shoulder. Is anyone watching us? There are other people in the room. Anatoly has a student and I think Quinn is here somewhere too. Does Nik do this with other women? Or is the scarf the sign of the most stubborn, the most hopeless, the ones who can't listen to reason and have to be treated like horses in a burning barn? Nik pulls his leg back from mine and settles into position.

"Breathe," he says sharply.

I exhale and we begin. Are we turning? I think we are but not very much. It feels slow and easy to follow. Maybe it's just like they say on the Discovery Channel — that when you obscure one sense the others become sharper — because I can feel every nuance of the floor beneath my feet and the music sounds more distinct, broken into units. One-two-three, Nik counts, or do I merely think it? The first step of the waltz is the big one, a surge of movement either straight forward or back. The second step is to the side and you rise with it, and then hover on your toes for a split second, stretched to your greatest height before you sink in the third beat. You sink, you rest, you settle, you wait. This is the tricky part of the waltz. This third beat, this part where you hardly move at all, where it is all energy and anticipation and shaping. The third beat is what separates the amateurs from the pros.

The blindfold is helping. I can feel the beats in the music as completely separate spaces, the one-two-three, the surge-rise-fall, and for once in my life, I don't rush the rest. This rhythm is like a wave that comes and lifts you and then there is another. Why would I fight this? Fighting this would be like refusing to float on the surface of water and it's easy to float, isn't it? If you let yourself, floating is the most natural thing in the world.

One song fades and another begins. The melody is different but once again I feel the beat beneath the notes. This must be what they call musicality and everyone says it's the hardest thing to learn. You can't practice it alone in your foyer, the way I practice the steps. Musicality is spontaneous, like God. It's either there when you need it or it's not.

At one point Nik slips behind me, pressing his chest into my back. This is what they call shadow hold, a high Bronze step or maybe even Silver, and I'm tentative at first but then quickly confident. Sure that the floor is there and Nik is there and that the world is safe and steady. I step forward and he turns me. I step again, we turn again, and we fall into a pattern that I cannot see but that I imagine to be like a braid, like two people weaving their way across the room. For a split second, life seems easy. For a split second, I'm rapturous.

"What do you call this step?" I ask him.

His voice is close to my right ear. "Water-fall," he says.

"That's right. I remember."

"We have never done."

We stop. Nik pulls my blindfold down and I blink.

"Better," he says.

I grin. I know I earned that "better."

When I walk to the couch to get my purse, my eye drags by the clock. We've gone over. It's ten minutes after three and Nik never goes over. A minute is money in this business. Every minute is two dollars.

The room is empty. No one else on the floor and no one at the desk. Nik seems surprised too. He turns the music off abruptly, not fading it out in that deejay way like he usually does, and he heads straight across the dance floor. There's a room somewhere in the back where the instructors take their showers and eat their lunches, a cot where they nap between lessons. I sign the schedule on Quinn's desk as I walk out. It's not like Nik to forget to say good-bye or confirm the time of our next appointment, but then it's not like him to go over either.

As I slide into my car seat, I realize I still have the scarf around my neck. It's such a strange thing for Nik to have in a drawer.

The edge says Hermès, and while it's probably one of those fakes that you can buy in the straw market of Nassau or on some side street in New York, it's still somebody's scarf. I pull the visor down and study myself in the mirror. It's tied badly, one big knot in the back like a noose, but it's nice and I don't know why I never wear scarves. I should get one like this, in a mix of blues and greens.

The studio is silent when I walk back in. I start to put the scarf in Nik's drawer, but that's presumptuous, to just go into his little cubicle and mess with his desk. Quinn would know what to do with it, but her desk is on the other side of the room and now that I've held it in my hands for a few minutes, it's dawning on me that perhaps this scarf is a true Hermès, because the pattern is exactly as clear on the back as on the front. In fact, there is no back or front. It isn't hemmed, it's carefully rolled at the edges so that both sides are completely identical.

I was wrong about it being a knockoff. Nik blindfolded me with someone's five-hundred-dollar scarf. This is not the sort of thing a woman would leave behind by accident and I can't just drop it on a desk by the front door. I can't stuff it into some random drawer and I sure as hell can't take it home with me.

I start toward the back room. Nik is probably in there, having his snack or maybe lying down on the cot. I'm holding the scarf out in front of me like it might bite and I'm at the door before I really think about what I'm doing.

One step in the room and I see them. Nik and Pamela.

They aren't embracing. They're standing very close and although Nik stands close to everyone, although people touching other people is pretty much the whole point of this place, I somehow know that dance is not what this is about. Nik lifts his head, but I'm gone before he can speak, back out the door before I'm fully in. It's probably the fastest turn I've ever made in the ballroom.

It's not like I walked in on two people having sex, I try to remind myself as I scurry back across the dance floor. I didn't even interrupt a kiss. But there's no doubt that I've seen something I wasn't meant to see. Pamela isn't as old as I am but she's certainly older than Nik and she gives off the vibe of a well-tended wife. Very dignified, very well dressed. She is, come to think of it, exactly the sort of woman who might own a Hermès scarf.

Quinn is just stepping out of the bathroom as I rush by, humming to herself and rubbing lotion into her hands. "I walked out with this scarf by accident," I say, but Quinn's hands are sticky and she pauses, still twisting them together while I slap the Hermès around in the air. "It's somebody's scarf and I think it's expensive and I'm sorry, I'm so very sorry."

Quinn looks at me quizzically. She must think I'm some sort of kleptomaniac, stealing apples and scarves and then immediately returning to the scene of the crime to confess. I suspect my face is very red.

"He used it to blindfold me," I say. "Because we were waltzing and I was being stubborn but then when I realized I still had it around my neck . . ."

In unison, we both look toward the back room. The lounge, they grandly call it, although it's no bigger than a closet. The instructor's lounge, and just in this moment someone inside is quietly closing the door.

"I should have knocked," I say.

She shrugs. "You were bound to find out eventually," she says. "Everyone does."

# CHAPTER EIGHT

"I want you to promise me something," Carolina says.

"If I can," I say. She's having a bad day. Her quesadilla lies untouched at her side and she's dozed off twice since I got here.

Cancer's ironic. Carolina had looked so good for so long that the supervising doctors had decided they might have been wrong about her. Not wrong about the diagnosis, but about the amount of time she had left. One of them ordered another course of chemo — extraordinary measures are usually verboten in hospice — and told us in the staff meeting that it might buy her a "bonus round." So Carolina has traveled by ambulance to the hospital for treatment and then back and the experience clearly exhausted her. You can't blame the doctor for trying. With someone this young, you always want to hold out hope, but hope is painful and chemo's a double-edged sword.

Now, just two days after it was declared she might get better, she looks much worse.

"It's about the pain," she says.

"Are you in pain now?"

She shakes her head. "When Virginia brings the boys . . . don't let them make me too groggy."

"Okay."

"Keep me right on that place where you're not really hurting but you're not drunk-on-your-ass-out-of-it either. You know what I mean?"

I nod. "The sweet spot."

One of the major responsibilities of hospice is pain management. By the time someone gets to us, they're generally in the last stages of their illness, at the point where doctors stop using verbs like "cure," "remove," and "eradicate" and begin using vague terms like "quality of life," "palliative care," and "keeping her comfortable." These patients are daily reminders of the limitations of medicine, so most doctors would prefer not to see them at all. It's the nurses who make this closing stage of life tolerable. But exactly how to do that is open to debate.

The true mission of hospice — at least in my opinion, although I've never stated this to anyone — is to give people a calm arena in which to think their final thoughts. Not everyone wants this opportunity. Some of our clients come in demanding the highest possible dosages of drugs, a premature sort of oblivion, which the nurses willingly provide them. At the other end of the spectrum are the people who fight any attempts at sedation, the ones who grip the steel bars of their bed frames with surprising strength, the ones who seem determined to suffer. We don't argue with them either. It's not our job to deny people pain any more than it's our job to deny people drugs. I've always figured that if death buys you anything, it buys you the right to stop explaining yourself to strangers.

But this scares the student nurses when they come through on rotation. Like the doctors, they have a surprisingly low tolerance for illness. At least this kind.

"Why don't you give them something?" they ask the staff, wide-eyed and frightened at the sight of such ostentatious suffering. What is it with these people, anyway? Are they religious nuts, deluded into thinking that pain in this life buys them a free ride into the next? Or are they paying the price for some private sin, trying to atone for some mistake they made sixty years ago, or maybe just the failures of last week?

The clients who want drugs are the easiest ones. They require nothing from their nurses but the plunge of a syringe or a pill on a tray. They die as if they have a train to catch. Those who refuse drugs aren't quite as easy, but at least they're understandable. All they want is a witness, someone to watch this final negotiation, to verify whatever deal they're striking with God and to stand at their bedside as impartial as a notary.

It's the ones who fall between these two extremes that keep me up at night. The ones like Carolina.

She's asking for consciousness without pain, and that's tricky. It requires chemistry and math, sure, but also an intuitive sense for each patient's limits and a careful observation of how those limits can vary from day to day. A dose that will send a burly man into a deep and dreamless sleep might have absolutely no effect on the hundred-pound woman in the room beside him. A cocktail that lets a person sail through Monday might leave that same patient trembling and weepy on Tuesday. At this point it's more about soothing the mind than soothing the body, and each human mind, I've come to understand, is a continent unto itself.

"Promise me," Carolina says again. "You'll make them keep me in my right head as long as they can."

"We'll try," I say, even though the nurses don't listen to the volunteers and the doctors don't listen to the nurses and the true trajectory of her care falls to the rarely seen supervising physician. This last round of chemo has left Carolina more morose than I've ever seen her.

"Virginia brings the boys by on Monday, Thursday, and Saturday," she says. I nod. I've seen them. Carolina psyches herself up for these visits. She begins tapering her medication the night before so that she can greet her sons sitting up, sometimes standing. The boys are boys. Two tall, embarrassed-looking teenagers, seemingly unaware of what these visits cost her. They poke each other's arms and complain about things at school, the way their aunt cooks, or about the A-hole coach that benched them. The minute they're gone she's flat on her back again, gripping the sheet with both fists, ready for the shot.

The nurses are for the most part sympathetic people, many of them with kids of their own, and they try to help her with the pain cycles. They know she wants to stay lucid for her boys, but experience has taught them to err on the side of overmedication. They've all been called from their stations by patients awakening in a sea of agony, drowning in it, screaming for someone to throw them a rope. I didn't know it would be this bad. Help me, help me. God damn you, help me, please.

And when things get that far out of hand there's nothing left but large doses, enough medicine to drop a horse. No option except to get them through this night and hope that in the morning some sort of equilibrium can be reestablished, that someone on staff can figure out the right combination. The sweet spot, the fulcrum of the seesaw, that elusive perfect dosage that will allow people to be present in a world full of pain without hurting. The dosage that will allow them to survive another day of being alive.

"Everyone here knows what you're up against," I say, although that's a damn lie. Nobody knows what anybody else is up against. The machines around the bed monitor every modulation of her body, counting breaths and measuring her urine, until the only thing in her life that's still private is the level of her pain. But Carolina has dozed off again and I sit there, picking at her quesadilla and thinking that maybe I really am better suited for hosting banquets and fund-raisers. I am promising this woman things I have no right to promise and I wonder, whether it's a month or a season or longer, if I will have what it takes to see this case to its end.

When I finally leave hospice, I'm drained. I decide to run by the grocery for wine and even, who knows, something sugary and soft. Anything to help me forget this hell of a day.

I pull into the parking lot and sit looking at the studio door. I could walk by like I always do, glance in and maybe wave, but things have shifted now. God knows, I'm in no position to judge Nik, or Pamela either, but I feel oddly complicit, as if by agreeing to keep their secret I have become secretive again myself.

Secretive is the last thing I want to be. My hands are resting against the steering wheel and I glance down at my wedding ring. When I put it on years ago I made a pact with myself to never again sneak around and I didn't, not really, not in any way that counted. I never cheated on Mark and my lies were only the lies of omission: the things I didn't say, those avoidances of truth that might even pass for kindness, especially once he got sick.

After a minute I go into the grocery, arcing all the way across the parking lot, weaving my way through the cars, doing anything I can do to avoid passing the studio. But when I come out, a few minutes later, I've decided I'm being ridiculous. If I want to keep dancing with Nik, and I do, I'll have to eventually go back in and face him. I decide to walk by the ballroom and wave as usual, to send a clear signal that finding him with Pamela in the instructor's lounge was no big deal.

But they're still in there. Dancing, just the two of them. The fact that I walked in on them did not compel her to flee, which surprises me. When I was having my affair with Daniel I was nervous and jumpy all the time, a woman who startled with every ringing doorbell or honking car.

They're doing the tango. I stand on the sidewalk, in the afternoon heat, and watch them through the smudged glass. Both have their eyes closed. The music sounds like a heartbeat, coming dimly through the walls of the studio, synchronizing with the rise and fall of my own chest. He holds her closely, in the Argentine fashion, and their feet weave, his among hers and then hers among his. Her head is on his chest and his arms are loose, embracing. He's lost his frame, I think, somewhat irrelevantly. He has let her give him her weight.

But this is not normal dancing. I am watching sex. It's what I gave up and what I gave up on, what I turned away from years ago. On one level they are dressed and in public and doing no more than a proper Argentine tango, and yet on another level, this is more raw and passionate than anything I might have witnessed in that curtained-off room, probably as sexual as anything they do in bed. He advances toward her. She pulls away. Only a little, like the quivering string of a violin. It is a slow and protracted sort of chase, for what one person wants, the other doesn't, at least not at the same moment. They take turns being the hunter and the prey. She comes up from behind him, slipping her hand beneath his armpit until it emerges, star-shaped and demanding, in the middle of his chest. He waits. Teases her, forces her to dangle in a split second of worry and then reacts swiftly, all at once. He whips around, pulls her in, dips her, and her legs buckle. She sinks all the way to the floor — limp, contrite, tossed aside. And then he flexes his shoulders and she springs, light and effortless, back into his arms.

I have stopped breathing. I am holding my breath, and my groceries, standing on the hot pavement, watching him drop to his knees. She bends back, a long unbroken stretch of feminine flesh, leaning over his waiting thigh. Drapes herself over him, bowed back until her head rests against the wooden dance floor. Extends one leg, slowly, toward the sky. He puts his hand behind her knee and turns his head as if to kiss her, but before he can, she has pulled up and away. God, I think. She's strong. That takes so much power, so much control, to be back on your feet in one fluid motion and moving away from the man. Her eyes are open now. She is walking toward herself in the mirror and she is smiling.

The waltz is rapturous. The foxtrot is playful and the cha-cha is flirtatious and Argentine tango is the dance of perpetually thwarted desire. It is the dance of a couple willing to forgo their individual balance and to lean into each other until they risk falling . . . until one or both of them ends up on the floor. This is a dance with no happy ending and I am stunned by the level of risk Nik and Pamela are taking, so much like the sort of risks Daniel and I took at the end. On some unconscious level they must want to be caught. They are tangoing here before this broad window, bragging of their passion to any stranger who happens to pass, slipping their true feelings inside the safe envelope of dance. Watching makes me feel things I don't want to feel, things I haven't felt in years. The appeal of the doomed affair. That strange beauty that comes when something is dying, the smell that roses give off in October. The freedom that comes from having nothing left to lose.

When I get home, I pour myself a glass of wine, sit down at the computer, and begin to look for Daniel.

There was a time when it was hard to find people. You lost them and they stayed gone. Elyse and I had shared a single afternoon with Daniel in Florence and he had kissed me good-bye at the station just before he hopped the train to Venice. A sweet kiss, memorable only because it was our first and our last.

Or so I thought. It had surprised me when he'd called twelve years later, announcing that he was moving to Charlotte. He said he'd gone to tremendous pains to track me down through my parents, aided only by the few casual facts that I'd mentioned in passing, including the fact that my father owned an insurance company.

"I'm surprised you even remembered my full name, much less that I told you what my dad did," I said on the phone. No one

141

had seemed to have a last name the summer Elyse and I went through Europe.

"Kelly," he said. "I remember everything you said to me. That day I spent with you was the best one of my whole trip."

It was? There was a split moment, I suppose, just then, when I was the one who held the power. He appeared to remember me far better than I remembered him. My kiss must have resonated profoundly, because I could hear something in his voice. Some tremor of nerves. He wanted something. I wasn't sure what. He had already made it clear that he would be accompanied on his move to Charlotte by a wife and children, and he suggested we meet at an IHOP near the airport. That sounded innocent enough. There's a limited amount of trouble a woman can get into at an IHOP.

"You'll never guess who just called me," I said to Elyse. I'd phoned her the minute that Daniel and I hung up and I was aware that my voice had already taken on the same tone as his — that I was struggling to sound casual and not quite making it. "The guy we met in Italy."

She was married by that time. Maybe even pregnant with Tory.

"We met a lot of guys in Italy," she said.

Maybe so, but I was already rewriting history in my mind, already making that single afternoon in Florence more than it had been. Telling myself it was indeed the best day of the whole summer, that I too had known with a single kiss that there was something special about this guy.

"The one we met in Florence," I said.

"Oh yeah. David."

"His name is Daniel."

"But we met him at the statue of David. He took our picture."

"Right. That's the one."

"What does he want after all this time?"

What did he want? What do we all want? I got to the IHOP early, as I always do. Sat by the window and saw him get out of his Jeep Cherokee and walk across the pavement.

"It was so hard to find you," he said as he slid into the booth. "It was like you had just fallen off the earth. But I kept looking."

I have spent years analyzing my affair with Daniel, but I've never come anywhere close to understanding why he had such a hold on me. There was that sliver of time, so brief, in which he wanted me more than I wanted him, in which I was the valued one, the pursued. But I gave the power away as fast as I could, tilted the seesaw in his favor, and it seems that all women have a story like this — the smart, the dumb, those of us in between. We choose some random guy and we put him on a pedestal. Imbue him with godlike powers. Our friends can see he's not worth it, but we can't. We can't see he's just a man, a man getting out of a Jeep at an IHOP, a man walking across a parking lot. We keep thinking of him years after the fact, even after we know the depths of his betrayal. We compare other men to him, and find even the kinder, better ones somehow lacking. And thus he stalks our life. The man who got away becomes the man we can't get away from.

There may have been a time when it was easy to lose people, but not anymore. I Google Daniel, search on Facebook, and there he is. A picture on the steps of what looks to be a church with his wife and his grown kids. For some reason I click on her profile first and from there it's easy to see her history, her likes and dislikes, the minutiae of her eerily relatable suburban life. We watch a couple of the same TV shows. She's a vegan. One of their kids is at Princeton. And yet, in the midst of all this middle-aged, middle-class domesticity, she has declared her relationship status to be "It's complicated."

So Daniel is struggling in his marriage. Possibly separated. I look down. My glass is still half-full, so at some point in the search I must have poured more wine without thinking. I have to be more careful. Nik is teaching group class tonight so I don't want to miss it, and I have a sweet spot of my own when it comes to wine, a place where the anxiety blurs but I'm still in control of my senses. I glance over at the pile of mail on the desk. Catalogs, bills, a statement from the lawyer. I should open it, but I don't.

Does Daniel look the same? I squint at the gallery of pictures but it's hard to say. More than two decades have passed since I've seen him and whenever I've allowed myself to think about what happened between us, I've never had much luck conjuring up his face.

The only thing that surprises me is that he's returned to the South. He always said he hated the South, that it was backward and slow, that people always tried to act like they were nicer than they were. But here he is, living in Charleston.

And that's entirely too close.

# CHAPTER NINE

Everyone's there when I arrive at group. As I walk by Nik to take my place in line he says, "You have had good day?"

"No," I say, "horrible."

He nods. "Me also."

He has come to the front of the room without turning on the music. This is a bad sign, an indication that he intends to torture us tonight with technique. The students are lined up before the mirror and Nik walks up and down the row like a sergeant, frowning, displeased in some way none of us can understand or fix. Valentina timidly asks if we can have music and Nik snaps back at her in Russian, then thinks better of it and translates. Apparently there's an old adage in their language: "When you learn how to swim better, then we will put water in the pool."

So, no water in the pool tonight. No music. Just Nik standing before us, slowly shifting from one leg to the other. The rumba can be fluid and sensual but when you break it down, it can also become a nightmarish sequence of micromovements, which are much harder to do slow than fast. You slide your weight to the left side of your body, then let it settle. As the weight settles, the hip releases. Shift, settle, release. And then you start all over again on the right.

We stare at our reflections, we bite our lips. It shouldn't be so hard. Shift on the first beat and then, on the half beat, release — just a little, just enough to allow the hip a slight swing to the side. It is subtle and when Nik does it, we can all see that it's beautiful. "It took me million tries to get right," he says. "Maybe a million one. Again. You are all too fast." The men are having more trouble than the women. They swing unevenly back and forth like a line of worn-out windshield wipers and Nik goes behind the group, putting his hands on each man's hips, trying to guide him into the rhythm of the dance. "Shift," he says. "Shift and then release. Is two separate moves. Again."

My mind wanders. In the mirror I can see that three men wearing business suits have come into the studio and are talking to Quinn. After a second, Quinn goes to get Anatoly, who emerges from the back room with a spring in his step and his hand already outstretched. Evidently the men are here to spend some major money. Because Nik has refused to put on music, I can overhear snatches of the conversation, enough to gather that they are with a French Canadian company. Come to talk about group lessons or some sort of incentive for their employees or maybe renting the studio out for a company party. Anatoly needs these sorts of people, the kind who can write big checks because the studio is barely breaking even. I know all this because of Isabel, who fills me full of dancing gossip that I can't understand, and who seems nearly as smitten with Anatoly as with Nik. She says she danced once with Anatoly at a Christmas party and it was the best experience of her life. Not just the best dance experience. The best experience, period. Better than sex.

"Kelly," Nik says sharply, and I snap my attention back to the rumba. He is either satisfied with the group's mastery of the shift and release or he's given up — hard to tell by his facial expression — and we're now moving on to the forward step. The key is to keep your knee locked, your toe pointed slightly out, and to shift all your weight onto the front foot in the instant that you step.

Very crisp. Very clean. Can we manage to do that?

It's a forward step. Surely we can all make a forward step. The very fact that we're here, in the studio, should be evidence that we are in fact capable of taking a sequence of forward steps — otherwise, we'd still be in the parking lot, trapped in our cars. But the skill seems to have deserted us all. Stepping onto a locked knee proves surprisingly difficult and to compensate I tend to turn my toe in. All wrong. Valentina's toe is beautifully turned out but Nik immediately sees that she's dividing her weight equally between both feet, another rumba no-no. Lucas has nice form, but he's moving too fast. Jane is so wobbly that she's flapping her hands to keep her balance. Steve refuses to try at all and checks his phone, and Harry steps forward confidently and then sways wildly to his left, almost falling off his feet and taking the whole domino line down with him.

"Again," Nik says. "A million more times. Which foot are you on? You say right? Prove it. Lift your left."

I'm so preoccupied with the intricacies of the forward step that I don't notice Anatoly walking across the room.

I don't notice him at all until I feel his

hand on the small of my back. When I look up he is standing behind me with his ramrod-straight posture.

And he says, "Kelly, will you help me demonstrate the waltz?"

I am balanced on one foot as it is, and for a second, I nearly buckle. I've never danced with Anatoly. Lessons with him cost more than those with Nik. His own students are afraid of him. Why doesn't he demonstrate with Pamela? She's right there in the corner and everyone knows she waltzes like an angel. But perhaps he's trying to show the French Canadians what an amateur can do, what they could hope to achieve in a few weeks.

Anatoly is waiting.

"I'd be delighted," I hear myself say.

Anatoly holds my hand high as he leads me to the center of the floor. We stand still for a second while he gives me the chance to settle in. To get used to the fact that he is much taller than Nik, that he holds his shoulders even farther back. That he gives a woman such a big frame that I will have to stretch to my maximum size if I even hope to fill it. Quinn goes over to the sound system and pushes a button. Too loud, too loud, the whole room is overwhelmed with music, but Anatoly remains perfectly still.

He gives me another second to breathe, to get the rhythm of the rumba out of my mind and begin to hear the waltz. The one-two-three, one-two-three, the rise and fall of a different sort of world. Although he does not watch my face, although he is in fact looking in the opposite direction, he seems to sense the exact moment when the rumba fades. Or, more accurately, the moment when everything else in the room is pulled from me fast, like when you hit the little picture of a garbage can on an iPhone and whatever you were looking at crumples and is sucked away. He gives me just enough time to settle, but not enough time to think, because he knows that if I think, I'll panic.

Later, when it's all over, this is what I'll remember. It was early fall. Just starting to get dark outside the door. I will remember the group class pausing, the students turning toward me, their faces serious and full of doubt. Nik's lips were pursed together as if he was mad at Anatoly for interrupting class, but of course he wouldn't be mad. Anatoly is his boss. He's probably just wondering, like everyone else in the room, why Anatoly had chosen me to demonstrate instead of Pamela. The teenagers lean against the back wall, shoulder to shoulder, as if they were expecting some sort of show.

The French Canadians consult among themselves. Anatoly is trying to make a sale, possibly one that could bring a significant amount of money to the studio, so why would he choose to dance with Kelly Wilder, a beginner? Someone likely to stumble or hesitate, someone likely to mar the stately and unforgiving rhythm of the waltz?

I'll remember all this but not the dance itself.

I will just sort of come to on the other side of the room. I'll have no actual recall of waltzing and yet apparently I did, because here I am, in a different place on the dance floor. It was like I passed out for a few minutes — perhaps because I'm scared of Anatoly, who is so tall and stern and expansive and grander than Nik. Nik tried to explain it to me once — he'd said Anatoly is a white Russian and he is a black Russian, a description that makes them sound like drinks. Which, in a way, they are.

But he must have taken me and we must have waltzed. Or rather Anatoly must have waltzed and my mind must have clicked off and allowed me to follow, and furthermore he must have led me into steps I don't know, because it's coming to me that there was a fall-away, possibly three, and that Anatoly had spun me — repeatedly and with more force than I'm used to. Not one turn like I've practiced with Nik, but multiple turns, and I still ended up the correct way. Facing the French Canadians, with enough presence of mind to curtsy.

Anatoly says "Thank you" and makes his little half bow. As if we are in Vienna or Prague or somewhere, as if it were 1826. Maybe I thank him too. He leads me back to the rumba line and the other students fold around me. Valentina says "You were great" and Isabel nods, although, being Isabel, she feels compelled to add, "Of course, Anatoly could lead anyone." When I look into the mirror, I'm flushed. Nik puts his arm around me, leans in to kiss my cheek, as if in congratulations. But when he gets close to my ear he whispers, "What the hell was that?"

Thirty minutes later I'm sitting in the dark parking lot. I've called Elyse but she didn't answer and I remember it's the night she teaches a pottery class at the university. I need to check on Carolina anyway and when I call the front desk number the nurse says, "She's out here in the TV room, wanna talk to her?"

"She's sitting up?"

"Yes, and she ate a full dinner. Doing just

153

a whole lot better." There's a pause and I can hear her carrying the phone across the lobby and the sounds of *Jeopardy!* in the background. Then Carolina's voice.

"What's up?"

"I wanted you to be the first to know I danced with Anatoly tonight."

She exhales with a fast "Whoa." She knows what it means. But of course she doesn't know how it happened, so I tell her, with every detail. And when I get to the end of the story, including what Nik whispered in my ear, she laughs and says, "So what was it like? Was that lady right when she said it was better than sex?"

"Promise me you won't laugh."

"You know I can't promise you that."

"Okay, well, it was magic. He had me doing things I don't know how to do. I've heard the other women in the studio talk about 'soaring,' but I never knew what they meant until tonight. It was like I simultaneously left my body and was hyperaware of my body. You know, looking down on myself from the ceiling but at the same time feeling every nerve and muscle. Like magic."

She digests this bit in silence, then says, "Sometime I want to see you dance."

"Sure," I say. I can hardly refuse her this small request. "My lessons are Tuesday and

I'm going to start going on Fridays too. I could come by and pick you up."

"I don't want to watch a lesson," she says. "I want to see you in a contest, wearing one of those dresses covered in crystals with your hair all up."

"It'll be months or maybe years before I'm ready to compete."

"Why?"

I pause. Look out across the rain-washed parking lot. The studio is closing. The front light has gone out. Someone is finishing up with the sweeping, then will go out the back door. The grocery is still open, and the Starbucks, but the pharmacy and dry cleaner are locking up too. The clock on my dashboard says 9:03. How can I tell a woman with cancer that I don't feel like I have enough time? How can I tell her that I am afraid of how I will look or what people will think?

"Here's the thing," I finally say. "I'm never going to be really good. I started too late."

"You said everybody clapped tonight."

"Yeah, but that's just in the studio. I'm not one of those people who are going to compete and win trophies. Nobody is ever going to see my name on a heat sheet and be scared to death. I just don't arch like the young girls arch anymore. I'm not flexible. I wake up in the middle of the night with cramps in my butt."

"Your teacher thinks you're good."

"They say that to everybody. They have to. If they tell you the truth, you'll stop writing them checks. Look, I know how this must sound to you, like I'm not grateful for the chance I have, and I'll be the first to tell you that there was a time . . . if I had walked through those doors when I was thirty or even forty and a young man like Nik would have told me I had potential, I would have sucked all that praise straight down like vodka."

"I'm not saying you have to be some sort of world champion. I'm just saying I want to see you dance. In one of those dresses with the shimmers on it."

"I guess you know you've got me over a barrel."

She gives a little hiccup laugh. "Don't they have a competition at Christmas?"

"That's way too soon," I say.

"Isn't there one in March?"

Does the woman take notes on everything I say? "Yeah," I admit. "The regional qualifier is in March."

"I want to see you there. In a fancy dress. Come on. You might not have as much time as you think you do."

"I can't believe how much better you sound than you did this afternoon."

Carolina begins to chatter that they might even let her go to the older boy's football game next week and I lean back in the seat and shut my eyes. My head is tilted sideways, my cheek against the cool glass of the window. Maybe that waltz truly was like sex, I think, for I am totally relaxed, my body loose and open in a way it rarely is. Is this what women feel like after orgasms? What they call afterglow? If so, I understand why you'd do almost anything to have it. After sex I used to get restless. I'd get up for water or to pee or get something to eat or check the locks. Sometimes, once I was sure Mark was sleeping, I would move to one of the other bedrooms and read. There was always some sense of unfinished business, the need to move and do something, but tonight . . . tonight I feel as if there is nowhere else to go, nothing to do, no other way I want to be.

The cadence of Carolina's voice rises and falls. I'm half listening and I know that I would not change anything about my dance with Anatoly. I would not change the music or the setting or the faces of any of the people who had stood and watched me. And I know that when it comes my time to die, that this is one of the nights that will make it easier to let go. That I'll be able to say to myself, "But you know, there was that one night, a long time ago, when I waltzed," and this thought will be a comfort. To know that there were times when I got it. When, at least for a few seconds, my life was not entirely wasted on me.

# CHAPTER TEN

By November I am indeed taking a private lesson each Tuesday and Friday and dancing group five days a week — six if they have a party on Saturday. I come to every class on the schedule, no matter who's teaching. Even on the nights when they bring in one of the local college dance majors to teach, even on the nights when they're doing something cheesy like the mambo or hustle. Any kind of practice is good, I tell myself. Every single movement brings you closer. Closer to what, I can't yet say, but I try especially hard to make the most of my individual lessons with Nik. And in order to squeeze every ounce of progress out of every hour, I decide that I must concentrate on the dances where I actually have some potential.

Talking to Nik about this won't be easy. The Russians are not big on conversation. If you ask them their opinion about anything, they grow wary, because they know if they give it, there's a chance you might say something else in response and then they're trapped. They speak primarily to convey information — it is not a culture of chitchat, and I suspect that at times Nik and Anatoly must feel as if the whole studio is spinning in a vortex of words.

At my private lesson the next Tuesday Nik leans back and asks me, "Who is leading dance?"

I'm ready for this one. "You are," I say. "You're the man."

"To dance is to create space and to fill space," he says. "When lady steps back, she makes space man steps into. He cannot be bigger than she will let him be. So who is leading dance, the one who makes space or the one who steps into it?"

He gets like this sometimes, kind of wonkily philosophical. It reminds me of those SAT questions from back in high school, the kind that go "If one train leaves Moscow traveling west at 100 miles an hour and another train leaves Paris traveling east at 80 miles an hour, which foot should you have your weight on?" Well, maybe that's an exaggeration, but Nik does make everything harder than it needs to be. And ever since I did that waltz with Anatoly, I get the feeling he's been trying to take me down a peg or two.

"I guess the one who creates the space is leading," I say.

"Wrong. Is trick. Man always leads."

"Screw you," I say, and he smiles, pleased with himself. Pamela is in the center of the ballroom floor. She's dancing with Anatoly today, and they're working on cha-cha. Her Latin clothes are sexy, even her practicewear, and it suddenly hits me that this is why Nik and I started with tango today, instead of warming up with the waltz like we usually do. There is a pecking order at the studio, one based more on finances than talent, and the sheer amount of money Pamela spends here in a week means that whatever she happens to be dancing at the moment determines what kind of music is coming out of the speakers. Pamela is doing cha-cha so the whole studio is pulsing with Los Lobos, and in turn I am doing tango because it is possible to do tango to the same beat as cha-cha. We all literally dance to the tune of the whales.

"Thrust the girls to the sky, darling," Anatoly says, and Pamela obligingly lifts her chest. Sometimes I wonder if he's gay. He supposedly slept with all his professional partners back in Russia, one right after another, but he makes outrageous statements to the women in the studio. The kinds of things only gay guys get away with. Or maybe this is all some sort of game Anatoly plays with Nik, hard to say. Flirting with his lover right before his eyes, but with this sort of tease-flirting that doesn't really have any teeth.

The music is fast, too fast for a tango, at least a tango at my level, and I know that I'm compensating by collapsing my frame. Just a little, but of course Nik has noticed. My legs are slightly apart, like a skier on the bunny slope, like someone who expects to topple at any minute. "Why do you sloop?" Nik asks me, with the exasperated tone of someone who's never fallen down once in his whole life. "I want you to stand like queen. Be the big lady." There's no good way to explain to him that American women don't want to be big, that we recoil from the word like a gunshot.

"Look at our girl," Anatoly says, right on the verge of a squeal, and Nik and I pause, still in tango hold, and watch him lead Pamela through a complicated set of swivels. All steps I haven't learned yet.

"Isn't she something?" Anatoly says.

"Very good," Nik says.

Pamela puts her hand to her chest and drops her head with a sort of exaggerated false modesty. Anatoly goes over to the stereo to start the same song again.

"I want to learn that step sequence," I whisper to Nik through gritted teeth.

"Later," he says.

"You don't think I can learn that sequence?"

"You learn later."

I sigh. He sighs too — loudly, as if he's mocking me — and we begin again, inching our way around the dance floor and all the time keeping an eye on Anatoly and Pamela. This whole lesson has been annoying. Nik's new thing lately is making sure that I'm always, at any point in the dance, balanced within myself and not leaning on him. He tests this by releasing me when I least expect it. Already today he has stepped back from me twice, letting me go in midspin and asking "Are you on your feet?" Quinn came in at some point and called out "Good job." Her compliments always feel a little random and today I was literally stumbling out of a turn when she said it.

I'd rolled my eyes and she'd said, "No, really. You're in the zone where people learn. Where you're uncomfortable with what you're doing but not so uncomfortable that you can't move at all. We call it optimal frustration."

Nik says, "We pivot again."

"God," I say. "You're relentless." He drops his palm from my shoulder blade and goes over to his little phone. He picks it up and looks at me expectantly.

"Re-lent-less," I repeat. "I bet if you try, you can figure out what it means."

"I love dancing with you," Anatoly coos to Pamela. All throaty, like some sort of porn star. "Does Nik ever tell you how good you are?"

I bet I know the answer to that. Nik never tells anyone she's good. I doubt he would even apply the word to the pros, because he knows dance is a slippery summit. You get your rumba almost perfected, but by the time you've done that, you've forgotten your waltz. So you work on that for a week but by then you've lost the foxtrot. And there is always someone younger, stronger, and prettier nipping at your heels. I suppose that's what makes dance addictive. This idea that you're moving toward something but never quite arriving. Of course they don't tell you any of this when you sign up. If you knew how hard it was going to be, you'd never have the heart to begin. "It costs too much," Isabel says as she gets out her credit card, literally crossing her fingers as Quinn slides it through the machine, and I nod, although the truth is, it's costing all of us different things.

Pamela's music starts yet again. She and Anatoly have reclaimed the center of the dance floor while Nik and I have been exiled to the Siberia of the far corner. The opening step of her competition cha-cha routine is flashy, a little impressive. But not, at least to my mind, all that hard. I could do that, I think, and my mind is drifting so that when Nik lets me go at the end of my pivot I'm not expecting it. I almost fall. I roll clumsily to a stop and look back at him, furious that he let me make such a rookie mistake in front of Anatoly and Pamela. He is standing with his legs apart and his arms folded over his chest.

"Dance your dance," he says. "Not hers."

"I could do that step," I whisper, even though I know they're not listening.

"Is Silver."

"What difference does that make? I already told you I'm not going to compete."

"You should. You know all Bronze steps."

"If I ever did compete, which I'm not going to, it would be in Newcomer."

He shrugs. "Is under you. And this," he adds, inclining his sleek, dark head in the direction of the spinning forms of Pamela and Anatoly, "is above you."

He's playing with me. He knows that today I am pissed about it all — about the incessant cha-cha music when I am paying to dance the tango. About the way Anatoly flatters Pamela and he does not flatter me — about the fact he almost dropped me, let me come out of that turn all a mess in front of a man I like and a woman I don't.

"I should compete on the Newcomer level," I say. "That's what I am."

"It is not supposed to be easy. You go up, you go down. Is your choice. Problems either way."

What he means is that Newcomers are only allowed to compete with a few very basic steps, which they do over and over again, and dumbing it down would frustrate me. And the bitch of the matter is, he's probably right. I do know all the Bronze steps — it was a Bronze level pivot that I fell out of just a minute ago — but to dance Bronze is to risk competing against women who have been dancing much longer than I have, women who I know going in are far better than me. The competitions are stacked with dancers who have taken lessons for years, who should have long since advanced to the Silver level with Pamela and such. Yet they hang back in Bronze, at the expense of people like me, and if I try to dance Bronze, Nik and I both know that these women will eat my lunch. They're nothing but a bunch of praise whores, I think, and I pull myself a little higher as Nik takes me back into hold, as we try that damn pivot yet once again. He's right about it all. Do I really want to dance Newcomer when I know I'm better than that? Or am I prepared to have my ass kicked by the Pamelas of the world?

"We need to talk," I say.

"Because of her?" he says. He is worried that I'm going to try to analyze the situation. To draw him into some discussion of the fact I know they're lovers.

"No," I said. "I wanted to talk anyway. Please. Just for a minute."

He hesitates. Last week when I had invited him for coffee he said no, that it was "improper," and I realized that he must have been quoting Anatoly. Evidently the instructors aren't just forbidden to go drinking with the students — they can't see us outside of class at all. Even if it's just a matter of walking across the parking lot to the Starbucks, even if the whole purpose of the meeting is to discuss a student's future in dance.

"We can just stay here and talk for five minutes," I say. "Please." Anatoly and Pamela have finished. He has walked her to the door and is holding it open for her and they are laughing about something.

"Okay," Nik says. "For minute." We cross the room and sit down at one of the small tables and I begin unbuckling my shoes. I persuade him to get his snack from the fridge and he comes back with an athlete's lunch — a banana, a tuna sandwich, and a ziplock bag with walnuts. I wait for him to unpack everything and take a gulp of water. Finally he looks up at me.

"You're talking about me competing," I say, "and we both know I'm not ready, but if I were, what should I be working on?"

"Everything," he says, an answer that makes me want to smack him. An answer that makes me want to weep. He glances around the empty room. Anatoly has also gone, presumably to lunch.

"Okay," I say. "Answer me this. What's my best dance?"

"You dance them all well," he says. "But there is house for improvement."

"I know there's room for improvement," I say. "There's always room for improvement. But I want to focus on the dances where I have potential. Come on. Level with me." I

168

reach across the table and squeeze Nik's wrist. He jumps.

We touch all the time on the dance floor. The pivot that we do in tango requires me to press my right thigh between both of his, and the crispness of the spin depends almost totally on how closely we press our hips together, how well we merge into a single point. It's a matter of physics. He has put a lot of pivots in my routine, because he knows I'm not shy about pushing my leg between his and Nik's not shy about accepting it. But here, off the floor and sitting at one of the tables, my hand on his wrist makes him jump.

"I know I can't be good at everything," I say. "There's not enough time, so I need you to tell me where the time I do have would best be spent."

He looks at me strangely. Where Nik came from, things were often harsh but always clear. There was a narrow window of opportunity to prove yourself in his childhood dance academy and if your chance passed, you were, as he says, "fooked." He has told me that many nights he had returned to his cot in the dorm with aching muscles and bleeding feet but it had never occurred to him to question one of his teachers. He danced for years without anyone telling him he was good; you knew you were good if they didn't send you home. And thus he struggles, as they all do, to remember that things are different here, that Americans dance for different reasons. There's no equivalent of the bored suburban housewife where Nik comes from. There's no Russian word for "hobby." I have seen a picture of Nik's mother. She is younger than I am but looks older and I suspect he finds us absurd, all of us overfed, overcoddled middle-aged women who do an offbeat underarm turn and expect wild applause. He is probably thinking that one of the failures of democracy is that a three-month student, a woman whose frame is dreadful, feels free to grab his wrist and question the methodology of his teaching. He knows I expect some sort of answer but still, part of him is hurt.

"All of my students are good at all of their dances," he says carefully and stiffly, putting in every conjunction for once. And then he looks down as if even he recognizes that this careful tone of voice is not completely his own.

"That's bullshit," I say sharply, and even though he knows it's bullshit, he looks at me as if I've slapped him.

I'm aware that my heart is pounding. This conversation may be painful for Nik but it does not come easily for me either. I am trying to tell a man what I want, what I really want, rather than what other people expect me to want, and it's like being thrown fully dressed into a swimming pool.

We sit for a moment in silence and then I try again.

"I'm not Pamela," I say. "I don't have fifteen years of experience under my belt. And I'm not the teenagers who compete, or Quinn either. I'm not one of those girls who are young and perfect and can bend and extend. My time is limited . . ." I glance at him to make sure he understands, but Nik is still gazing gloomily down at the table, as if I'm describing his limitations and not my own.

"I want to get better," I say. "I want you to tell me how to get better. I need to . . ." Here I bring my hands to my face and point them in front as if my nose were a beak. "I know I need to focus. That's the only way I'll improve. So tell me, I'm begging you. If I could only dance two or three dances, what would they be?"

More silence. From the back room we can hear the faint sounds of samba music. "You do not need to shake your ass," he finally says. "You need to stand straight and open your arms and be . . . the big lady. I would

171

say waltz. Foxtrot. And tango."

For a minute I'm stung. He's telling me I shouldn't do Latin. That I'm better suited for the old-lady dances, the fat-lady dances, the last ones you give up before you retire, or die.

"What about cha-cha?" I ask. Pamela is close to my age, maybe a few years below, but not that much. And she competes in cha-cha.

"Not cha-cha," he says, nodding as he often does when he tells me no.

My face is hot. I know without looking in the mirror that I've gone all splotched. "You're saying I shouldn't cha-cha," I say. "Which is pretty damn interesting considering that when I came in for my free lesson the very first dance we did was the cha-cha and I got the lock step on the first try and you said that was great and you told me, the very last thing you told me before I got out my checkbook, was that the cha-cha was my dance."

"I did not know you then," he says simply.

"And now we've danced together maybe three months and you know exactly what I need."

"Yes. That is right."

I've asked him a question and he's answered it . . . so why am I angry, so irrationally hurt? I've done this before, now that I think of it. I've assured men that I wanted the truth and then, when they tried to give it to me, I've started to cry. I've upset him too, but Nik, to his credit, for once is looking me right in the eyes. "You already have rhythm," he finally says. "You come here to get something else."

"What else?" I ask, although a dim part of my mind sees what he's getting at. When I was young I shook my ass a lot and I'd been pretty good at it. When I was young, then yes, it had been my go-to mode, what I did when I couldn't think of what else to do. But how could Nik know this? How could he know that while he was a little boy in that militaristic dancing school somewhere in the eternal night of Siberia, obeying his teachers and trying so hard to be good, that I had been shaking my ass for any number of inconsequential men?

"I'm pretty good at the cha-cha," I say again, for emphasis, even though I know this is no longer the point.

"So yes," says Nik. "Yes, yippee, we say. Kelly can shake her ass and some women cannot do this and so they must start there. Women must know that they can shake their ass before they know that they do not have to shake their ass, but you already have shaked your ass and it is over. Put it down on the floor. Now you must —"

"Stand up straight and be a big lady."

My tone of voice is petulant but he ignores this. He puts his hands to his nose and points them, fingertips together, in a parody of my earlier gesture. "We will, yes, focus," he says. "First on how to enter and take the floor because you . . ." He stops again, searching for the words, but I understand his meaning. The fact that I had known, almost by instinct, how to do the steps of the cha-cha had been a sure sign that it was not my destiny to do the cha-cha. People do not come to the dance floor to learn what they already know.

"Because I have to get okay with people seeing all of me, not just my ass."

And then in that moment, we both laugh. We are fond of each other, despite it all. I could keep talking, try to push for more understanding, a wordier and more American-style meeting of the minds. But he has answered my question completely. And so I will waltz, and foxtrot and tango and possibly talk him into the quickstep. My fate is the romantic dances. My fate is to be the big lady.

He slides my folder toward me and I sign my name.

"This was a difficult lesson," I say.
He nods. "Hardest yet."

# CHAPTER ELEVEN

The last round of chemo appears to have done the trick. They agree to let Carolina go home for Thanksgiving and possibly Christmas. They're very careful with the words. They never say "cure" and they don't say "remission." They say "a few weeks." They say "We'll keep checking in."

So much of her hair has come out that she makes the same decision a lot of cancer patients do — to shave her head. There's something defiant about baldness, especially in a woman, the implication that you have chosen your fate and not had it thrust upon you.

Hospice keeps a variety of clippers and razors just for this purpose and I help Carolina with them on the Wednesday before Thanksgiving. I have brought her every scarf I could find in my house, then picked up a few more at Target. The nurses and other volunteers all stop by to wish her well, and to make predictable comments about her having a lot to be thankful for this year. She looks better bald than most women do, since she doesn't have any of those lumps or ridges most people have in their scalp.

"You have a very symmetrical head," I tell her.

"Just one more thing to be thankful for," chirps a volunteer, and Carolina makes a face at me in the mirror.

After that there is nothing left to do but pack her bag and drive her home. We have timed it so she will arrive just after lunch, giving her a chance to rest before the boys get home from school. She lives in a neat little tract house with perfectly round boxwoods lined up around the front, and the first thing I see when I push open the screen door is one of those plaques that say AS FOR ME AND MY HOUSE, WE WILL SERVE THE LORD. It surprises me a little. I've never heard her mention God.

Virginia has fixed lunch and, despite the fact we ate at hospice, we eat again. There are pictures of Ritchie and Josh all over the breakfast nook — in baseball uniforms, Boy Scout uniforms, football uniforms. I always thought they were just embarrassed when their aunt forced them to come to hospice, but now I see that embarrassment is their natural facial expression, captured in a whole line of photographs, starting from birth. On the refrigerator, Virginia has drawn herself a chart marking their team practices and school functions in different colors of ink, each color meaning, I presume, something significant to her. She seems to be managing all this as well as she can. She's a shorter, harsher version of her sister, with a face lined from cigarette smoke and direct sunlight and God knows how many disappointments. Other pictures in the room are further proof that Carolina was always the pretty one — an overly bright Olan Mills shot of the three girls when they were little shows Carolina on the end, the youngest and possibly the most favored, since she is the only one with a bow in her hair and the only one in the picture who is smiling.

There have been times when I've thought that Virginia was jealous of my closeness with her sister and now, when Carolina starts to droop in exhaustion, Virginia is quick to say she'll help her to bed. She jumps up, pushing her chair back with a scrape, and escorts Carolina down the dark hall, as if the woman doesn't know the way through her own house. I hear the soft sounds of their fading conversation and put my fork down. While we were eating, another thing caught my eye, a folder stuck on the refrigerator door along with the boys' schedule calendar. It's marked with the word MAIL in big black Magic Marker letters, but I suspect MAIL means BILLS. I walk over to the folder and pull out the envelopes inside. Something from the bank, from the electric company, water, cable, a dentist office, and the used-car lot we passed on the drive over here.

"I'm going to take these," I tell Virginia when she gets back into the kitchen.

She looks at the envelopes in my hand and then away. "Carolina . . ." she says. I wait, but she doesn't finish.

"She might not even ask about them," I say.

"Did anybody tell her . . ."

"They didn't tell her anything. They don't know. Just to keep her away from germs. I realize that's hard with the kids coming and going, but her white blood cell count — we need to make sure she doesn't catch a flu bug, anything like that."

Virginia nods, sighs, and looks back at the folder in my hands. "I guess this is the part," she says, "when I'm supposed to thank you."

■ ■ ■ ■

"Now don't freak out, but I found Daniel," I tell Elyse. "I looked him up on Facebook."

"I'm surprised you didn't do something like that a long time ago."

"You don't think it's pathetic?"

"You're talking to a woman who never lets go of anybody," she says with a laugh. Elyse has been having an affair with the same guy on and off for years and she takes a sick sort of pride in the fact she's close friends with her ex-husband.

"But considering the way things were left . . ."

"Oh, he was a right bastard, no doubt about it."

"He's in Charleston."

Now that gives her pause.

"That's too close," she finally says. "You're not tempted to go down there, are you? Hide behind one of those Civil War statues and jump out at him? Because that would be a huge mistake."

"Why would I do that?"

"Maybe you want to show him how wonderful you ended up."

"I don't think I ended up all that wonderful. You're still coming at Christmas, right?

And bringing Tory?" When she hesitates with her answer I feel a moment of panic rush in. "I know she probably thinks she should stay with her dad, but tell her I'm counting on you both being here. What's the point of having six bedrooms if nobody ever comes to your house?"

"You could move, you know. That neighborhood was always full of Mark's friends, not yours. Get a little condo or something. Decorate it however you want."

"I'm not ready."

"I'm just saying that as long as you're in that house —"

"Have you eaten dinner?"

"Yeah. A couple of hours ago."

"It seems like it's been a long time since we've had dinner together on the phone."

She pauses. "You've been taking group lessons almost every night and then going out for drinks with your new friends afterward. You're a lot busier than you used to be. And that's a good thing."

"Is it? Sometimes I feel like dance has eaten up my whole life." Now it's my turn to pause. There's something wrong in that sentence but I'm not sure exactly what. "You were always the one who was too busy for me," I finally finish lamely.

"Kelly, it's fine," she says with a laugh.

"As it should be."

"You don't think we're growing apart?"

"Don't be silly. We don't have to talk every night just to prove we're friends. We're not in high school anymore."

"But you're still coming at Christmas, right?"

"Of course I am. You're my home. Always have been, always will."

I hang up the phone unsettled and craving a taco salad. They were one of my private indulgences during my marriage, one of the things I would sneak out to eat when Mark was playing golf. Now all of a sudden I want the whole guilty thing, with the jalapeño ranch dressing and the sour cream and tortilla chips and dark meaty chili with cinnamon and garlic.

I've never gotten the hang of asking for a table for one, so I just take a seat at Esmerelda's bar, wedged between a young girl who keeps tossing her hair on me and a sour-faced man who never looks up from his food. Happy hour has started and the speaker above my head is pumping out music with such force that the whole bar is vibrating. They have one of those big glass containers on the corner of the bar that's approximately the size and shape of a beehive but instead of honey it holds vodka and many wedges of pineapple, intricately stacked. It's all lit from below so that it looks like it's glowing and I noticed it the first night I came in with the group class. Alcohol as art, I guess.

"What do you call that drink?" I ask the bartender. "The one with the vodka and pineapple juice?"

"Vodka and pineapple juice."

"Oh," I say. "Okay, I'll try it."

The drink is strong, sweet, heavy on my tongue. The backs of my knees are hurting, like they do all the time now, and as I reach down to rub them I see, of all things, Steve sitting in the corner. He is having dinner with a woman who looks like a young Mary Tyler Moore. He notices me too and nods.

"Would you like a drink?" the man beside me asks.

"I have a drink," I point out.

"What I mean is, I'd like to pay for your drink," he says. "In celebration of the fact I'm getting to sit beside such a beautiful woman."

"I'm not sure my husband would like that," I say, pointedly twisting my ring.

He backs down. They always do. The size of this ring is kryptonite.

"Well, you're still pretty," he says, and

183

then he leans back, presumably to take a shot with the hair-tossing woman on my other side.

Just then Steve's date squeezes by us and disappears down the bright orange hall, evidently in search of the ladies' room. She has her purse with her, which is normal, but she also has her jacket with her, which is not. And she's walking just a little too fast.

She's bailing on him.

I can read it in her body language. She may be acting like she's headed to the bathroom but she's really going to walk out that back service door at the end of the hall and just keep going. I look over my shoulder. The waiter is delivering the food to Steve's table, and judging from the way he's smiling and joking with the guy, I don't think he's realized anything has happened.

I wonder how long it's going to take him to figure out that she's gone. It pains me to watch him in the mirror, looking about the room, obviously unsure if he should start eating his own food or wait for her to return. He makes some comment to the people at the table beside him, giving them his big, full-throttle billboard smile, but I've seen this man anxious before and I recognize that slight pucker between the brows.

It's beginning to dawn on him that he may have to finish this meal alone.

It's hard to eat alone, true. But not nearly as uncomfortable as it was on those times I went out to eat with Mark and he simply wouldn't talk. He never had any of my social self-consciousness. If Mark had nothing to say, then he said nothing — which I suppose is admirable if you're a Zen master but which did me little good in restaurants, where I always imagined other diners were looking at us with pity. "What a sad couple that is, eating with their heads down, sitting there in silence," I would imagine them thinking. "She's utterly failed to enchant him — that much is clear."

Once I told Mark about this little trick Elyse and I used to have when we were in high school and they were taking pictures of us for the school paper or yearbook. One of the side effects of popularity is that you're in a lot of pictures, and in them you want to be chatting and laughing and talking — like you're the sort of funny, clever girl who deserves to be so frequently photographed. So we came up with a little ruse. While we were waiting for the kid to take our picture, Elyse would turn to me and say, "ABC?"

And I would answer back "DEFGH," then pause for a second and add "IJ." We would carry on like that for as long as it took, saying the alphabet back and forth to each other while the camera flashed, creating images of two girls who were full of lively conversation, who always had plenty to say.

Mark had been nothing short of flabbergasted by the suggestion. "You want us to sit here," he said, "in a perfectly lovely restaurant having a perfectly lovely meal, and keep saying the alphabet back and forth to each other? All because you have it in your head that the busboy feels sorry for us?" And then he sat back in his seat and leveled the same condemnation he had directed toward me so many times before.

"You expect too much," he said.

Did I? Was I really that much like Elyse by the end or was that bit about expecting too much just something all men say to all women? Now, sitting here alone in a Mexican restaurant, I pull a dance shoe from my purse, where I stuck them after today's lesson. I hold it in my palm, turn it from side to side under the bar, admiring the elegant, torturous arch in the sole. I want this, I suddenly think. I haven't wanted anything in a long, long time. The vodka has hit me like a truth serum and it's scary to think that I might want something that Mark's money can't buy for me, something that being the pretty girl won't help me get either. Scary to want something that I can only give myself. I take another sip of the drink, roll it around in my mouth, and beneath the bar I stretch my legs. Developing your flexibility is the most painful and dangerous part, Nik says. Much harder than becoming fast or strong.

My salad comes and I cram the shoe back into my purse. Yep. I want this. I want this and no one else can give it to me. But, it occurs to me that if you want something that no one else can give you, then no one else can take it away from you either, and there's a certain comfort in that. I'm going to have to figure out a way to stand tall and give Nik the sort of frame he's asking me for. I take a bite out of the chili and look around the bar. Except for the man who wanted to buy me a drink and now possibly Steve, I'm the only person in the whole room sitting alone. Everyone else has a friend or a lover or at least someone they work with. Elyse likes to eat alone but I've never understood that, never understood her penchant for solitude in public places. I feel vulnerable, I think, and I can almost imagine Nik whipping out his iPhone and saying, "What is this 'vulnerable'?"

"Hey," says Steve. He's come up behind

187

me. "I know this is a little out of line, but I have a favor to ask you."

"You want me to go to the bathroom and look for your date?"

He grimaces and shakes his head. "I don't think you'd find her. I was wondering if you would just pick up your salad and come sit down at my table. The waiter feels sorry for me. And so do the people beside me."

"She might come back. Maybe she went on the sidewalk to make a phone call."

"I doubt it. That door leads to the loading dock. This isn't the first time this has happened to me."

"Well . . . okay," I say slowly, but I'm wondering what the waiter is going to think when he comes back and finds a whole new woman at the table. I slide off the bar stool and Steve grabs my salad and my vodka and pineapple juice. When we get to his table, I notice Mary Tyler Moore's plate has already been cleared and that the couple beside us does indeed seem to be taking a lively level of interest in the unfolding drama. Or maybe they're just happy to have a distraction, something to focus on other than each other.

"So what happened?" I say to Steve when we get everything settled and I'm in my seat. "Did she get pissed off or something?"

"I have no idea," he says, raising his margarita to his lips. "It was a setup. You know, a blind date. All of mine are."

"Come on."

"Trust me, being known as Dr. Boob of Charlotte makes dating a challenge." And then he proceeds to tell me that a lot of women refuse to date a plastic surgeon on principle and that this, along with his ex-wife's efforts to get him blackballed from the city's elite social clubs, has driven him to do the unthinkable — to sign up for a matchmaking service. A discreet one, of course, and he has carefully instructed the women working there to describe him only as a doctor, without elaborating on the exact nature of his practice.

"The whole dating after forty thing," he says, "is impossible."

I've misjudged him. Maybe I've misjudged lots of people about lots of things. So I sit there steadily eating and let him tell me all about the women he's met through the dating service. Women, not girls, he insists. He won't go below thirty, that's just sick. Quinn is like the daughter he never had, the daughter he was too busy to have, and he loves her for the very fact that she doesn't care how she looks. He dates at least twice a week, he says, but it's tough. Thanks to the billboards, some of the women recognize him on sight. Others walk into the restaurant or bar and when they see him they frown and start wondering why his face is familiar. And then at some point in the evening, it hits them. He dreads this moment, dreads the self-consciousness that inevitably follows. Sometimes he feels like he's spent the year since his divorce buying strange women drinks and listening to them apologize for the size and shape of their breasts. He's been trapped in one-sided arguments about feminism and the La Leche League and *Baywatch* reruns, he tells me. He's been the subject of very amateur and very unfair Freudian analysis.

"That's awful," I say, although while he's been telling me all this, a couple of times I've snuck a look at my own cleavage. My breasts used to be quite good but now I've got a bit of asymmetry and tons of age spots on my chest and most definite sagging.

"And you want to know the joke of it all?" he says. "I'm an ass man." He sighs, puts his empty glass down, and gestures to the waiter that we'll need two more. "So what brings you out to Esmerelda's?"

He doesn't say "What brings you out 'alone,' " but I feel the word, sitting between us on the table just as plain as the basket of chips.

"Nik told me I'm too old to do the cha-cha."

Steve stops midbite. "He did not."

"Well, not in so many words. But the more I think about it, the more I think maybe he's right."

"Why do we do this to ourselves?" he asks, waving his fork around.

"Do what? The dating?"

"The dancing. Why do we keep trying?"

"Because it's our new religion."

"Quinn calls it optimal frustration."

"Yeah, she said that to me too. Just today." He sighs again and looks around the room as if he's still somewhat embarrassed by the situation.

"Oh, come on," I tell him. "Don't get all morose just because Mary Tyler Moore ran out on you."

"You want her burrito to go? I told the waiter to box it."

"Sure," I say. "Tomorrow's lunch."

"You really think she looked like Mary Tyler Moore? Because if I'm going to get dumped in a Mexican restaurant, I'd like to think that at least I was dumped by Mary Tyler Moore."

I laugh and pick up my second drink.

Earlier I thought that I felt "vulnerable," but now I'm thinking that wasn't the right word. I have sore knees and I'm too old to shake my ass and I want something that I probably can't get, and here I am eating dinner with some other woman's discarded date and the word for what I'm feeling is "happy." I'm happier than I've been in a long, long time.

# CHAPTER TWELVE

Mark and I went to the MS Holiday Auction every December for years and the tickets automatically arrive the day after Thanksgiving, in the mail — two of them. I stick them to the refrigerator with a magnet.

And about a week before the event, the calls start. Some from the ostentation and some from people I haven't seen since Mark's funeral. He was one of the big donors to this particular charity and it seems important to the planning committee that I be there. Several couples offer to stop by and pick me up so that I don't have to find my way to the big, bad hotel on my own. "We thought you might not want to drive at night," said one woman, as if I were the one who was eighty, as if it weren't widely known throughout our gated community that her own husband/chauffeur was half-blind, half-deaf, and in the early stages of dementia.

In the end, I agreed to go. I wouldn't be helping with the auction this year, or setting up the tables, but I would attend. "It's the least you can do," another woman told me, rather artlessly, and never let it be said that Kelly Wilder Madison didn't do the least that she could do. I didn't think about what to wear until the evening of the event and then I dug an old gown out of my closet. Dark blue, that kind of clipped velvet that looks almost like suede. Off one shoulder with an interesting play of the straps in the back and it had once been one of my favorites. But it's snug when I pull it on. It makes puckers across my thighs and strains in the hips. I glance at the clock. I'm cutting it close on time as it is, so I don't want to dig around trying to come up with something else. I find a pair of heavy-duty Spanx, the kind that start just under your breasts and end at your knees, and heave my way into them and then put the dress back on.

I look in the mirror. I feel miserable but I look okay, so I wiggle my way into the car and drive uptown to the hotel, trying to keep myself as diagonal as I can in the driver's seat so that I don't make a whole new set of creases in the dress. My decision to come was prompted more by guilt than anything else. Just as I've stopped calling Elyse every night, at some point in the last few months I've stopped thinking about Mark. Trying to preserve his legacy by going to this stupid auction — it's a half-hearted stab at best. I'm sure I look ridiculous at stoplights, with my head pushed back and my butt in the air, and I wonder vaguely just how much weight I gained during that year I lay in bed and ordered takeout, and how much of it I've so far managed to dance off. I need to lay off the margaritas at Esmerelda's, that much at least is clear.

I valet. Toss five bucks at the kid and wobble inside. There are only a few name tags left on the table outside of the ballroom. One for me and one for Mark, I notice with a small pang. When I sent in the RSVP, did I respond for one, or did I just mail the form back without looking? It must have been the latter, because there it is, his name staring up at me.

"I'm Mrs. Madison," I say, tapping my own name tag with a fingertip.

"Good evening, ma'am," says the young girl working the desk, with the kind of overblown enthusiasm I've noticed is typical among nonprofit employees. "Is your husband parking the car?"

"No, it's just me," I say.

"Oh, that's too bad. I hope Mr. Madison isn't ill."

"He's dead."

This shuts her up, if only for a minute. She seems confused as to why I am attending a charity event in an overtight dress when my husband's just died, but I take pity on her and add, "It was a long time ago. I made a mistake on the RSVP."

"I see," she says, crumpling his name tag in her hand, as if that somehow makes it all better. "I'll get someone to escort you to your table."

Oh God. It just hit me that there will be an empty seat beside me. I'll be as bad as Steve at Esmerelda's. All the society ladies will gaze upon me with expressions of smug compassion. But the usher is already there. He holds his arm out to me, much like Nik does when we're taking the floor at the studio.

"Mrs. Madison?" he says.

When Mark Madison proposed twenty years ago, it was an escape chute.

Because after Daniel had left town — or, more to the point, after Daniel had left me — I went through what Elyse called the Year of Many Boys. Which is a nice way of saying I was a slut. I've heard someone explain — Oprah maybe, or Dr. Phil, or Dr. Oz, or Ellen, some disembodied voice I've overheard in passing — that a lot of "sexually impaired" women go through periods of promiscuity, much in the way that compulsive gamblers believe one more roll of the dice will change their luck. And my job at the bank was tailor-made for brief, meaningless affairs. There were so many men and so few women on my level, the hours were so long, the business trips so frequent, the bars always so close at hand.

The fling that ultimately ended the Year of Many Boys was with a guy named Ron McSomething and the fact that I don't remember his name is telling, because he's a very small part of the story.

But I do remember the night we went back up to the arbitrage floor after dinner and found ourselves utterly alone. That in itself was rare. It was the eighties and people were ambitious. They worked all hours, they did cocaine in the bathroom, they did each other in the stairwell, and the money came so easily that I think we were all high on the smell of it. I know I was.

The arbitrage floor had that strangely haunted quality that normally busy places have when they're empty, that echo of silence. Ron started to pull me back toward his desk but I said no, not here, and we ended up sneaking into one of the corner offices, where we knew there would be a couch and pillows. The one we chose happened to belong to a man named Mark Madison.

The next morning Mr. Madison's secretary called the secretary for my division and invited me to lunch. I couldn't think why. Mark Madison was not directly over me and I hardly knew the man. So my anxiety had steadily grown all morning and by the time I joined him in the executive elevator — the one that went directly to the top floor, where the private lounge and gym and restaurant were located — I was convinced that I had been summoned there to be fired.

The restaurant was tasteful in that sort of "nothing's untasteful" kind of way. We sat at a table with white chairs and a long, white tablecloth, ordered white wine and white fish, and then made small talk. Where I'd gone to school, renovations he was making to a vacation home in the mountains, the local sports teams. God help us, I think we even discussed the weather. We were seated right beside a window, fifty-two stories up, and this unfamiliar view of my hometown city was scary.

Then finally he brought out a manila envelope and handed it to me, saying, "I believe this may belong to you."

It was my silk camisole, lost somehow in the cushions of his couch the night before.

A strange thing for me to forget and probably the proverbial cry for help, although why my subconscious had decided to cry out to this particular man, white-haired and elegant and a little stern, I do not know. My reputation preceded me, I suddenly realized. For him to assume without question that the camisole was mine meant that even the executives in the corner offices knew who I was and what I was about. And then I did a highly uncharacteristic thing. I began to cry.

He patiently ate his Dover sole and waited for me to finish. I was so shamed, sitting there among all that whiteness, so high in the air, with my underwear folded and tucked neatly into one of the bank mailers. I knew he wasn't really going to fire me. He wasn't my boss, and besides, you can't fire someone for having sex on a couch. If they did that, they would have had to shut down the whole sales department. But I wasn't prepared for what happened next.

He said, "You deserve more for your life, Kelly."

And then he began to tell me about himself, in a linear and measured way, as if we were on a job interview. It took my guilt-addled mind a while to figure out that I was the one interviewing him and that the job he was applying for was that of my boyfriend. No, not my boyfriend. Something more. He was explaining to me why he would be a good husband. At the time I thought of him as old, but now, looking back, I do the math and it kicks me right in the gut. Mark was fifty-five when I met him, barely older than I am now.

He finished his litany by saying, very simply, "And I furthermore promise you that I will never cheat."

Furthermore? I just stared at him. My own fish was untouched, the envelope with the camisole was on my lap, and there were streaks of mascara on my napkin. This man knew the worst thing he could know about me, and it didn't seem to make any difference. He still wanted me. Was it only because I looked the part of a corporate wife? I tried to think back to the only occasion in which I'd ever really spent much time with him. A fund-raiser for the Special Olympics. I had played basketball with the kids. So had he. Not everyone in the office had ventured into that violent and illogical game. Most of them had just given money and sat in the stands, drinking bourbon out of thermos bottles and cheering.

"I'm not saying this to brag," he said. "It's just something I don't do, you know. I don't cheat."

He sounded so sure of himself. Exactly like Elyse. Sometimes standing in the presence of that much certainty weighs you down . . . and at other times, it feels like a lifeline.

"Is it because I'm pretty?" I asked.

"Partly," he said, which was the right answer. I appreciated the fact he didn't try to bullshit me, even though we both knew he was the one holding the cards. He smiled and blotted his mouth with his own perfect napkin. "If you say yes, will it be because I'm rich?"

We laughed then. I finally ate a bite of fish. "Because that's what everyone will say," he said, leaning back in his chair. "They'll say we got together because you're pretty and I'm rich. I hope that sort of gossip doesn't bother you."

It didn't. Just a few weeks earlier I had gone by Elyse's house and she had been baking Christmas cookies. She had sworn to me that baking cookies was hard, infinitely harder than it appeared on the surface, and she had been babbling about making 144 of them for a church cookie swap and how I couldn't possibly understand the sort of pressure she was under. But I had leaned against her sticky counter and absorbed it all — her tree, the carols on the sound system, Tory toddling around underfoot, the smell of cinnamon — and I had known that this was what I really wanted. The allure of the bank was fading for me. A woman can only own so many red jackets. She can only drink so many bottles of cabernet. The Year of Many Boys had come to an end. It was now January and I was sitting here, across the table from a man who had suddenly opened a door.

Mark and I set down our wineglasses at the same time and they clanked against each other. Very gently, but the sound rang out with such pure clarity that we both jumped, and so you could see it as an act of chance, or maybe something deeper, as if the universe itself was toasting our deal, even if we were too tentative to do it ourselves.

We break ourselves against men. Break ourselves like waves against rocks and we can't seem to help it, or even explain it. Elyse had never liked Daniel, never understood why I'd spent the twilight of my twenties going in and out of a hopeless relationship with a married man. Well, maybe at the beginning, when it was all sort of light and charming, she got it a little bit. Saw it as one of those movies with Glenda Jackson or Audrey Hepburn being all fey and carefree and wearing great clothes. But then at the end . . .

At the end I know I scared her. By the end I was scaring myself.

And then came the Year of Many Boys, which was actually more like the Eighteen Months of Many Boys, and the longer that madness had droned on, the less amused Elyse had been. "Do you know what you're doing?" she asked me once, and I'd answered, "Sometimes I don't even know who I'm doing." She hadn't laughed.

So I thought she would be thrilled to meet Mark. He was so different from Daniel — respectable, honest, eager to marry me and save me from myself.

We made a plan to have lunch at a café on a spring day. Mark and I were sitting outside, drinking wine, and Elyse had walked toward us pushing Tory in her stroller, a balloon tied to the handle and a big smile on Elyse's face. It seemed like it would go well. Mark insisted the lunch was his treat and Elyse has always liked men who pay — it's one of her little inconsistencies, one of many. He made a great fuss over Tory too, who with her wispy blond hair and fat cheeks always looked like a baby in an ad for something wholesome, like yogurt.

"Do you want more kids?" Elyse had rather pointedly asked him, as he'd made a puppet with his napkin and Tory had chirped and cooed.

"No, this part of my life is over," he said, his eyes never leaving Tory's face. "So we'll all have to share this beautiful little girl, if you don't mind."

It was like a thunk hit the table, a thunk that only Elyse and I heard. She glanced at me, trying to read my reaction. Although Mark and I had discussed the children by his first marriage, and the fact that he wasn't sure he had the heart to, in his words, "do that shit all over again," hearing that direct and flat "no" was a shock. I tried to cover. Act nonchalant, as if I were unsurprised by the certainty of his answer.

The thing is, I was never sure I wanted kids either. I imagine that many women who've had an abortion carry a niggling sense of unfinished business, but a niggling sense is quite a different thing from a full-blown desire to be a mother. So I had nodded and said yes, that Tory would have to be enough for us all, and Elyse just sat back and absorbed it, with the slightest little frown on her face.

Later, walking her and Tory back to the car, I said, "So what do you think? He's different, right?"

I didn't have to say "different from Daniel" because she knew what I meant. The very fact that Mark had been prepared to meet us at a café in broad daylight was different from Daniel.

"Yeah," she said. "Totally upstanding . . . but Kelly . . ."

"What?" I said, dreading the answer but figuring we may as well get it all out now.

She stooped to lift Tory from the stroller and put her into the car seat. A lot of strapping and buckling, with Tory fighting her the whole time, and then she cranked the car to get the AC going so that the baby wouldn't swelter while we talked, and then walked back around to the other side of the car to fold up and store the stroller. There were so many steps, I thought, so many steps to being a parent. Even going out to lunch was a procedure.

"It's like," Elyse finally said, slamming the door and leaning against the side of the Jeep. "It's like you ran off the road on one side and said 'Well, that sucked' and so you

205

got back in the car and drove it off the road on the other side, you know what I mean?"

"You think he's too upstanding."

"Maybe. Sometimes it's nice to, you know . . . lie down a tiny bit and wallow." She looked at me directly, chewing her lip.

"But I won't judge you," she said. "Even if I don't completely understand it, you know that I would never judge you. That's our deal."

It was a nice little lie and it got us through the next few months. Planning the wedding, my moving into his house. "The big house," we called it, which was what my daddy used to call prison, and I was astounded by the size of the place and its emptiness, the fact that there were whole rooms that would echo when you walked through them. The first time Elyse came to see me, they wouldn't let her past the gate. I had failed to understand the system, which is that you have to leave a guest's name down at the guardhouse before they are admitted, and this was in the days before cell phones, so Elyse had to abandon her car by the side of the road and walk into the little stone guardhouse. It was covered in ivy and always reminded me of a place where elves or dwarfs would live, and she had them call me from there, all the while bouncing Tory on her hip.

"I'm with the guards," she said, her voice dripping with exasperation and exhaustion, "and they won't let me through the gates. Will you please, please, pretty please tell them that you know me?"

After that I took a picture of her down there for them to post on the wall, for the guards were old and changed shifts frequently, and I wanted to make sure that they all knew her face and would wave her through on sight. I wrote LET THIS WOMAN IN ANYTIME on the bottom of the picture with a black Magic Marker and we never had that problem again.

Mark gave me free rein to do anything I wanted with the house. He knew that it echoed, and that an echoing house was sad, and that beneath the granite countertops and oak floors, the place cried out for a woman's touch. He had built it, but it would be my job to make it come to life. I started with the garden. Hired a landscape architect and an arborist from the local college and the result was so beautiful that when the time came for the wedding, we decided to have it there, among the roses. This meant a small ceremony, with a much larger reception to follow, and I liked the notion of taking our vows privately and fulfilling all the social obligations later, at the country club. Tory would be our only attendant. She could barely toddle but she would walk before me down the cobblestone path, throwing petals.

"She might mess up," Elyse fretted.

But there was practically no one to see her if she did, and besides, I love it when children act up at weddings. That's how the morning of the ceremony found me and Elyse and Tory dressing in the master bedroom. She'd brought a CD of old music to keep me calmed down. The stuff we listened to as kids — Joni Mitchell and the Eagles and Neil Young. We started by drinking mimosas, but then the orange juice ran out.

"Just as well," said Elyse, who has always liked drinking champagne straight from the bottle.

"You threw them away, didn't you?" I asked, calling out from the closet where I'd gone to slip into my own dress.

"Threw what away?" she asked, although I suspect she knew.

A couple of weeks earlier I had taken Daniel's letters out of the glove compartment of my car, where they had ridden around with me for over two years, and given them to

Elyse. "Burn them," I'd said. "Flush them. Bury them in the yard and play the bagpipes. I don't care. Just get rid of them." But of course all the time I had known she would keep them. Elyse is the curator of my life, just as I am of hers. It's not enough to keep the pom-poms from cheerleading or the first stubs from our first big-girl paychecks. We are required to hold all of each other's history, the good and the bad, and Elyse could no more throw away Daniel's letters than an archivist could forget the Civil War.

"Of course I did," she said. She was lying on the bed where Tory was playing with some sort of box toy where you push a car forward and back. Tory was already dressed in the filmy little blue dress with all its tedious buttons, sitting on the pouf it made like a cherub on a cloud, and Elyse had taken a dozen pictures of her already.

And when I finally came out of the closet in my Italian silk dress, she said, "My God, you look gorgeous."

"It's right for a second wedding?"

"It's right for anything. Seriously, I've never seen you look better."

"Then why do you have that look on your face?"

"What look?"

"You seem sad."

"I don't know," she said, standing and scooping up Tory, as we began to move slowly toward the bedroom door. Down the long staircase, through the wide doors, into the garden and my new life. "Maybe I'm a little bit jealous."

Immediately after the wedding, I began my slow excavation of the soul of Mark Madison. There was kindness beneath the gruffness — but I suppose a lot of people knew that. Over time I furthermore found the shyness beneath the kindness, the small wounds that only women detect in men. I tried to look past the abruptness, the occasional rush to judgment, the political incorrectness and the awkward jokes, toward the boy he once must have been. Before the alcoholic mother. Vietnam. The first wife, who had moved to California with his sons. Before he had begun to suspect that even the very heart that pumped within his ribs would someday betray him.

There's a sweetness there, I thought. There are treasures just below the surface, and thus for almost twenty years I devoted myself to a kind of emotional archaeology. Striving to unearth all the clues from my husband's past and analyze everything that made him what he was. And after he had the heart attack and retired I took on a second task, working to make his days pleasant, agreeable, just stimulating enough to be purposeful, but always shielding him from the small irritants of life, diverting problems before they landed in his lap. The things he couldn't quite feel, I felt for him. And this, I fear, was where I was truly a typical woman. Not by falling in love with a worthless guy who abandoned me. Not by faking in bed. Not even with the Year of Many Boys. A lot of women have those experiences, but what is truly universal, what truly aligns me with all other human females past and present, is my stubborn belief that by saving a man I could also save myself.

The weird thing is, it partly worked. Mark softened during our marriage and he never spoke of the morning he found the camisole — not even in anger, which a lesser man might have done. He found himself in the charity work and by the time he died he had more friends than I did.

"Are you still in mourning?"

The person asking the question is the wife of Mark's lawyer. They were sitting at my table when I was escorted there, along with two other couples. There was a bit of a scuffle but a chair and a place setting were swiftly removed and the gap at the table is not so noticeable now.

"Diane . . ." her husband says warningly.

"I'm just asking," the woman says, waving a well-manicured hand in my direction, "because navy is a vague color. And she would be so perfect for John Carlyle, don't you think? Are you ready to date, my dear?"

"Not yet," I say.

"Stay out of it, Diane," says her husband, who still hasn't told me how rich I am but who now seems to at least be aware of my discomfort, and the awkwardness of the situation.

"Well, she has to get out and about eventually, doesn't she?" the woman chirped on. "And, Kelly, you shouldn't feel one bit guilty about it. You gave Mark a lovely home while he lived. That's all that matters."

Is that what I did? I've barely grazed over the first and second courses but already I feel as if the Spanx are about to give way and fly around the table like a released balloon. My collar is scraping my neck and the earrings feel ponderous on my lobes. Another thing I haven't worn in a year — these golden drops so heavy and serious, a gift for my fifteenth anniversary, I think, or maybe my fiftieth birthday. I remember Mark claiming he chose them because they were so understated. "Nothing is more gauche than showing off wealth," he would say, and this room is full of people who evidently agree with him. For we are all understated, elegant, restrained. Even our faces, which have a uniform expression of polite boredom. As if it's a sin to try. A sin to want anything too much.

"What are you doing to fill your time?" asks another woman at the table. "We haven't seen you on any of the planning committees."

Is that an implied criticism? I can't remember her name, or that of her husband.

"They could have used you here," she goes on, with a little laugh, and everyone looks at the centerpieces in unison. A round bowl of roses sitting on a round mirror. Pretty sad.

"I'm dancing," I tell them. "That's how I fill my time."

"Well, that's nice," says Diane. "Dancing is a great way to meet men."

"No," I say. "My teacher is my partner."

She swallows this, along with an oyster.

"I waltz," I say. "At the Canterbury Ballroom."

"Doesn't Steve Mesovic dance there?"

someone asks someone. "The plastic surgeon?"

"Have you run across Steve?" Diane says.
"Tall, good-looking man with a —"

"I know him," I say. "But I'm not looking
for a way to meet men. I find it impossible
to be in a romantic relationship and still be
a whole person. When I'm with a man I'm
not curious and authentic and big and you
know, questing and all that."

Now where the hell did that come from? I
sound like Elyse. The six people, the three
couples, at my table all stare at me. About
half with curiosity, the other half with concern.

"Are you all right?" asks the woman whose
name I don't know.

She means "Are you drunk?" but I'm not.
I do feel a little breathless, more the result
of this damn dress than anything else. I have
a sudden urge to rip it off my body, to toss
my shoes into the centerpiece of roses.

"What time is it?" I ask.

"Almost seven," Diane says with a peek at
her watch. "Entrées any minute."

Not yet seven? I had forgotten how early
they hold these dinners, in concession to
the fact that the median age of their donors
is somewhere in the seventies. If I hurry I
can still make tango.

214

"Excuse me," I say. I am up and away before anyone can respond. Out of the ballroom and through the lobby, and then the revolving door, until I am at last on the windy street where the valet parking boys are huddled beneath their umbrellas. I hand them my claim and a twenty and the car appears before me with stunning speed. I grab my duffel bag out of the backseat, ask the kids to hold the car for five minutes, and run back into the hotel, where I find a ladies' room and lock myself in the handicapped stall.

The dress is trouble. The Spanx even more so. But I get them off and my black Lycra practicewear on, exhaling for the first time, it seems, all evening. Pull off the heavy earrings and put them in a side zipper compartment in my duffel bag. Leave the stall and wash my face, then take down my hair. Finally I drape the dress and the Spanx over one of the stuffed embroidered chairs in the lobby part of the restroom, with the matching shoes beneath it, and I leave the little jeweled bag in the lap of the dress. Maybe someone will want them. It looks like the woman wearing these clothes must have been teleported somewhere, like we're in one of those movies where the aliens come and take some humans but not others. It will confuse the hotel maids, just as it will confuse Mark's lawyer and the others when I do not return to their table.

But life, after all, is an extraordinarily confusing thing. They'll get over it.

# CHAPTER THIRTEEN

Nik makes one more attempt to persuade me to compete at the Holiday Classic, but I promise him I'll dance at the Star Ball in March instead. It's in Charlotte, it's easier, and I'll be more ready. For the Classic, I'll just be Quinn's helper, a sort of all-purpose handmaiden to the other dancers. He warns me I'll be sorry. When I get there, I'll get the fever and wish I were out on the dance floor too. He might be right, because I've already begun to curse my lack of nerve. The studio has been nuts for weeks, with people booking double lessons to get ready, and the female students modeling their newly rented dresses.

We pack Quinn's ancient little VW bug and drive to Atlanta on Friday afternoon. Or Hotlanta, as Isabel keeps insisting on calling it from the backseat, until I for one am about ready to scream. The studio has gotten us a block of rooms on the same floor

217

of the hotel and Anatoly has laid down strict orders that there will be no drinking until after the competition is over. It's my first hint that while this road trip is considered a vacation by the students — they're spending anywhere between six hundred and six thousand dollars depending on how many heats they're dancing — as far as Anatoly is concerned, it's nothing but business.

We're barely in the room and unpacked before Quinn begins spray tanning the teenage girls who are doing Latin. They get in our bathtub one at a time and stand there, grimly nude, with their eyes squeezed shut, while Quinn goes up and down their bodies with a sputtering little machine. Judging from the shrieks and yelps coming from the bathroom, it's a miserable process — cold and sticky — and after each one is finished, she walks around the room Frankenstein-style, with her arms and legs splayed out, waiting for her armpits and inner thighs to dry. When the girls are finished, Quinn packs up her machine and heads out to do the boys in their own bathtubs.

My task is relatively simple: to go from room to room among our block collecting coffeepots so we can keep a steady supply of caffeine flowing tomorrow morning. Quinn is doing several people's hair and makeup, which I gather is a significant source of extra income for her, and she has them stacked up to arrive in the order they'll be competing. Valentina, who is dancing in the Newcomer division, has to be down at the ballroom at six-thirty in the morning and she's coming to our room at five. Holiday Classic is a one-day event, meaning it's an absolute marathon of competition with heats scheduled every two minutes. I carry the coffeepots back to our bathroom, which has brown outlines of human body parts all over the shower stall, and fill them with the Starbucks Breakfast Blend I brought from home. I get Quinn's sewing kit and thread a needle with each color we might conceivably need, sticking them all in an orange from the welcome basket. Then, even though Quinn isn't back yet, I get into bed and try to sleep.

Evidently I succeed, because the next thing I'm aware of is an alarm going off and the sound of Quinn cursing and crashing to her feet. I roll over in the darkness. The clock glows 4:30. "Rise and shine," Quinn mumbles, then she goes down the line of coffeemakers, flipping each switch before she gets into the shower. The room begins to gurgle like an aquarium.

I pull on yoga pants and a T-shirt that says

"It's not a mistake, it's a variation" and go down to the buffet to bring back plates of food. The entire hotel has been taken over by the competition, and because of the insane start times, our welcome brochure said they'd begin putting out a continental breakfast at four o'clock. No one is actually sitting and eating, but there are a fair number of people in line, scavenging like me. I pile fruit and toast on a plate, put five containers of yogurt in a plastic bag, and, when no one is looking, snatch an entire gallon of orange juice. It's cumbersome in my arms but when I get back to the elevator, a man in a tux pushes the button for me. I ride up with women swathed in feathers and sequins and lace, all giggling like schoolgirls, and when I turn the corner of our hall I see Valentina is already there.

Quinn has instructed the women to dry their hair with as much mousse as they can handle and Valentina has evidently taken her seriously, because she is knocking gently on our door with a halo of wild, witchlike hair. She's wearing the hotel bathrobe, fishnet hose, and large red fuzzy slippers and is carrying a little sack in her hand that I assume holds her hair accessories. For months before the competition the dancers have been collecting jeweled barrettes and sparkly combs and even little tiaras. "I am very scared," she whispers, as Quinn opens the door and lets us both in.

Quinn and I discussed it on the drive down. She's going to show me how to put the foundation on with a sponge so that when the women begin arriving in droves we can get a production line going. Quinn carries all her stage makeup in a big fishing tackle box, which is open on the bed. She watches while I practice with Valentina, slathering her with the dark brown liquid. It seems like a ridiculous amount of gunk on poor Valentina's pretty face, but when I finish, Quinn immediately says, "She needs more."

"Are you serious?" I'm more worried about the obvious line of demarcation where the makeup stops an inch under Valentina's chin, but Quinn brushes aside my concerns.

"Don't worry," she says. "When we get the bronzer on her it will blend right in."

"She's doing ballroom. I thought only the Latin dancers had to be brown."

"Only Latin dancers have to spray tan, but everybody has to be brown. Look at her. She has that fair Russian skin and she's going to wash right out under the lights."

Valentina is sitting trustingly, with her

back to the mirror. There's a knock at the door and Quinn lets Isabel in, with Jane right behind her.

"Hurry it up," Quinn tells me. "Another layer on Valentina and Isabel goes next." Jane takes a banana from the welcome basket and stretches out on the bed, and Isabel is chattering wildly. They have the same stiff hair, the same bedroom slippers and fishnet hose. I appear to be the only one concerned about the weird color of Valentina's skin.

We get into a certain pattern. Coffee, yogurt, bananas, foundation with me, and then hair with Quinn. Then a pee and back to me for cheeks and mouth. Quinn is amazingly fast, so if I want to keep up with her, I can't be so cautious with the makeup. She takes one side of their hair and pulls it back slick to their heads, then does the same with the other side and forms a little French twist. I can see from across the room that these hairdos are too hard and tight to move, not even if the women turn cartwheels or run through fountains. Another knock at the door and a gaggle of teenagers spill in. I didn't know Quinn had agreed to do them too. Big clouds of hair spray periodically fill the air, until we're all choking and even the orange juice tastes like

Final Net. If the woman has short hair, like Jane, Quinn has come prepared with hairpieces and she's turning them over at a rate of seventeen minutes per dancer. I'm managing to keep up with her, painting every nationality in the studio a uniform shade of adobe brown. At one point Wilhemina arrives, fully dressed in her gown, and everyone moves over to give her the best chair.

Quinn trusts me to do the foundation, blush, and lipstick, but she brings them back to her chair for the eyes. She applies a long swoop of black gel eyeliner with a remarkably steady hand, followed by big arcs of shadow and then the false eyelashes. Huge spiky things like sea creatures and some of them have small crystals or glitter attached to the ends or even bits of fur. Quinn runs the glue line along the base of the woman's existing lashes, places the false lashes on top and then tells her to hold them there until it all dries so she can start on the next lady. When Jane stands up from the makeup table, she is completely unrecognizable.

"It's a costume," she says, to no one in particular. "We're all just characters in a play."

For the last step, the woman stands up and I brush bronzer all over her neck, back, and shoulders. Most have brought their dresses with them, so that I can bronze them all the way down to wherever the fabric starts. The dresses are low either in the front or back or both, so it's a challenge to cover all that skin. To stop in the middle is to risk making it uneven or clumpy, so I soon learn that I must brush them in long strokes, as if their flesh were the wall of a house. Others return to their rooms to dress and then come back to us for the final touches, a few more dabs of bronzer around their cleavage or the hollow of their backs. The room begins to fill with swirls of color. The bright fuchsia of Valentina's gown, the midnight blue of Wilhemina's, the lavender of Isabel's, the mint green of Jane's.

The protocol is obvious. Valentina and Jane rented their dresses, which is not as good as owning, but Isabel is trying to do it even more on the cheap, so she bought a prom dress at a consignment shop and had Quinn stone it for her with a glue gun. Swarovski crystals are apparently the ticket — both Valentina's and Jane's dresses have a few scattered across the bodice and shirt. If you add enough of them, the crystals alone can up the price of a gown by a thousand dollars. But Isabel's are Korean crystals and while I would have laughed at this designation weeks ago, something about the thin little flecks of light on her gown now break my heart. They are already falling off as she moves about the room. Crystals are on the bed and scattered around the toilet. It doesn't seem to bother her. This is her first competition, and Isabel is literally trembling with anticipation. "Quinn," she calls from the bathroom. "Do I need more lip gloss?"

"Listen up, ladies," Quinn calls back. "In ballroom, the answer to do I need more of anything is always yes. If even a part of your brain considers asking that question, you need more."

The women are too nervous to think for themselves, so I find myself barking orders. Sit there, bring me this, inhale. If you have to drink coffee, at least drink it through a straw. Quinn tells me I'm a good assistant, and I know I am, but Nik was right. The women look bizarre and unnatural but somehow they are beautiful too, and I'm a little jealous. The room is full of Cinderellas who have just put down their brooms and laundry. Their dresses are due back when the clock strikes midnight and there's something frantic just beneath the surface of their giddiness, a desire to squeeze as much glamour out of the day as they can.

When the last woman is finally finished and back out in the hall, Quinn begins getting ready for her own dances with Steve, who, despite three years of private lessons, is still competing on the Newcomer level. Although no one really ever sits you down and explains these things, I'm beginning to understand how it works. It's not just a matter of the people who "dance down," competing on levels beneath them in order to guarantee they'll place well. It's also the fact that instructors try to load their students into heats where no one else in their gender or age group is dancing, so that although there may be other couples on the floor at the same time, the student is in essence competing with no one. An uncontested win still counts as a win, and I gather this is what Quinn has carefully engineered for Steve. A bit of store-bought glory, the ego stroke of being called up at the awards banquet tonight for a handful of ribbons, not to mention guaranteed points for the studio. Anatoly has been talking about it for weeks. We brought down a large contingent and the whales are dancing lots of heats; Pamela alone, I believe, is doing eighty. If our people place well — as they can hardly fail to do considering the way all our instructors have been poring over the heat sheets, looking for the perfect slot in which to place them — we have a shot at Studio of the Year. And evidently that matters too.

Quinn's gown suits her, although it's a bit renaissance fair, with large patches of pink and purple, and she has attached a nest of braids to the top of her head. I help her cover her tattoos with the thickest makeup we've used yet, something she digs out of the bottom of the tackle box that comes in a medicinal-looking tube and that she says was developed in France after World War I to cover the scars of burned veterans. She dashes out of the room, her heels in her hands, and I strip naked and collapse back onto the bed.

I'm exhausted, but I can't rest. I keep looking at the clock. If I had the guts to dance, I'd probably be dancing about now. I wonder how much competition I would have, how many people would be in my division. It seems that being both in your fifties and a Newcomer would be a bad combination, that I might be teetering on the edge of the ridiculous. Yet, Wilhemina is thirty years older than I am and she's down there giving it a shot. Her hair was so thin that Quinn whispered it would have broken if she'd tried to pull it back, so instead she'd given her a strange little wig with bangs and a flip, similar to the one she must have been wearing the first day I came into the studio. Quinn had almost glued Wilhemina's eyelids shut with her weighty lashes and had drawn her eyebrows into the high arch of permanent surprise. But her gown was covered in crystals, more than all the other dresses in the room combined, and when she had stood to go, Wilhemina's face had been as excited as those of the teenage girls.

There's no way I'm going back to sleep. In fact, my heart is pounding. I debate taking a Lexapro, something I haven't done since Mark died, but then I look again at the clock: 6:35. It's still dark outside and it feels like I've been up all day or maybe like it's somehow still the night before. Valentina's warmed up by now and the first heats have just begun. She's in number nine, she said, and at two minutes a heat that means she'll dance soon. Maybe it's the old cheerleader in me, but I feel guilty. If I get up and hurry, I can be down in time to watch her dance.

I pull my clothes back on and follow Isabel's glitter trail to the elevator. The ballroom is bright and loud when I get there, and full enough that it takes me a while to find the table with our studio's name. My timing is perfect, since they're just wrapping up the sixth heat. People of all ages are leaving the floor, from children to the elderly, and I can see Valentina in the corner of the ballroom, practicing her Viennese waltz with Nik. Since she couldn't afford many private lessons, she decided to only compete in one dance for all ten of her heats — the Viennese waltz, her favorite. The heats before hers blow by fast and Valentina and Nik line up at the corner of the stage. When the music starts, it's "My Favorite Things," the classic Viennese waltz tune, the first one on the iPod shuffle at our studio, and her face splits into a wide smile of recognition.

Somehow I thought watching a ballroom competition would be like going to the opera, a sedate affair, but I soon learn that all the tables hoot and holler for their dancers, and it's really more like NASCAR. Valentina's nervous, taking small steps and making tight little turns, but she's smiling as they spin past us, the painfully young Internet bride and her dance instructor. Her husband is taking pictures, but it's hard to say whether he's getting Valentina in any of the shots. He doesn't stand up — maybe he can't — and he is aiming his camera toward the dance floor in an unsteady fashion. He seems more like a father watching a daughter go off to the prom than a husband, and it's both sweet and kind of sobering. Did Mark and I ever look like that?

As her last heat concludes, Nik escorts Valentina back to the table, where we all stand and cheer, and then he immediately goes to warm up Isabel in the corner. I almost didn't recognize him when he came in, stained dark as coffee with his hair slicked back and knotted at the nape of his neck like a vampire's. Quinn and Steve are coming up in eleven heats. How could I have thought of sleeping through this? It's fascinating, it's fabulous, it's like reality on steroids. I wonder what Elyse would think if she were here, if she'd think I was nuts to be sitting among all these feathers and tiaras at seven o'clock on a Saturday morning in a two-star hotel on the outskirts of Atlanta. But Elyse would probably treat the ballroom dancers like the Hopi or Navajo, just one more aboriginal tribe for her to study, with their own brand of ritual and adornment. Or I wonder what Mark would say about so much silliness — if he would consider it a noble kind of silliness, or if it would just look to him like an ostentation that's found a whole new way to spend their husbands' money. If he would consider these men no more than gigolos, paid to fuss and flatter.

Paid to prop up sagging marriages the way a buttress shores up the wall of a house.

Jane has pulled her chair beside mine. She's got the program open in her lap and is panicking because she's just realized that Nik has put her into heats that have six or seven dancers in her age group. This couldn't have been by accident — we've seen him carrying around the entry forms for weeks — so she and I both know he's testing her. Her lover, Margaret, hasn't come to Atlanta, something about a sick dog back home, and that might be one reason why Jane seems so agitated. I can't say I'm surprised Nik has pulled something like this. He's ambitious for his dancers. Not competitive — I don't think trophies or ribbons mean anything to him and he isn't like Anatoly, a compulsive point counter, determined to push the studio higher in the rankings. Nik would rather one of his dancers come last in a hard heat than win an easy one. He has said as much to me, that you only improve through that sort of pressure, so it makes sense that he's loaded Jane into crowded heats. He doesn't want her to just be the first of one.

"Oh God," she says, flipping through the program. "There are seven women in my tango and six in waltz. I don't care about being first. I'd be thrilled with fourth or fifth. I just don't want to be last."

"Nik won't let you be last," I say, although that's exactly what I'd have been thinking if I were in her shoes.

"Who are these women?" she says fretfully, peering at the listings through her reading glasses. "Shit, two of them are from California."

"That doesn't mean they're any better than you."

"If you weren't good, why would you bother coming all that way?"

She has a point, so I turn my attention back to the dancers and leave her to worry her way through the book. It's easy for me to think this, since I'm not the one whose ass is on the line, but I'm proud of Nik for not stacking the deck and I agree with him that placing his students in hard heats will make them better dancers. A lot of things are becoming clear to me as I watch the competition, in fact, because everything Nik's ever said is being acted out before my eyes. He's always telling me to put power in my steps from the start. This goes against my natural inclination, and probably everyone's natural inclination. When something is new and you're uncertain, you want to keep it controlled and careful, at least until you're sure you've memorized the sequence. Nik won't let me do this. He says things like "We go across room in five steps," without telling me what those five steps are going to be. And when I beg him to let me learn the routine before I put in the power, he shakes his head.

Power first, then finesse. If you don't have energy from the very start, then it's hard to put it in later. By that time you're proud of your pretty little steps. You don't want to mess them up or change something that seems to be working, and so you stay small, and now, here before me, all over this ballroom, I can see the truth of what he's been saying. People who started out careful and never figured out how to get bigger. Their form is correct. Their timing is accurate. They don't make any obvious mistakes. They're trying hard not to come in last. But they aren't really dancing.

Quinn swoops in and says, "Time for round two." She's finished dancing with Steve so we're going back upstairs to get Pamela ready for the Silver heats. Word is she's even doing a few Gold and I respect her for it, a bit grudgingly.

"I've got to go help Quinn," I tell Jane. "I'm sorry, but I don't think I'll get back in time to see you dance."

"Good," she says, still staring into the program, her pink high-lighter in her hand. "I don't want anybody to see me. I don't know why I ever agreed to do any of this. I'm in hell."

Pamela, needless to say, owns her gown. It is stunning, heavily stoned, a bright red chiffon with a low back that reaches almost to the dimples of her butt cheeks. The sort of thing a woman wears when she is no longer afraid of being noticed.

"It's amazing," I tell her.

She shrugs. Pamela and I have only had one conversation in our entire lives, that night in the Esmerelda's bathroom when she tried to warn me off Nik. I wonder if she even knows I'm the one who walked in on her that day in the instructor's lounge. "I'm thinking of getting rid of it," she says.

"Really?" Quinn says. "I'd take it off your hands, but I'm too fat."

"It might fit you," Pamela says. It takes me a second to realize she's talking to me.

Quinn has Pamela in the chair, putting up her hair, and I walk over to the dress hanging on the door. It's a Doré, which is one of the best. The price of ball gowns seems ridiculous until you learn how much engineering goes into them and then the price

234

still seems ridiculous, but a little less so. They're sewn together over a skeleton of girdles and bras so that nothing ever slips, even if the dancer does lifts and splits. Looking inside one of these dresses is like opening the hood of a sports car. You see at once where the money went.

"It's a professional dress," Pamela tells me, which, thanks to Quinn, I know means that it's superconstructed, even by ball gown standards. "I saw someone wearing it last year and pitched such a fit that Bob got it for me for Christmas." She laughs, a high, tinkly sound like a bell you'd ring for a maid.

"Pamela's husband," Quinn says, so many bobby pins in her mouth that I can barely understand her, "owns the shopping center the studio is in."

"Canterbury Commons is one of his properties," Pamela says primly, a note of correction in her voice.

"Really?" I say. "That's very cozy." And then I lift the hanger off the doorframe and nearly drop the dress. Between the beading and the interior construction, it's much heavier than I would have figured and I've been carrying ball gowns around all morning. If you were to put this dress in the corner, it would probably be able to stand there a minute on its own.

"It weighs sixteen pounds," Pamela says, as if reading my mind. "Do you want to try it on?"

"There isn't time," I say, but I hold it up to myself in the mirror and for a second my reflected image gives me pause.

"Red on a blonde is unexpected," Quinn says. "I've never thought about it before, but you two look a little bit alike. You're both about the same height, I mean. And the hair."

This is an observation that probably doesn't please either one of us, but Pamela shifts a little in the chair so that she can see me in the mirror. No one wears dresses like this at the Newcomer level, or even the Bronze, where most of the dancers are still renting or making their own. A dress like this is a statement, a demand for attention, a sign the dancer takes herself seriously. Maybe a little too seriously.

"I'll let it go for three thousand," Pamela says.

"Think of it as an early Christmas gift to yourself," Quinn says, spinning her around in the chair so that she can face the mirror at last. "I bet it would look great on you."

"And there's room to let out the seams if it's tight in the hips," Pamela says. She is frowning at her reflection and when Quinn hands her the smaller mirror so that Pamela can scrutinize the back of her hair, she catches my eye. She mouths the word "bitch" and I hang the dress back on the door.

Pamela may be a bitch but the artistry of her dancing astounds me. She and Anatoly begin their quickstep with a running leap into a slide — very tricky, but their timing is perfect. Pamela's dress flares like a Chinese fan when she leaps.

It's late in the day, the last heats of the afternoon, and Pamela and Anatoly clearly have it in the bag. The rest of us sit around the table in various states of disrepair. One of Isabel's eyelashes has come off and the other is still on. Jane stares straight ahead in a kind of stupor. Wilhemina has gone to her room to take a nap and Valentina and her husband have left to drive back to North Carolina. Which is a shame, since Nik just learned she got a first and three seconds. I believe that going up to the judges' table to get her ribbons would have pleased Valentina very much.

The mood of the ballroom has changed throughout the day, become more business-like as we've moved on to the Silver and

237

Gold heats. People have stopped cheering or lining the floor to take snapshots of their family and friends and started drinking instead. The moves on the floor are getting harder, much more athletic, and at Quinn's direction, I have brought down a Styrofoam cooler filled with ziplock bags of ice. The pros are exhausted. They are icing themselves every time they come off the floor. Everyone on this level has competed many times, and they've met everyone else in their divisions. They seem to know the circuit almost too well, and who is supposed to beat whom. A woman from another studio has just walked by our table in tears, talking loudly into a cell phone. "Tricia took two of my tangos," she was sobbing to whoever was on the line.

"Well, this is just a great big bucketload of drama," Isabel says. "Every direction you look. What do you think that woman's dress cost? Probably more than my car." I laugh, a little guiltily. Isabel's gown looks especially shabby in this company, now that most of the newcomers have begun packing and leaving and only the whales remain in the room. "Seriously," she goes on, "if I'm going to keep doing this, I'm going to have to find a civilian partner. Paying for the heats is one thing but when you add on the instructor fees, it's killing me."

"And just where do you plan to find this civilian partner?" Jane asks.

"The group class, of course," she says, and we all start to giggle, picturing Harry and Lucas decked out in tuxedos and taking the floor.

"Well," I say, "there's always Steve." And this makes us laugh harder for some reason. We've all gone punchy with some combination of nerves and vodka and hair spray fumes and sleep deprivation.

"Dr. Boob wouldn't dance with me if I was the last woman on earth," says Isabel. "I might make a mistake and God forbid he ends up with a partner who makes a mistake."

"Steve's not quite as bad as you think," I say, and then I ask Jane, who's been keeping a running total of who's placing where on her program, how we're doing on overall points.

"Good," she says. "But I don't know about Studio of the Year." Anatoly really wants that silly trophy but we're probably too far off our native turf. Some ballroom in Georgia will more likely take it. For the first time in a long time I feel like I'm on the inside of a group. I wish Carolina could be here. I should get my phone and send a few pictures to her.

Nik has been standing right at the edge of the dance floor, watching Pamela compete with Anatoly. She's one of the dancers whose name is known around the region and it means a lot to the whole studio, but still . . . he shouldn't be hovering so close or watching her so obviously. The rumor is her husband might show up. Apparently that's always the rumor, at every comp and showcase, that Pamela's husband might just swoop in at the last minute and start shooting or something. I glance around the ballroom. The judges are bent, conferring over their score sheets, and Nik rubs the back of his neck. He's spent, I think. They all are.

I should have danced. Why didn't I? What am I waiting for? It is just like Nik warned me it would be. I've run around all day like one of Cinderella's mice, sewing rips and painting lips and fetching orange juice and being helpful and hesitant, just like I've always been. I may as well scoop up some of these molted feathers and dropped sequins from the floor and make them a goddamn tablescape. I'm the worst kind of hypocrite. I knocked Valentina for taking small steps when I didn't take any steps at all.

At the table beside us, a woman has sat down while she waits for the callbacks to be announced. She puts her foot on a chair and I can see that she's bleeding through her shoes. She's wearing the pretty competition kind, which are made of pale gold silk. They're designed to be flesh-colored, at least if you're Caucasian, to imply one long stretch between your foot and leg. But apparently she didn't break hers in enough before competition and she's popped blisters. A pattern of blood has run across the top of her shoes, making the outline of each toe distinct.

"God," I say, "I'm so sorry. Do you want an ice pack?" The ice packs are for our dancers, and she's probably Pamela's competition so maybe I shouldn't have offered. But it comes out of my mouth automatically.

She shakes her head. "No time," she says. And just then they announce a string of numbers and she rises, her shoe growing redder the moment she puts weight on it. She gives me a look somewhere between a smile and a wince and says, "Only the strong survive."

They have called Pamela's number too. Anatoly takes her hand and she seems to glide to the center of the ballroom, the red floats of her gown billowing behind her. She's smiling even though there's no guarantee of anything, not at this level, where everyone is good.

Nik is suddenly beside me. He puts his arm across the back of my chair.

"So," he says, "you are bitten with bug? You will compete next time?"

"Not only that," I say, "but I'm going to buy your girlfriend's dress."

# CHAPTER FOURTEEN

Carolina is back in hospice. They took her in last night, after exactly what they warned might happen did. She caught a cold, probably from her kids, and her white blood cell count zoomed out of control. She treats it as a temporary setback, but she's too smart to misread what this really means. Her immune system is shot. She can no longer screen out the everyday toxins of life, so she will spend her last Christmas in Hospice House after all.

"She seems defeated," the client coordinator told me, but after I saw her, I would have said a better word was "fatalistic." A lot of cancer patients are like this. People who come in from strokes and heart attacks often have a startled expression, as if they were ambushed, but most cancer patients have been stalked by their disease for months, even years. They've tried to hold the truth at bay: skipped tests, ignored symptoms, made excuses for how bad they've felt. But deep inside they've heard the rustling of the leaves and felt the breath of the beast. When he finally catches up to them, they are not terribly surprised.

"We need to come up with a dance quick," I tell Nik. "It doesn't have to be good, it just has to be fast. Something we can perform in front of people who don't know anything about dancing. People who have other things on their minds."

He considers this for a moment. "We will waltz," he says. "And we open with three unsupported spins."

"I don't do unsupported spins," I remind him.

And so we spin. My whole private lesson is forty-five minutes of just the opening, practicing how we will get across this broad, flat floor to meet in the middle, and I am still, despite all his council about spotting by looking at a fixed place on the wall and keeping my abdominal muscles tight, coming out of the turns weak and wobbly. Almost falling into his arms.

This has been a frustrating session, but Nik is superstitious. He never lets me move on until I have at least somewhat mastered the step in question. I suppose I can understand it from his point of view — he doesn't want me to get it in my head that certain steps are impossible — but on the flip side, this philosophy of teaching means that sometimes the lessons never end.

"What are you afraid of?" he asks me.

"Falling. Everything. I'm weak in the gut," I say. But it's more than that. I don't have the stamina I once had and my lungs are aching with effort. My knees are even starting to hurt although I'd die before I'd admit that part. The older women at the studio are always complaining about their knees.

Nik is unimpressed. "You just need practice." He demonstrates again. A perfect 360.

This time I'm so nervous I underspin, not making it quite all the way around. If we had been in hold, Nik would have been able to use my hand to help rotate me, tugging me the rest of the way through the circle. But in competition, a judge would catch that in a heartbeat, and besides, I can't always depend on Nik being there. In group class the guys don't help you at all. It's every dancer for himself, with half the people overrotating and the rest of them underrotating. Once Lucas and I came out of a spin back to back.

Nik is trying hard to make a point. He spins and tells me to call out a number while he's turning: 180, 360, 405, 540. No matter what number of degrees I call, he stops right on it, beautifully and without the slightest wobble. He isn't doing this to show off, but rather to prove to me it can be done.

"Now," Nik says, "you will push on pole." We've come to the end of our forty-five minutes and he leads me over to the stripper-style pole in the corner that the young girls use to work on their backbends. I need to at least nail the 360, he says, before we can go further. I feel like a kid kept behind after class for bad behavior, and besides, we've spun a thousand times and my right foot is already hurting.

"I'm in a bad place with this," I tell him, and I can feel myself starting to cry.

"Just for a minute, then you can stop," he says.

"Sometimes people come to their personal limit, you know? My friend Elyse says everybody has a limit."

"Yes. True. This is not your limit."

"What makes you so sure?" I say, and to my horror I realize I am truly crying now. It's not the spinning, or at least not just the spinning. It's Carolina and finding Daniel on Facebook and the fact that I'm staring down the barrel of another Christmas without Mark. It's everything.

I stomp out onto the sidewalk and leave him there, frowning at me, probably thinking I'm just one more self-indulgent American who's never really dug in and worked for anything in her life. I'm so rattled that I've walked out in my practice shoes with their suede bottoms and risked ruining them on the sidewalk, so I sit down on the nearest bench to unbuckle them. Steve's car is in the parking lot. I don't know many cars, but I know his, this red BMW that screams out everything you need to know about the man. It's three minutes after three and he's just sitting there, alone in his car. I've always assumed the way he hurries in a few minutes after the hour was an affectation, his way of reminding us that his time is far more important than anyone else's. But now I see him late but still waiting, until finally, at five minutes past three, he jumps out with his dance shoes in hand and dashes in the door as if he's just arrived.

He's scared, I think. He has so much trouble talking to people that he pretends to run late so that he has an excuse for not hanging out.

Maybe I'm a coward but I'll be damned if I'm as big a coward as Steve. I push to my feet, grab my shoes, open the door, and walk back in. Nik very pointedly ignores me and

I ignore him. I walk over to the pole and push off it. I go around in an almost circle, maybe 330 degrees, something like that. Not 360. I push again.

Quinn is working with Jane and apparently everything about her upper body is a disaster. Quinn is running her hands down the length of Jane's arms, pulling some parts down and others up in pursuit of that elusive thing called frame. In waltz, the shoulders should be relaxed, the upper arm lifted — this in itself is hard enough — with the elbow in perfect alignment with the shoulder and the wrist dropped flat against the man's bicep. Who knew the human arm had so many parts? Or the hand? The middle finger is key, extended straight out as a natural continuation of the arm. The second and fourth fingers are slightly elevated, and the pinky a centimeter higher still. You can do it, if you think about it. You can do it in the mirror, before class. But when the music starts and there are a hundred other things to remember, it's easy for your hand to forget its graceful task and become a grasping claw. Pawing the air in search of any solid surface — preferably your instructor.

But frustration is what we're paying for. Frustration is what we all want. Quinn guides Jane's arm up and down, and I spin again, over and over, trying to find that still space in myself. It's a type of meditation. It drives out all emotion and makes me forget everything. I have almost forgotten the sight of Carolina lying pale and motionless on her narrow bed.

Isabel has the next lesson after mine. She demands certain songs and certain dances during her private time with Nik. She likes to rumba to Chris Isaak's "Wicked Game." When she told us this once, over drinks, every woman in the group had giggled a little slyly. "Wicked Game" is such a fantasy song for women. We have all imagined running across that white beach, toward that lanky, squinting boy. Nik tries to get her to dance to something else. He puts his iPhone in the stereo cradle and punches up this thumping Eurosound, pretending that he's going to lead her into something modern and formless. But she just puts her hands on her hips and refuses to budge.

Maybe I should throw more fits, because Isabel is certainly not afraid to be a pain in the ass. She knows the instructors call her high-maintenance, but that can be said about most of the women at the studio, and besides, Nik likes her. She isn't his favorite. She doesn't pick up the steps the quickest, she doesn't have the best form, and she certainly isn't the easiest to get along with. But Isabel seems to understand that it isn't necessary to be everyone's favorite and I would imagine that realization must feel like manacles falling from your ankles. She stands in the middle of the floor with her hands on her hips until Nik laughs indulgently and puts on "Wicked Game."

I spin. I watch them. It amazes me how different he is with each of us, how he brings a different part of his personality to every client's dance. He treats Pamela, at least in public, like a china doll. He kids around with Isabel like a sister, speaks Russian with Valentina, and with me and Jane . . . he is harsher, more pedantic. Take it as a compliment, Quinn has told me. He doesn't waste his energy on people unless he thinks they have promise.

Students come and go. Jane leaves, Steve leaves. Valentina stops by with some papers. Her English is a little too formal but otherwise perfect, and Quinn told me once that she had been a translator back in Moscow, that she still does some work for the studio. She leaves a folder on Quinn's desk, waves at me, and I wave back. I'm covered with sweat by this point and my heart went into the aerobic zone about fifty spins ago, but

I've come up with a system. I do five spins holding on to the pole and then five spins without holding on to the pole. Then a break for the vertigo to subside. When I use the pole for leverage, I can make it the full 360 most of the time. Without it, the turns are more of a crapshoot, but I won't have a stripper pole beside me when I waltz at hospice.

By the time Isabel pays and leaves I can do ten unsupported spins in a row, about three of them good. Nik comes up to me and says "Enough spin" and asks me to tango. Just asks me, like I'm a regular person he met at a party. He knows how hard I've been working. This is a little reward. Two free minutes of tango.

We pivot, we corte, and it all feels easy after the spinning. I try to tell him that I'm sorry I got upset, but he stops me and says, "Everyone cries. Some cry and come back."

That night I go on Facebook again. I've gotten into the habit of doing it whenever Carolina is in one of her sinking spells or I've had a bad day at dance. It's a small private pleasure, comforting like a cup of cocoa, and yet each time when I log out, I take care to obliterate my trail. Mark taught me how to do this when we started to bank online. He said it was important that if someone stole your computer, they couldn't reopen the last thing you were looking at.

It struck me as paranoid at the time — what was the likelihood someone would steal our computer? — but now I do it whenever I visit Daniel's profile. Just in case I die in my sleep, I guess. I don't want someone, most likely Elyse, to go through my things and find this last guilty secret: that even in the end, I was still trying to figure out Daniel.

In my favorite picture, he's leaning against the side of a boat. He has a fishing reel in his hand and the harbor behind him is clearly Charleston. He is laughing, looking happy, relaxed, fit for fifty-three. I play with the idea of messaging him. I write something silly — "Catch anything?" — and then erase it. I also backspace over the slightly accusatory "So that's where you ended up," the downright terrifying "I've got a few questions," and the totally pedestrian "How have you been?"

In the end I decide that the best message is a picture of my own. The faded one of me and Elyse standing at the feet of David. I had scanned it into my computer to make a copy for Tory as a Christmas gift, and I look at myself, so young and confident, pushing back my sunglasses and squinting into the Italian sun while Daniel's shadow, even after all this time, is still lying on the floor between us.

I attach the picture and press Send.

Pamela's house is probably twice the size of mine but oddly situated on its lot, sitting a bit catty-cornered to the street to accommodate a ravine running through the property. The landscaper has tried to hide the fact that the house is so precariously perched with an abundance of bushes, but there's still something unsettled about the place. This is the lot the builder takes, I think, as I park my car in the street and begin the long trudge up her driveway. The unsalable, half-assed lot that's left over after everyone else has had their pick.

She greets me at the door with the normal small talk and then the two of us climb again, this time up a broad staircase with a chandelier dangling overhead. We pass a series of bedrooms that seem to belong to teenage boys. There are tangled wires on the floor connecting stereos and video games and shelves crammed full of silver trophies, most likely won for soccer or tennis or lacrosse. The hall leads into the master suite, which we transverse in silence, until I am at last in Pamela Hart's closet, an enormous and well-lit affair with an entire wall of mirrors.

"Do you practice in here?" I ask her.

"No," she says, sounding surprised. "I only dance at the studio." Then she pauses and asks, "Do you want a drink?"

Now it's my turn to be surprised. I've never had anyone offer me a drink inside a closet. I guess there's a wet bar somewhere within the master suite.

She yanks open a pair of double doors and there they are — her ball gowns, their collective sparkle enough to blind a sinner, and each one hanging so that it faces out straight ahead. There are at least ten of them.

"God," I say, "they're dazzling."

"You're wondering how the rods manage to hold them up," she says. I wasn't wondering any such thing, but I nod and she goes on. "Bob had his men build in extra supports. Otherwise, the strain on this wall would be so much —" She breaks off and I have a vision of the dresses slowly pulling down the rods, the closet, and then the room and the hall, until the whole house falls, piece by piece, into the gulley.

"And that's why you need to marry a builder," she finishes, with that tinkly little laugh, which I guess could be either charming or annoying, depending on the situation.

"Maybe I will take that drink," I say.

She turns and walks out of the closet and I sit down on one of the step stools, which were evidently placed there to help her reach the pocketbooks and shoes stacked on the shelves behind me. I've brought three thousand dollars, in a mix of hundreds and twenties, neatly tucked into a manila envelope. It's a bit like a drug drop, but the fact that she specifically asked for cash gives me hope. Elyse began to hoard cash before she left Phil. Hiding small amounts of money here and there is apparently standard behavior in migratory females and so maybe Pamela ultimately does plan to leave Bob. Maybe she does love Nik. All of which is none of my business, but he seems so exposed to the winds of fate with nothing but a phony student visa standing between him and deportation.

"I'm on to you, you know," Pamela says.

She has walked back into the closet and is coming toward me in the mirror, holding out a clear drink over a mound of shaved ice. I taste it. Gin and tonic.

"The setting on that ring is way too modern to be a family heirloom," she says, sipping her own drink as she leans against

255

the mirror. "And with the size of the stone I can pretty much guesstimate what it cost. You're one of us, aren't you?"

"My husband left me an allowance, if that's what you mean."

"Well, you don't have to look so guilty about it. And it wasn't just the ring. I saw you at the MS ball. In fact, I think my husband used to serve on the board with your husband. He's another one of the check writers."

"Wait a minute. Robert Hart's your husband? God, I'm so stupid, but everybody just kept saying Bob and I didn't make the connection. I've sat on a board with him too. Hospice."

She wrinkles her nose. "Hospice is depressing."

"MS isn't exactly a barrel of laughs."

"Agreed. That's why I went with the symphony." She lifts her drink to her mouth and flicks her tongue over the mound of ice like a cat. "Because we have to do something useful, don't we? We can't just dance."

I can't think of a damn thing to say to that, so it seems like it's time to get my dress and go. "The money's in the envelope," I say, inclining my head toward the place where I left it propped against one of the mirrors.

"And the dress is on the hanger," she answers, pushing herself abruptly away from her own mirror. It's the same sort of gesture I watched her make during the tango — a sudden surge of energy following an almost unnerving beat of stillness. It's what makes her a good dancer, this willingness to wait, to not forecast her intention before that split second when she actually moves. There's something animalistic in it, and something enviable as well.

She hands me her drink and then slips a gray silk bag over the dress, stuffing the skirt a bit roughly and pulling up the long zipper. I hand both drinks back to her as we make a clumsy transfer and then I follow her out of the closet, through the master suite, down the hall, and to the top of the stairs, where I stop to grapple with the ungainly weight of the dress bag. I don't want to trip and go tumbling all the way down this faux-historic staircase with a sixteen-pound red ball gown in my arms. So I inch my way slowly, step by step, and as I reach the bottom I hear a voice boom out from one of the rooms to the side.

"That you?"

"Yes," Pamela said. "Of course it's me."

I shift the dress again to look in the direction of the voice and see Bob Hart standing in the doorway of another room. His study, evidently, although perhaps "study" is not the proper word, for over his shoulder I can see a gun rack full of rifles. Do men have hunting rooms anymore? If I stepped closer, would I find deer heads on the wall or little stuffed foxes running along the tabletops? Bob is holding a tumbler of the same size and shape Pamela handed me, but his is empty. Which means that even though he must have gotten home just minutes ago, must have entered during the brief time Pamela and I were in the closet, he made his first drink of the night and threw it back immediately. Pamela's right about me, in a way. I am one of them, and the first thing a woman who lives in a big house learns is how to gauge how fast a man is drinking.

"Honey, this is Kelly Madison," Pamela says. "I think you knew her husband, Mark, from MS."

"Fine man," Bob says, leaning against the doorframe. "I haven't seen him lately."

"Neither have I," I say. "He died a year ago last summer."

"Oh," says Bob. "Real sorry to hear that."

"Kelly is borrowing one of my dance dresses," Pamela says, a little too quickly. "The red Doré, you know, the one you gave me last Christmas?"

He nods without interest. She's a trophy, all right, but he won her years ago, in a contest he's long forgotten. Now she sits on a high shelf, like the collection in his sons' rooms, representing his past glory, gathering dust.

Speaking of the boys, there's a portrait of them on the wall. Handsome kids, all three, which is another way of saying that they look like their mother. But they're bigger than I would have guessed and I'm trying to readjust my thinking with each new piece of the Pamela puzzle I find.

"You have fine-looking boys," I say.

Now this gets his interest. He turns and considers the picture. "The twins are at Duke and Carolina," he says proudly, rattling the ice in his glass. "Youngest one goes next year and he's thinking State."

"Good for them," I say, shifting the dress bag yet again, for my shoulders are starting to ache. With three in college, Pamela must be older than she looks or else she had them white-trash young. Neither of which is the image she wants to give out at the studio, and she must have been following my thoughts, because she springs back into action, in that abrupt way of hers, moving toward the door as if she's suddenly eager to hustle me out. I've seen too much — the

259

alcohol, the guns, the age of her kids, the fact that this house, while enormous, has a slapped-together air. Bob's a clever one — now that I know who he is I can remember the people at hospice talking about him. Came into the real estate market at just the right time. Bet on Charlotte before the banks exploded and this sleepy little burg became a boomtown. Built left and right while everybody else was saying "Wait and see." And now he's got wealth, but it's a certain kind of wealth. The type the South looks down on, what my granddaddy used to call "money so new the ink's not dry."

"Well," I say. "I've got to go. Thanks for letting me borrow the dress."

"Think nothing of it," she says, and opens the door.

# CHAPTER FIFTEEN

People always ask me if I have children, a question that should be simple enough, but I have trouble answering it. The reason is Tory, who is technically Elyse's daughter, but, just as Mark predicted we would, through the years we've shared her. And in my role of honorary aunt, I suppose that I've been overly indulgent — the giver of extravagant gifts, the planner of trips to Disney World, Broadway, Paris, and Cancún. This wasn't really a problem when she was little and Elyse welcomed the break, but after her divorce . . .

No. No, not really. That's too easy an explanation for what went wrong between Tory and Elyse. All girls come to resent their mothers as they approach puberty, not just those who have been forced to sleep on air mattresses in a series of apartments in which their mothers throw pots and hold soirees and summon tribal spirits, and slip farther and farther from the epicenter of respectable suburban life. If I stepped in at a few key times — if I was the one who bought Tory her first bra, who took her to get her hair styled for the prom — it was only because we both knew how much Tory craved normalcy and how ill-equipped Elyse was to provide it.

"You're the un-mother," Elyse has said to me on more than one occasion. We still find it funny when strangers think that Tory is my daughter, an assumption they stupidly base on the fact that we both have blond hair. Any glance beyond the superficial would immediately show that Tory and Elyse have the same facial structure, the same upturned almond eyes. They are alike in the bone. But most people just make assumptions because of our coloring — except for this waitress who once asked Tory if she wanted her soup brought out at the same time as her mom's salad. "How did you know which one was my mom?" Tory had asked, and the waitress had answered, "Because you were going to get the chipotle chicken special too, weren't you, I could see it on your face. You were all set to get the chicken until you heard her order it and then you said you wanted something else." Perhaps this is indeed the crux of the mother-daughter relationship — you wait and see what your mother orders and then you ask the universe for something else.

I have seven gifts wrapped for Tory, including a check with a number of zeroes that will probably make Elyse mad. But I've always liked giving her things, and it wasn't just me — Mark doted on her as well. The two of them had their own little private history, ever since she came into the bank on her own, the summer between her junior and senior year of high school, and applied for a job as an intern. Mark hired her at once. He said it wasn't because he knew her parents, but because she was clearly the best of the batch. "She's a sharp kid," he said the first day, without my having to ask how things had gone. "A damn miracle, considering . . ."

Considering what? That unconventional Elyse was her mother, that stony-faced Phil was her father, that she was a child of divorce, that she had spent her life shuttling between two divergent worlds? He didn't bring it up again, but later that summer we bumped into Elyse and Tory at a restaurant and Tory had run across the patio, squealed, and plopped down into Mark's lap. "How's my best girl?" he said. And then, the next spring when Tory graduated from high school, I asked him how much money we should give her and he said, "She wants to go to Scotland."

How did he know that? More to the point, how had he failed to know that I'd always wanted to go to Scotland? Things began to break apart that year, as if Tory was the linchpin holding us all together and when she left we flew off into different directions. "Scotland," I'd repeated, and he'd said, "Yeah, so give her two or three." Meaning two or three thousand. I gave her four. Elyse had been astounded and even Phil had sent us a thank-you card. Across the bottom he'd printed, "You two always did know how to make me look like shit."

"I guess he's kidding," I said. "Do you think he's kidding?"

"Of course he's kidding," Mark said. "That's Phil's sense of humor."

"I never thought of Phil as having a sense of humor."

"Any man who'd marry Elyse would have to have a hell of a sense of humor." Which sounds mean, but Mark smiled when he said it, and over the years I have gradually been forced into the knowledge that even Mark and Elyse actually got along in a certain way. They used to pick at each other, but there was never any rancor in it and

Mark flat-out loved Tory. That wasn't even an effort. I'm stranded with the knowledge that it was my presence that made everyone uncomfortable, my anxious assumption that they couldn't all possibly get along, that I was the only thing they could ever have in common.

Tory and Elyse both headed west three years ago, but not together. Tory had been accepted at the University of Texas and Elyse was finally making good on her long-time threat to move to the desert. But despite the fact that we've scattered, we still have our holiday rituals. They fly in mid-December and stay the week leading up to Christmas with me. Right after the holiday Elyse moves on to her mother's house and Tory leaves with Phil and her stepmother to celebrate New Year's in some sunny place. This time I think it's Aruba.

Last year was somber, overshadowed by the rarely acknowledged fact that it was the first Christmas since Mark's death. Despite the fact that there are nine beds in this house, Tory had insisted on sleeping on the couch in Mark's office. "It still smells like him in there," she'd said, and once I heard her crying through the door. Since it was just the three of us, I made Cornish game hens instead of a turkey, put up only the tabletop tree, and hung our little stockings. But this year I'm determined to pull out all the stops.

Elyse is due to arrive this morning, but first I'm meeting the other girls from group class to give Nik his Christmas present. Apparently he once told Isabel he wanted a black leather jacket and she'd never forgotten. When I saw how quick everyone was to donate to Nik's gift, I realized that I'm not the only one who feels protective toward him. "Where's he going to go on the actual day of Christmas?" Steve had asked, with the concern one bachelor feels for another, and Harry had reached in his wallet, pulled out a fifty, and said, "Poor kid."

We'd ended up with enough money for a seriously nice jacket and Isabel has it in the trunk of her car. She didn't wrap it or put it in a box, but rather just left it on the hanger, swathed in great expanses of red tissue paper. It looks like something James Dean would have worn. It's the American dream cut out of leather.

We know we can't present it to him in front of Anatoly and Quinn, who are getting gift certificates and bottles of wine, so a few of the women have agreed to converge in the parking lot at 9:50 a.m., before he meets

Pamela for her ten o'clock lesson. Our timing is good. We've only been sitting bunched up in Isabel's car for a few minutes when Nik pulls into the parking lot.

I don't particularly like seeing Nik outside the studio. He looks younger in the daylight. Small veins are visible through his pale skin and he slumps a little when he's wearing his jeans. Isabel honks her horn. He walks over slowly, blinking with uncertainty, and we all get out as Isabel pops the trunk. The jacket lies there, zipped over a headless red torso. It's a little alarming really, as if we've all collectively stumbled upon a crime scene.

But he knows at once what we've done, and he startles me by squealing. It's a sound like a little girl would make — high and pure and full of unfeigned joy.

"Thank God you're here," Elyse says when I meet her at the airport. An odd remark considering that I'm the one who never left. I'd sat in the cell phone parking lot waiting for her to call and tell me she'd landed, and then I swung around to the arrivals lane, which was insanely busy. She tossed her suitcase in the back and jumped in fast, amid honking horns, so we didn't get the chance to hug. We just patted each other's shoulders.

"This place is a zoo," Elyse says as I weave among the stopped cars. "I'm sorry we're going to have to come back in two days for Tory."

It's been a sore point for weeks that Tory is arranging her travel plans around a party her boyfriend's parents are hosting back in Austin. She's dating the son of a conservative pro-life senator, something I suspect is an attempt to jab at her mother, to prove to the universe she sure as hell isn't getting the chipotle chicken. But who knows, maybe she loves the boy. Her e-mails are full of references to the wonders of Jason.

"She's got to find her own path," Elyse says vaguely, as if we've been discussing it. "Evidently she was a big hit at the senator's holiday party."

"Why wouldn't she be?" Thanks to a father who's a dentist and a stepmother who's a dermatologist, Tory has flawless skin and teeth. She wears her thick golden hair pulled back in a headband that makes her look like Alice come straight from Wonderland. She's perfect breeding stock, the ideal daughter-in-law for a politician, an asset to any family Christmas card. "You don't think she's going to marry that boy, do you?"

Elyse shakes her head. "She won't push it

that far. Nobody in their right mind marries the first man they ever sleep with."

"You think she's sleeping with him?"

Elyse pauses, then murmurs, "Well, it never occurred to me that she wasn't . . ." which is a reasonable response, unless you factor in that the ultimate way for a girl to rebel against a mother like Elyse would be to remain a virgin.

Throughout the years I've been on the receiving end of many late-night weepy phone calls — some from Elyse and some from Tory, but they have all begun with the line "You can't believe what she said to me this time . . ." For a while I fantasized that I would mediate between them, that I would be the one to broker a compromise, but of course that was never my place, and besides, things are shifting. Ever since Tory has gone off to college, Elyse has thrown in the metaphorical towel and they seem to be getting along better, as if the sheer geographic distance has brought them some peace. I do my part to give them this neutral place and to make it nice, stocking up on the strange peppers and herbs that Elyse likes to cook with, going overboard with the decorations, cranking down the heat to the stone-coldness that Tory's hyperrevved metabolism requires. I don't mind sleeping with an extra blanket if that's what makes the girl happy.

I feel for Tory. I understand how hard it is to not be Elyse.

"Well, at least Wonderboy won't be joining us around the holiday table," Elyse says. "For a while I think she planned to spring him on me and Phil at the same time. Oh and Janet," she adds, remembering the woman who replaced her like she always does, as an afterthought. "I didn't tell Tory that Jason wasn't welcome, of course. That would have been like waving a red flag in front of a bull. I told her he was completely welcome and that's when she said he couldn't make it. I think she's trying to use him to shock me."

Elyse and I break into the giggles. Trying to use a man to shock Elyse would never work. Men like Elyse. Let me rephrase that. All men like Elyse. Even the ones you don't expect. Let me rephrase again. Especially the ones you don't expect. Someday, when the moment comes that Jason and Elyse do eventually meet, they will undoubtedly become confidants by the end of the first glass of wine and poor Tory will be forced to throw herself into the Rio Grande.

"That's pretty," Elyse says. She's dragged

her suitcase as far as the dining room and is staring at what I think of as "my last tablescape." One for the road, the end of an era, but I'm still a bit proud of it — a line of red ribbons and irregularly shaped crystals and dried brambles from the rose garden, running the length of the table in what I consider an artful snarl. "Of course you always did . . ." Her voice fades as she wanders her way into the kitchen and I hear the pop of my refrigerator door opening.

I stand frowning down at the tablescape, wondering exactly what she had been starting to say. I suspect Elyse finds my interests trivial. One Christmas, sometime after Elyse moved to Arizona, I'd decided to throw a dinner party in her honor. The old gang was coming, friends from years ago whom I hardly saw myself anymore. I'd gone into the pantry for something. I guess I'd been dashing around, but no more than usual. Is it a crime to want things to be nice? I'd burned a CD of light jazz for the background because sometimes there's a lull in conversation and that always goes better if there's music. It makes it seem almost like the lull was planned. I'd screwed up the crab cakes the first time and had to remake them and maybe I fussed a little more than I should have. It was about an hour before everyone was due and I came out of the pantry to find Elyse and Mark laughing. "You know what she called you?" he said, leaning against the counter and swirling his scotch. "She said you're like a geisha. A geisha on amphetamines."

"Do you think I've overdone it?" I ask Elyse, shaking myself out of the memory and following her into the kitchen. "I was at this party a couple of weeks ago and the centerpieces were actually roses on mirrors, if you can believe it, and I started thinking thorns were better, and jagged crystals, so it would be sort of like the same idea deconstructed, you know, like the boring old centerpiece had blown apart and the roses had died and the mirror had broken. Deconstruction is very big right now."

"Right," she says absentmindedly, staring inside the refrigerator.

I persist. "There's art in that, you know, things falling apart. You said it was pretty, but it's not supposed to be pretty. It's supposed to be real."

"Right," she says again, either too bored or too polite to point out to me that she's the actual artist, the one who really knows about these things.

"It's just that last year was so gloomy and this year I wanted things to be more festive.

Back to normal."

"Are you having your usual big party?"

"No. Of course not. Who would I invite?"

"What about your dance studio buddies?"

"None of them have ever been to my house. It doesn't work like that."

"Why?" Elyse leans away from the refrigerator door and looks around my big, shiny kitchen. "Are you afraid they won't like you if they know where you live?"

Actually I'm afraid they might like me more. Or at least like me different. I look around the kitchen too, and through the doors into the dining room with that monstrous tablescape running down the center of the table. "You think I've overdone it, don't you?"

"Of course not, baby, why are you getting upset? Everything's beautiful. You want to make some salad?"

"We could go out for lunch."

"Do you mind if we wait until dinner?" I shake my head. She got up at God knows what hour this morning, of course she just wants to shower and relax. She slams the refrigerator door and a Christmas card flies off the front, one I'd stuck on with a snowman magnet.

"It's from Nik," I say.

She picks it up and looks inside. "See you

son," she reads.

"Isn't that cute? He meant 'See you soon,' because I haven't told anybody this but I'm doing a little recital while you and Tory will be here. Nik is meeting me at the hospice Christmas dinner and we're going to waltz to 'Silver Bells.' Carolina has been after me to dance for her for weeks and this seems like a good time to do it. You'll come, won't you? Do you think hospice will freak out Tory?"

"Of course we'll come."

"I thought you and I can go over there tomorrow and watch a movie. I want you to meet Carolina. And maybe you can come with me to my dance lesson too, if it's not too much —"

"Kelly," Elyse says, her voice firm but kind. "What are you doing? There's no way in hell I'm going to miss the chance to meet Carolina and Nik. You talk about them all the time. Why do you get so jumpy like this whenever two parts of your life come together? Tory will be fine at hospice. She's a big girl. And we both want to see you dance."

The kitchen is suddenly blurry with my tears. "I don't know what's wrong with me. I cry all the time lately."

"Christmas makes people emotional."

Elyse sticks Nik's card back on the fridge. "See you son," she says softly. "That's a funny mistake to make."

"Are you sure we want to watch something this sad?" Elyse says when she notices the movie I've picked out for our visit with Carolina.

"This isn't sad."

"You don't call a brain tumor sad?"

"She gets the brain tumor in *Dark Victory*. In *Now, Voyager* all she does is fall in love with a married man."

"Oh yeah, right. A comedy."

"How is Gerry, anyway?"

"He's great. He's always great. He doesn't know how to be anything else." Elyse looks up at the crooked wreath on the Hospice House doorway and her face tightens a little. "This is going to be hard, isn't it?"

I'm used to the house of death, since I come here five times a week and sometimes I forget the effect it has on other people. I link my arm through Elyse's. "You're going to like her. And yeah, that's exactly what's going to make it hard."

We find Carolina in her room. Getting her back on the IVs and meds has stabilized her a bit and she hugs us both and grins when she sees the bottle of wine Elyse has smuggled in her purse. She won't drink much of it. With so many painkillers in her system, a thimbleful of alcohol is enough to get her looped. But she likes the idea that I bring it on movie nights, along with the bag of popcorn and the oversize box of Raisinets.

"Oh good. Bette Davis," she says when she sees me open the DVD case.

"I'm teaching her about the heyday of Hollywood," I tell Elyse as we all climb into the bed together. Carolina is so thin now that she lies between us like a child; Elyse unscrews the wine cap while I fiddle with the remote. "We've done Marilyn Monroe and Joan Crawford and we're halfway through the classics of Miss Bette Davis."

"You need to get her going on Elizabeth," Elyse says. "Or maybe Lana." She has always referred to movie stars exclusively by their first names, as if they were old childhood friends of hers.

"Elizabeth is up next."

"I like Bette Davis," Carolina says, her mouth full of popcorn. "She's so real."

"That she is," says Elyse. "And I've got to tell you, it totally gets on my nerves."

Carolina laughs delightedly and I can see Elyse has already charmed her. She pours glasses of syrah for me and her, a smaller one for Carolina, and the movie begins.

I always forget how disturbingly plain Bette is at the beginning of *Now, Voyager,* with her tight bun and wire-rimmed glasses and sensible clothes. I gulp the first couple of inches of wine and hold out my glass. Elyse tops me off, her eyes never leaving the screen. It's not like we haven't seen this movie a hundred times, like I don't know that within minutes she'll go to the sanatorium and have her big makeover. There's no reason to worry that the movie is going to somehow change course and Bette will get stuck in ugly-land or that she'll never get on that cruise ship and fall in love.

Elyse suddenly picks up the remote and hits Pause, freezing Bette with her mouth open and her eyes bulging.

"Is this the one where the guy puts two cigarettes in his mouth and lights them both at once?"

"Yeah."

"And she says 'Forget the moon and keep the stars'?"

"The actual line is 'Don't ask for the moon, we have the stars.' "

"It's coming back to me." She picks up the remote again but I find myself blurting something before she can press the button. It pops out in a little hiccup.

"I don't think I've ever been in love," I say.

Carolina and Elyse both shift in the bed to look at me.

"I know what you're thinking," I say to Elyse. "You're thinking that if I wasn't in love with Daniel, I sure as hell gave a good imitation of it, but that wasn't love, it was obsession. He was like some itch right in the middle of my back that I couldn't scratch. And then poor Mark . . . there was a woman at a charity dinner who said I gave him a lovely home and that's all that matters, but do you think that's really all that matters? Because I've been faking, faking it my whole life, and I think Mark sort of knew that. I'd catch him looking at me sometimes like a dog who doesn't understand why you put him outside in the yard, and I don't want to be like this but I always have been, and I don't know how to stop and now I'm fifty-two, which seems significant, because it's like the number of weeks in a year or the number of cards in a deck. It's a big number. So that has to mean something, don't you think, although maybe it just means I'm getting old. The kind of old where it's too late to change. What do you think?"

Elyse seems strangely frozen, much like

278

Bette, but when I come to the end of my speech and take a big, defiant swig of wine she exhales slowly and considers her answer. "I don't think it's too late," she finally says.

"Time's running out. I know that. I'm not delusional. But I think I have to try."

"Try what?"

"To not be fake."

Elyse nods, slowly and carefully. I've lost my fucking mind, that much is evident to everyone around me. Last week I made that crazy speech at the charity dinner about how romantic love keeps women from going on a quest and everyone thought I was drunk and now I'm here at hospice, drinking again and talking about putting dogs out in the yard and I don't even have a dog, which is probably just one more thing that's wrong with me. I feel like I'm on some flat, open territory, some prairie in a state where I've never been before. Emptiness and possibility stretch out all around me, in every direction. I start to say that I don't want to be one of those women who lies on her deathbed and repents for what she does not do, when I remember that Carolina is right here between us, looking up at me with wide, solemn eyes.

I try again. "I know I was a bitch to you, Elyse, when you fell in love with Gerry and left Phil and I kept telling you to be careful. I know that's not what you needed to hear. But the truth of it all is that I was jealous, so jealous I couldn't see straight. Because you knew what you wanted and you went for it and now look at you, you got love. Meanwhile I'm still sitting here waiting and wondering if I even know what love is."

Elyse shakes her head. "I swear, Kelly, sometimes it's like you and I aren't even watching the same movie. I got love? That's what you think?"

"You got Gerry."

"I don't have Gerry. Gerry comes and goes." Elyse looks at Carolina. "I'm sorry, honey, Kelly and I are being rude, talking over the top of you like you're a piece of furniture. Gerry is a man I met years ago on an airplane and after that I left my husband — he's the one she means when she says Phil. Everybody thinks I traded my husband for my lover but it's way more complicated than that."

"Oh, I know the whole story," Carolina says confidently. "Kelly says that you had the safe man but you wanted the bad boy."

"Good God," Elyse says. I drain my glass and hold it out. She ignores me.

"And Kelly's bad boy dumped her," Carolina continues, her voice a little ragged.

"So she married a safe man and she says that's because there are two kinds of men in the world — the ones who make things easy and the ones who make things hard. You and her started out choosing the opposite, and then the two of you sort of crisscrossed somewhere along the way, and now she lives in a big house but you've had a lot more sex."

"Really?" Elyse says. "That's what she said?"

Carolina smiles and takes a dainty sip of syrah. "Some of it I figured out for myself."

Elyse gives a big hoot of laughter, which relieves me. "Well, it's right as far as it goes, Carolina, but let me tell you, my life is about one-tenth as exciting as Kelly makes it out to be. Yeah, I left my husband because I was bored and lonely, but what I didn't realize was that all the other women who were bored and lonely but didn't have the guts to leave their husbands were going to crucify me. It's all anybody ever says about me, that I left a nice man. They're going to carve it on my tombstone: *Here Lies Elyse Bearden. She Left a Nice Man.* And yeah, I have a boyfriend, but he pops in and out of sight like a kid on a water slide. Meanwhile selling a bowl every once in a while doesn't pay the rent, so I teach pottery at a community college. I bet you know how glamorous that can be. And that doesn't pay worth a shit either so I just signed up to teach three classes a week at the senior citizens' center."

"You didn't tell me that," I say.

She shrugs. "They just offered it to me. The class starts after New Year's. They've warned me that some of my students will be in pretty bad shape, but touch is the last sense to go. Even blind people can feel clay."

"You could do that at hospice," I say. "The hospice in Tucson." Elyse complains sometimes about money but I didn't know things were this bad.

"Hmmm," says Elyse. "What about it, Carolina? Do you want to throw pots? Do you think that would fulfill you?"

"I've never thought about it," Carolina says, looking up at the clouds. "I've never thought about what would fulfill me."

"Then tell me this," Elyse says after a minute. "Have you ever been in love?"

I'm ashamed to say this is a question I've never asked. I know odd things about Carolina, like her white blood cell count and the amount of her weekly car payment, but I don't know what happened to the father of her boys. Whether she loved him, whether she married him, where he went, or even whether he was the one who truly mattered. I roll over to where I can hear her better.

"A long time ago," Carolina says.

"And was he one of the safe men or one of the bad boys?"

"Hard to decide," Carolina says. "And what difference would it make either way? Like my grandma used to say, they're both no good."

Elyse shrieks again with laughter, rocking her knees back and forth on the bed. I reach over Carolina to hand her my glass and this time she lifts the bottle to pour in more but then she stops, leaving me with my hand and my glass out there in midair.

"I guess you've noticed," she says to Carolina, "that this one still wears her wedding ring."

I turn my hand, dropping a couple of drips of syrah on the sheet in the process. All three of us study my ring.

"I can't seem to take it off," I say.

Carolina frowns. "You mean it's stuck?"

"Not exactly. What does a ring like this say to you?"

"It says, 'I'm rich.' "

"No, it says, 'I married a rich man,' " I say. "Which, trust me, is a totally different thing."

The size of my diamond seems to get Elyse's mind back on Elizabeth Taylor. "We should have brought *Suddenly, Last Summer,*" she says. "It's the best movie ever." She proceeds to tell Carolina why Elizabeth was the last of the true American movie stars and I put my head back on the pillow and shut my eyes.

*Suddenly, Last Summer* is at the top of the pile of movies on my bedside table. It's the movie I most associate with Elyse and I did indeed start to bring it today. Elyse and I first saw it together on one of those Saturday nights at the drive-in when we had our eyes on the screen and the four hands of the Pressley twins up our skirts. It wasn't until much later, looking back, that it occurred to me I'd been watching all those old movies because I was desperately trying to get an idea of what a desirable woman might look like. And when I'd seen Elizabeth Taylor in *Suddenly, Last Summer,* a film in which she is so beautiful that Montgomery Clift can't stop himself from falling in love with her, even though he is her doctor, even though she is so obviously crazy and he is so obviously gay . . .

Elizabeth was a goddess of sex and Elizabeth scared me. Look where sex got her — locked in a mental hospital on the verge of getting a lobotomy. I switched my allegiance to Marilyn Monroe, a woman who seemed — what did we know? — too giddy and innocent to ever be destined for tragedy. But even after I started to model my behavior on Marilyn, I couldn't stop sneaking peeks at Elizabeth, who I knew, for all her flaws, was a more accurate reflection of what female desire really looked like. Elizabeth wearing heels and a white slip, Elizabeth in a speeding car, Elizabeth sprawled across a messy bed, more beautiful in black and white than she would ever be in color. Of course Montgomery couldn't help himself. Her eyes were half-closed. Her mouth was half-open. This was the face of sex, somewhere between death and pain. I knew it then and I know it now, which is probably why I picked up *Suddenly, Last Summer* today and then put it back down.

"But for now we need to catch up with Bette," Elyse is saying, reaching for the remote. We've all slid down in the bed, and the wine bottle on the table is empty. We're bunched, but it's also kind of cozy. "We've left her in a bad place."

"Who needs the moon when you've got the stars?" I say. It's such a great line.

"I've never understood what that means," Elyse says.

"It's bittersweet," I say. "Because the man who changes her life isn't going to be there with her when the new one begins."

"No matter how many times you say otherwise, I still think this is a fucking sad movie," Elyse says.

We sit for a moment in silence.

"Maybe it'll end different this time," Carolina says.

"Maybe it will," says Elyse, and she presses Play.

# CHAPTER SIXTEEN

I decide that Pamela's red dress would probably be too much for the dance at the hospice Christmas party. I'm not good enough yet to carry the responsibility of that many crystals. Plus it's too tight in the hips, just as Pamela predicted. It hangs in my closet and I see it every time I open the door.

In the meantime, I have a long practice skirt and a pretty boat-neck top in a color that the dancewear company calls "pewter," but which I think looks a lot like silver. It will be festive enough, and if it's corny to wear a silver dress to waltz to "Silver Bells," that's okay too. They aren't really looking for subtlety at the hospice Christmas party. Carolina wants to put up my hair with a rose in it, and even though I haven't seemed to have much luck with that particular flower, I don't have the heart to say no. Nik is meeting us there. He offered to bring his tuxedo, but I assured him that his nice black suit with a red tie will be more than enough.

I called the grocery two days ago to order a cheese tray, which we'll pick up on the way. Tory and Elyse seem excited about seeing me dance, but I'm trying very hard not to think about it. There will only be thirty or so people there, forty at the most, and I keep telling myself that none of them are likely to be connoisseurs of ballroom dancing. But still, I'm a little shaky as Elyse and Tory and I walk into the grocery. Elyse goes to look for wine and Tory left her razor back in Austin, so I'm alone when I go back to the deli counter and ask for my cheese tray. "There's supposed to be a rose with it," I say to the sad-looking stock boy, who's obviously not pleased to be working the Friday before Christmas. "Just one single rose."

He finds the cheese but not the flower. I send him back to look harder. "Silver Bells" comes on over the sound system, which I decide to take as a good sign. The boy comes back roseless yet again and I tell him not to worry, that I'll just pick up one. Carolina will be able to clip it down and get it in my hair. I'm humming along with "Silver Bells" and trying to unobtrusively practice my heel leads as I work my way to the crowded floral department, where, in honor of the fact that they've themed it to look like Provence, they're playing "Joyeux Noël." And it is there, among the flowers, balancing an unwieldy tray of cheese in one hand and reaching for a rose with the other, that the crowds suddenly part and I see Daniel.

He doesn't have a cart. Of course he doesn't. He's wearing a navy sweater and jeans and he has paused before the artichokes. He reaches, plucks one from the treacherously stacked pile, and considers it before placing it in his basket. For this is the kind of man he is. The kind who knows how to cook artichokes. Who doesn't think they're too much trouble, even if he's just at home by himself. The kind of man who makes every moment a small celebration, who knows how to find sweetness and purpose in the smallest acts of daily life.

What is he doing in Charlotte and not in Charleston? And alone, rather than in his complicated marriage?

He turns. It isn't him.

Now that my eyes have cleared I can see that the man moving toward me in the navy sweater isn't Daniel and, in fact, looks nothing like Daniel. He has caught me watching him and he smiles, almost apologetically, as he brushes past. I've picked up two roses by mistake and I try to put one back, but for some reason I cram it down among the carnations. Elyse is a few feet over, pondering the chilies, and I sidle up beside her and say, "You're not going to believe this, but I thought I just saw Daniel."

"Daniel's here?" Elyse spins around, actually looking. Of course she would take me literally. Things like that happen to Elyse. She lives in the kind of world where lost lovers reappear without warning, just suddenly manifest among the artichokes.

"No," I say. "A man who looks like Daniel." Not even a man who looks like Daniel. They had the same curly dark hair, that was all.

"All that stuff you said in Carolina's bed," Elyse said. "About wondering if it was too late. What were you talking about?"

"Nothing. I was drunk."

"Not that drunk."

I look wildly around the store. "All of a sudden I don't feel so hot."

Tory has come up behind me while we're talking. She takes the tray from my hand but leaves me the rose. "You're just nervous about dancing."

"Yeah," says Elyse, willing to let it slide for the moment, although I know eventually she'll be back on me like a hound on a scent. "Tory's right. You're just wound up about dancing and that's why you thought you saw Daniel."

Tory tilts her head. "Who's Daniel?"

"He was the love of your aunt Kelly's life."

"No," I say. "He's the man who broke me."

Carolina does a good job with my hair, weaving it up into a high mass of curls and anchoring the rose above my ear. Nik texts me that he's waiting in the lobby, right on time, and I walk down to meet him in my clogs, with my dancing shoes in my hands. He looks very handsome in his black suit and he smiles as he sees me coming toward him.

"You are ready," he says. It's a statement, not a question.

"I know." We have practiced three extra times just for this and — other than the fancy spinning entrance — we're doing the most simple of waltzes. "Silver Bells" is a slow song, an easy pace. I'm more than ready, and as I take his arm and we start down the long, cloudy hall I feel calmer than I have all day. He's the one who seems nervous.

People applaud the minute we come into the room, which seems to throw Nik further.

Teresa makes a few announcements and welcomes everyone and while she talks, Nik drops to one knee and helps me buckle my dance shoes. The sight of this boy kneeling before me — I keep forgetting how pretty he is, how much he looks like the prince in a child's book of fairy tales — seems to flummox Elyse. She frowns and studies the little one-page program, as if she might find some sort of explanation there. The room is full and I feel the pulse in my neck beating a little stronger now. All ten of our current clients, a few of the volunteers, and their families. Virginia and both of Carolina's boys.

"They die soon, these people?" Nik asks quietly as he rises, his eyes darting along the row of seats.

"Most of them."

"You not pay me for this."

"Of course I will. You got dressed up and drove out here. Don't be silly."

"No. This is Christmas gift."

Teresa looks at us and I nod yes, that we're ready, and she may as well dim the lights and cue the music. We go to our opposite corners and begin. My opening spins are good — not perfect, but straight and well paced — and once I am connected to Nik it becomes a gentle dance, leaving me plenty of time to observe the audience as I pass them. Tory is smiling, Elyse is taking pictures, and Carolina seems transfixed, leaning forward with her elbows on her knees. Or maybe it was all the other way around, hard to say, but I feel that we are moving easily and well. I'm soaring, I think. I've heard other women at the studio talk about soaring and I imagined it would feel something like that night I waltzed with Anatoly, but I was wrong. That night I had left my body and tonight I am acutely aware of every cell and every nerve. It seems natural to be the one in the center of the room, the focus of the attention, and it's like being back in the old days of cheerleading. Like I have all the time in the world. I remember to smile. I keep my pinky lifted as I settle my hand on Nik's shoulder. There is only one small mistake, a moment when I come slightly off balance in a twinkle. But Nik rights me, and we continue.

When the music ends, Nik unfurls me, and I feel the soft rush of the fabric around my thighs, sounding like angel wings or prayers. I curtsy, and Teresa turns the lights back up.

Everyone claps. Louder than I expected. All my girls are there, surrounding me with hugs, and chairs are being dragged against the floor. The pastor volunteer says a prayer and Teresa starts a CD of general Christmas music as people begin to eat. Wheelchairs go first. I'm too high on adrenaline to be hungry so I sit down and let the crowd pass. I would have expected Nik to bolt at once but he hangs around for a while, getting a plate of food and talking to Tory.

"Your name Victoria?" I hear him ask her. "In Russia, we call Vika."

"I like Vika," Tory says, dazzling him with the full power of American orthodontia. "It's a much better nickname than Tory. Much better."

When "Jingle Bell Rock" comes on, he puts down his paper plate and teaches her a few steps of the East Coast swing. They're beautiful together. I don't know why it's never occurred to me that the two of them are so close in age.

"Don't do it."

Elyse has come up beside me. She hands me a cup of coffee.

"Don't do what?"

"Don't turn him into the son you never had."

I look at her.

"He's about the right age, isn't he?"

Only people who have known you a long time can hurt you like this. "That's not what

I'm doing, but so what if it was? What's wrong with trying to get a second chance? You did. Lots of people do."

"It could all be gone in a second," she says.

Anything we love could be gone in a second, a fact Elyse knows just as well as I do. She and I stand there, surrounded by people who won't make it to the New Year, and I think of Mark, lying on his hospital bed with his face as gray as my dancing skirt. "He has a paper-thin heart," the doctor had told me, as we watched him through the glass, but sometimes I think all our hearts are paper thin. Nik spins Tory and she laughs. He does too and it hits me, hot like coffee down the throat, that this is the first time I have ever seen Nik laugh.

Carolina gets tired during the party. I can see it on her face. I tell her I'll walk her back to her room and she protests. It's my night, she says. I should stay and mingle.

But I'm pretty much mingled out by that point and eventually she succumbs to her exhaustion and lets me lead her back down the long unlit hall, the Christmas music fading as we walk. I help her pull off her clothes, noting that her body is even thinner than it was the last time I saw it, and button up her nightgown. I take the rose from my hair and float it in a glass of water on her bureau. Then I lie down beside her, just for a minute, because now that the juice of the dance is fading, I'm tired too.

"Go back," she mumbles. "It's your night."

"I'm more comfortable here," I say, which is true.

Elyse finds us an hour later, shoulder to shoulder in the hospital bed, both dozing, me in my silver dancewear and Carolina in her nightgown. She shakes my arm, and I swim from my shallow nap back to the shore of consciousness, looking up into her worried face.

"Come on, baby," she says. "It's time for us to go home."

"Did you like my dance?" I ask her. "Do you understand why I do it now?"

"Kelly, if I could do that . . ." Elyse hesitates and for a moment I think she's going to cry. "If I could do what you did in there, if I could be graceful like that or I had that kind of courage . . . well, it would be all I ever did. I'd say to hell with the rest of the world and waltz all day long."

I roll over and look at her, surprised. Elyse doesn't think she has my kind of courage? Her life has always been the bigger one, painted with great slashes of color against a broad landscape, while I have kept myself smaller, more careful and finely realized, a still life. But her face in the shadowy room is serious, her expression tinged with appreciation and even a bit of envy. It scares me. What happens if I outgrow her?

# CHAPTER SEVENTEEN

"I want you to tell me all about him, this guy you thought you saw in the grocery," Tory says, spreading the towels across the counter and draping one over my shoulders. She's convinced me to let her color my hair. I'm not sure why it means so much to her, but I suspect I've changed noticeably since she's seen me last and that my obvious aging has frightened her somehow, maybe made her think about the mortality of her own mother. "Hmm," she adds, looking down, "your towels are way too nice to get stained. Do you have at least one crappy one that we can use to wrap around your head?"

"I can get one of Mark's old golf towels out of the mudroom," I say.

"No, I'll do it," she says. "You just sit here and think because I want the whole story." She dashes out of the room and I can hear the soft thud of her feet going down the

298

staircase, the pause and louder thud as she skips the last step and lands in the foyer with a little hop. Tory has descended staircases exactly the same way her whole life. I stare at my reflection with my hair brushed straight back and the towel clipped around my neck. She doesn't want the whole story. She just thinks she does.

"So he sent you letters," Tory says, back with the crappy towel and a plastic grocery bag besides. "I know that much because Mom says she kept them for you all those years, like you asked her to do. But why were you and this man writing so many letters? Did he live in another city?" She twists the caps and lids off a collection of little bottles and, without consulting the directions, begins to mix them. I can only hope she knows what she's doing.

"No, back then he lived in Charlotte too," I said. "The letters were just his way of courting me. Daniel was a great letter writer. And I gave them to your mother because they were the only proof that any of it really happened."

Our eyes meet in the mirror. "I guess he was married," she says.

"I guess he was." It feels funny talking to Tory about it, but there's no point in being coy. She's twenty, goes to a big school. I doubt I could say anything to shock her.

"It started in Italy thirty years ago," I tell her, pulling off my jewelry as she begins to squirt her cold, gelatinous concoction across my hairline. "You know that picture downstairs? The one with me and your mother and the statue of *David* but you can't see *David*?" She nods. "Daniel's the one who took the picture. We met him in Florence and we were all together for a few days and then — well, it was the middle of August, almost time for school. He went back to Georgia and we came back here."

"But you knew there was something special about him even then?"

"I have the feeling this story is going to disappoint you. I mean, if my affair with Daniel were a movie, it would be on a channel with a high number. If you happened to stumble across it late some night, you'd pick up the remote and keep looking for something better. It wouldn't star somebody like Bette Davis or Elizabeth Taylor. I'd be played by, you know . . . one of Charlie's lesser angels."

"I'm not expecting *Dr. Zhivago*," she says, then flushes a little. Elyse and I have been teasing her about Nik ever since the dance. "I'm not a child. In fact, I'm probably the same age you were that summer in Italy."

"Come to think of it, you are. Well, okay then, no, I didn't think he was so special when I first met him. He was cute and he was nice but it didn't really all start until maybe ten years later. He got transferred to Charlotte and he remembered your mom and I lived here and looked us up."

"Both of you?"

I try to shake my head, which is almost impossible with all the towels and hair clips. "Elyse had forgotten he'd ever existed. There were a lot of boys back in those days, Tory, there was a lot to keep straight in your head. I don't think she would have even remembered that day if I hadn't shown her the picture. He's in it, or at least he sort of is. You can see his shadow."

Tory sets the timer on her iPhone and pulls the vanity chair next to mine. "That's the only picture you had of him?"

I nod. Strange but true.

"So you met him in Italy and then, ten years later, you meet him again," Tory prompts.

"Right. By the time he gets to Charlotte we're all just past thirty and he's been married five years or more to a woman he knew from college. We were just going to have breakfast and chat up old times but the minute I saw him . . . I don't know what it

301

was. We were at a stupid restaurant. I think it was an IHOP and I got there early because you know what a nerd I am. Twenty minutes early for everything. I remember sitting there in the booth looking out the window and wondering if I'd even recognize him and then I saw a man get out of his car and . . ."

"And you recognized him," she says.

"There wasn't any doubt. One look and boom, I was gone, just like that. Maybe I should write a country song. 'I Lost My Heart in an International House of Pancakes.' "

"Has that ever happened to you since?"

"Nope. Never before and never since."

"And because you'd known him before, it was like you were back in that earlier time. It probably didn't even seem to you like he was married. You couldn't picture it, so it was easy to just act like it wasn't true. Like nothing had changed and you were just that same girl and guy back in Italy all over again."

"That's a very generous interpretation of events, Tory. Let's go with that."

"And he seduced you gradually, wore you down with the letters."

Actually he had seduced me in a nanosecond. Arousal has never been my problem.

Arousal's the easy part, and on that day in the IHOP, I don't think we even finished our pancakes before we were scrambling out to his car. The letters came much later and perhaps that's why I really kept them all those years. Because they'd proven that Daniel had continued to want me even after he'd had me. That I wasn't just a fling or a conquest, but someone worthy of romance.

Tory mistakes my silence for agreement.

"So where did you guys . . . meet?"

"The first year we would go to all sorts of places. The country sometimes. You know the hiking trails at Kings Mountain? They're pretty much deserted on weekday mornings. That was where we were the first time, on a picnic table, which sounds ridiculous, but at the time it felt kind of wild and glorious. I had never made love outside. He would do little things . . . he brought a kite one time and marshmallows, like we were kids. We went to a planetarium, if you can believe it, and just made out during the show. And another time we drove all the way to the beach in the middle of the night. I remember that we found this catamaran, sitting on the sand, and we stayed there on that wet canvas until the sun came up."

She digests this in silence, her head tilted thoughtfully to the side. She's made that gesture ever since she was a little girl. "All this happened the first year? How long did the affair last?"

"Three years. But by the end he wasn't planning things as much. It wasn't quite so romantic. We mostly met in his car."

"His car? Really? That's kind of cool. I mean in a different way, kind of retro."

"You think?" It wasn't a car, it was a mini-van. The sort of vehicle a man drives when he has two kids under the age of five. I have a sudden flash of myself lying in the back of that van, tangled in a nest of jumper cables and children's toys.

I pick up the timer. "Are you sure we should leave this on the whole time? I only want to cover the gray."

"Give it five more minutes. Why didn't you go to hotels? That's what Mom and Uncle Gerry used to do when they had their affair. In fact, even now that they've both been single a million years, they still do it. He comes to Tucson and half the time they still end up going to hotels because her pottery dust makes him sneeze and she says it's easier to be sexual when you're not in your own bed."

That sounds like something Elyse would say. She's always liked hotels. She has a million bathrobes she's snitched from Marriotts and Hyatts all over the country. "No, we talked about going to one of those pretty little inns they have in Charleston but we never made it. Daniel and I weren't anything like your mother and Gerry. They've made an art form out of trysting, but we never seemed to have that much time." Or money. Daniel was terrified of having to explain away credit card charges or missing cash.

The bell dings. Tory indicates I should bend my head and I do, tilting my forehead down into the sink so she can run warm water down my neck and all over my scalp, her slim hands separating the strands of hair to make sure all the dye washes out. She pats my hair dry with Mark's golf towel and dabs on conditioner. It doesn't look much lighter, which is good. I don't want to get kidded at the studio. There's nothing more pathetic than a woman who's trying to be what she's not. Unless it's a woman who's trying to be what she used to be.

"So it was all really impetuous," Tory says.

"More like frantic. The big thing I remember is that it was important that I was always ready. I shaved my legs twice a day, I wore my good bra even to the library because I never knew when he would get a free moment. I used to take my phone with me into the bathroom, and balance it on the side of the tub in case he called."

"Lunch in five minutes," Elyse yells up the stairs.

"Watch how much oil you put in it," I yell back. "I've got a size-four red dress I have to fit my size-eight butt into."

"It's olive oil," she hollers. "It keeps you from having heart attacks or going senile."

"Maybe so, but it's still a hundred calories a tablespoon," I shout for the final time, and then I say to Tory's reflection, "Your mother has a heavy hand with the oil. Her food is suspiciously shiny."

"Rinse."

"What?"

"The conditioner needs to come out."

"Oh." I bend my head again and let the water run. Why did I even start this story? It isn't my job to warn her that there are heartless men in the world. Men who throw women back like shots of liquor, getting bolder and meaner with each one they take.

"How did it end?" she asks when my head is back up.

"He dumped me."

"In his car?"

"In a bathroom of an Exxon station at the corner of Providence and Rama. Go ahead, your mom's lunch is almost ready so we have to hurry. Blow me out."

She picks up the hair dryer and I close my eyes as the hot hair blasts around my ears. Even after twenty years I can still feel exactly what it was like to be perched on the edge of that Exxon station sink, with one foot crammed against the toilet seat for balance and one hand reaching behind to clutch the soap dispenser. My angle is awkward. I'm slipping. I look at myself in the mirror, the dirty men's room behind me. The urinal — that nasty thing no woman ever wants to see, that sign you must have somehow somewhere made a wrong turn. My eyes lock on it. Something inside of me is already beginning to suspect that it isn't the man I love, but the attention. I've always needed to be noticed and Daniel understands this. Uses the fact against me. He knows that I crave attention so bad that I will agree to meet him in the men's room of an Exxon station on my lunch hour. Each time Daniel thrusts into me, pale pink suds squirt into my palm. Foam runs between my fingers and drips onto the cuffs of my silk blouse. I've lost a button. How am I going to go back to work now?

My eye falls on my purse, precariously dangling from the broken towel dispenser so I wouldn't have to set it on the sticky floor. A manila envelope is poking out the top. It is late in our affair, at the point where you have to make some decisions, have to push things one way or another. He'd been talking about interviewing for another job. He and I could go somewhere else, he said. His wife was a lunatic. Cold and harsh and there was a good chance, he thought, that he and I could get the kids. He wouldn't leave them with her, couldn't live with himself if he did, but maybe we could try Winston-Salem. That was all it had taken and I had set to work researching Winston-Salem. The best school districts, the average price of houses, job openings in our fields. I had put it all in that manila envelope, God help me, and brought it when I'd gone to meet him in the Exxon station.

When it was time to go I'd handed him the envelope and told him everything we needed to start was inside. He thanked me. He said, "Not just for today, but for everything," and then he slipped out the door. A rather formal departure and unlike him. That should have told me something right then and there. His leaving first was our pattern, and I would slip out a minute later. I always hated this part, standing alone all by myself in a men's room, giving him time to get into his car and drive away. I had asked him once why we couldn't at least use the women's room because it was cleaner, and he'd been shocked. He couldn't go into a women's bathroom, he said. I must be kidding. But he could leave me standing here, smoothing down my skirt, looking for my lost button, a little queasy from the combined odors of urine and cigarette smoke and diesel fumes.

Tory gently pushes my head down toward my knees and begins to blow the back of my hair dry, flipping it around her hand with an expert touch. I shouldn't have told her so much. Or maybe I should have told her more.

That afternoon was the last time I saw Daniel. I waited a couple of minutes and wrenched open the bathroom door and boom, there was a woman standing right in front of me. I almost screamed. She'd pulled her car around the back of the gas station to put air in her tires and she had turned when she heard the door open. Saw me coming out of the men's bathroom, me in my suit with my little heels, and she'd known what I was up to in a split second. I could tell by her face. I must have flushed with shame, and she froze for a minute, just gaping, before she turned away. Went back to putting air in the tires of her minivan, where her children were squirming around, poking their fingers out the windows and talking to her over the glass, asking if they could get out and get a Coke.

Tory clicks off the dryer and I raise my head.

"It looks great," she says.

Jesus. I am way too blond. My hair is as light as hers, uniformly golden. "Oh God, honey," I say. "This is more than I expected. I'm so —"

"Pretty," she says. "What you are is pretty and that's okay, Aunt Kelly. We've got about a minute to finish your story before Mom starts screaming again. What happened to Daniel?"

"He packed up his wife and his kids and he left."

Tory's eyes narrow. "You never tried to find out where he went?"

"Someday you'll understand. Everybody's got a story like this. Mine's nothing special."

Another head tilt. "And that's really all there is to it?"

That's all there is to it. He left. I waited for him to contact me and tell me where he was and when to follow, but that call never came. I drove by his house after the first awful month and saw the "For Sale" sign in the yard, the empty garage, the curtainless windows staring out at me. Staring blankly, just like the woman who'd been putting air in her tires. What would Elyse think of me talking to Tory like this? I have barely managed to stop short of telling her the true end of the story — that it had been Elyse who drove me to the abortion clinic two months later when the sum total of my stupidity had finally been tallied. Tory had been about six months old and napping in the back of the car. I don't tell her how on the way home she'd started to cry and Elyse had said to please dig in the diaper bag and find her pacifier, and that when the time came to turn in my seat and put the pacifier in her mouth, I had been unable to do it. She'd been too perfect, too perfectly formed and human, and I didn't think I could touch her. I had started to cry myself and Elyse had been forced to pull off the road and take care of both of us.

When I had finally sobbed myself out I said, "We will never talk of this, never," and Elyse had said, "Of course not." What would Jason and his father make of this little story? I may have told Tory too much today, more than I should have, but I will stop short of telling her the most wildly inappropriate thing of all: that when my grand love affair had finally ended, really and truly ended, she herself had been there.

Tory and I are looking at each other in the mirror. "Don't be offended," I say. "But we might need to go back in with some lowlights. Tone it down a bit."

"It's perfect," she says, with that same irritating certainty her mother has, that same self-satisfied little toss of her head. "It's like you've gone back in time." She begins to gather up the towels, to throw all the little combs and bottles in her plastic bag.

"The omelets are ready," Elyse yells up the stairs. She's put on "Santa Baby," Madonna's version, and it's so loud I can barely make out her voice.

I give myself one final glance in the mirror before I push to my feet. Like it or not, Tory's right. I do look younger.

# CHAPTER EIGHTEEN

It is the Christmas of strange gifts. When she sees the size of the check I've tucked inside a card for Tory, Elyse literally throws her hands up in the air. "Kelly," she says warningly, "you're too generous." But the truth is I can't seem to spend the money fast enough. My checking account is like a bathtub always on the verge of overflowing. I paid Carolina's mortgage in November and it was lower than my power bill, and I'd asked myself yet again why I have such a big house. Isabel had invited us all over to her apartment one night after group class for a Christmas party. We sat on the fireplace and stairs, balancing paper plates on our knees. And it had been fun, but I still didn't have the guts to invite everyone to my house the next time and just let them see that okay, yeah, I'm one of those gated-community types.

For Elyse I found a beaded clutch purse

on a Hollywood auction site; they claimed it had once belonged to Elizabeth Taylor. She gives me a bowl. The latest theme of her pottery has been Native American gods, mostly Hopi ones based on kachinas, and my bowl shows this knobby little figure that she swears is the god of dance. She has modeled only his face, putting him down in the bowl and looking up, like he is at the bottom of some horribly deep well.

"He looks like he's screaming," Tory says, which isn't far from the truth. Elyse's pottery has always scared me a little. It's rough and wild and she often puts odd things together so that her figures come out deformed. Now she launches into one of her long and rambling explanations about how children were initiated into adulthood and this god, whose name is Tunwup, snaps at them with his whip until they dance, and the dance is their transition into adulthood. Or something like that. Elyse's Native American legends never make any sense, but this one is especially odd and Tory and I sit on the couch passing the bowl back and forth while she talks.

"Well, gee, Mom, that's just a swell little story," Tory says when she finishes.

"It's sort of like a Native American version of Santa Claus," Elyse persists. "Because the god isn't real, of course, it's just some man from the village with the tribal mask on. And he jumps around and flicks at them with his whip and then when it's over, and they've danced, it's revealed that he's only a man dressed to represent the god. You know, he takes off the mask and it's Uncle Joe or somebody. Explain it to her, Kelly."

"I wouldn't know where to start," I say.

"Mom," Tory says, laughing until she wipes her eyes. "That's nothing at all like Santa Claus. I can't believe Aunt Kelly gave you a vintage purse and you gave her some fake uncle god who beats children. It's not a fair swap."

"Of course it is," Elyse says, leaning back against the couch, smiling. "She gave me something from a goddess and I gave her something from a god."

"No, I get it," I say. "Dance isn't easy. I like the part about the whips and the initiation."

"Precisely," said Elyse. "You see, honey, your aunt Kelly and I understand each other."

"And another thing," I say, smiling over Tory's blond head at Elyse. "Each time I look at this bowl I'll remember that the god of dance is really just a regular man in a mask."

"I still think it's a weird-ass Christmas present," Tory says.

Two days after Christmas, Isabel and I meet at the food court in the mall. "I'm worried about Nik," she says, as we huddle over her Panda Express and my Jamba Juice. "I guess you heard his car got keyed."

"What?"

"He didn't tell you? Now see, I thought if he told anyone, it would be you. But maybe that's not so weird because he was embarrassed about it. He wouldn't let Quinn call the cops. And Builder Bob keeps showing up at the studio . . . I don't think he's going to rest until he gets our boy out of the country."

I feel like she's kicked me. "Start at the top. I don't know half of what you're talking about."

"Okay," she says. "Pamela's husband is the guy who built the shopping center with the studio, right? Bob Hart. He owns half this side of town."

"Yeah, I know him," I say, thinking back to the pasty-faced man leaning on the doorframe of his study, with all those guns lined up behind his head. "He used to be on the board of hospice."

"That doesn't surprise me. He's big noise. Wants to be in the paper all the time and everybody says he's not the type who'll just stand there while his wife runs off with some immigrant kid."

"Bob Hart must be worth millions. I can't see him keying somebody's car."

Isabel took another bite of cashew chicken. "Me either. But he has a bunch of roughnecks working for him and somebody might try to suck up to the boss." She looks at me archly through the wild tufts of her hair. "And don't think because he's always throwing money toward charities that makes him a good guy. He's already threatened to raise the rent on Anatoly."

"I don't think giving to charities automatically makes you a good guy. Are you saying he's trying to get Anatoly to fire Nik?"

"Well, of course he wouldn't say that, he'd just announce that it's time to raise the rent. But Anatoly isn't stupid. He told Quinn he knew way too many men like that back in Russia and that Bob could just suck his cock. I was standing right there when he said it. I mean, these guys talk like Boris and Natasha chasing moose and squirrel half the time but the minute they cuss, they become completely American. The accent goes right down the drain. When Anatoly said 'Suck my cock,' I swear it sounded like he was from Kansas."

"I don't understand," I say. "You can't have somebody deported because they're sleeping with your wife. Not even Bob Hart can just call up the government and say 'I don't like this guy. Get rid of him.' "

Isabel smiles, but there's an edge to it, a bit of an eye roll. She's dealt with this stuff a lot longer than I have. "Nik is on a student visa, but he isn't a student. Ordinarily, things like that can slide, for months or even for years, but if anything happens that draws attention to the person. You know, they commit a crime or get even halfway involved in some sort of trouble . . ."

"What sort of trouble?"

She shrugs. "I don't know. Anything. Anatoly got a stupid speeding ticket last year before he was legal and just about lost his mind. So Bob could inform the authorities that Nik's student visa was a hoax or even just keep cranking up the rent on the ballroom until . . ."

"You don't think Anatoly would cave, do you?"

Isabel violently shakes her head. "Builder Bob doesn't know who he's messing with. This is Anatoly's business. His little world.

He's gone through hell and back twice to have his own studio and now he's the king. And he's not going to let some redneck, even a rich one, come through his door and tell him who he can employ and who he can't. No, I'm not worried about Anatoly selling Nik out or even the shit about the car. I'm worried that Nik is going to feel so guilty that he does something stupid."

"I can see that." Nik knows how much the studio means to Anatoly. And when it comes to making a dramatic gesture for the sake of Pamela, yes, I can see that too. It's not hard to imagine plenty of scenarios in which Nik's fatalism would outrun his common sense.

"He's a romantic," Isabel says, spooning up the last of her rice. "And you know what that means. There's no telling what he might do."

"I guess you feel like you have to bail them all out," Elyse says.

"Bail who out?" I ask warily, although of course I know. I've just left the mall and her voice sounds kind of tinny and weird over the car speakerphone.

"Carolina. Nik. All of them. Whenever people get into trouble, you rush in to fix it. It's just what you do."

"Rich is the new pretty."

"What the hell does that mean?"

"I don't know. But I couldn't bail them out if I wanted to. It's tied up."

"They told you that? Did you ever even ask?"

The light has changed and the car behind me honks, startling me. "I'm not talking tied up in a legal sense. It's just that I still think of it as Mark's money."

"My grandmother always said that whenever a woman marries for money, she ends up earning it in the end."

"I didn't marry him for his money."

"I know you didn't. I'm just telling you what my grandmother said."

When I get home, I call my lawyer. I'm thinking he might say something about the way I ran out of the charity event. I've always wondered how they explained the clothes I abandoned in the ladies' room.

As it turns out, he doesn't mention it at all. In fact, he comes on the line sounding jovial and a little hungover.

"Let me guess, you overspent at Christmas," he says.

"Do you have an immigration attorney in your practice?"

There's a pause. "Not specifically. Why?

320

Are you having some problem with your housekeeper?"

I can't believe I ever invited this ass to my house for dinner. "No, I need some advice for a friend."

"A friend," he says doubtfully. "We do have someone on staff with a bit of experience. I think he did an internship in Texas."

"I need to make an appointment with him. And about the money . . . I can go into the principal if I want to, right?"

Another pause. Longer. "Is there some kind of problem? Perhaps you and I should have a private talk."

"There's no problem. My housekeeper is fine and I'm fine and I have a ridiculous balance in my checkbook. I'm just asking if I could go into the principal if I wanted to."

"It's your money," he says, a slight edge to his voice. "You can do anything you want to with it."

"Good," I say. "That's exactly what I thought."

# CHAPTER NINETEEN

January is tango month in Nik's group class. After everyone assembles he says that in honor of the New Year, we're going to try a harder routine and it will open with two pivots into a promenade and then a corte. I know the sequence he's talking about — we worked on it just the day before in my private lesson. The same thought must have occurred to him because he pulls me out to demonstrate.

Tango is my best dance, but I've never been the model before. Nik puts on the music we'd practiced with, the Bon Jovi song "You Give Love a Bad Name." It's surprisingly good for tango, the way lots of old rock music is. He whispers "Three times through" and then we're off, ripping through the step sequence once, then again and again.

I feel good. When I drive my thigh between Nik's for the pivot I am more solidly on my feet than I have ever been. He has me demonstrate again, both the right way and the wrong way, and afterward he says "Thank you," two words I do not believe I have ever heard come out of his mouth.

But it isn't just the pivot. I'm strong in everything tonight. Just strangely on, and it all feels effortless, a runner's high. People dance weeks and months and years hoping to hit a night like this and for some reason I'm given one. When I go down the line of men, every single one of them is able to do the pivot with me, even though they struggle through the move when they're with the other women. They struggle so badly that we don't even get to the promenade and the corte. We spend the entire forty-five-minute class just trying to pivot.

"Once again, see how Kelly pushes her leg," Nik is telling the class. He has started adding pronouns and conjunctions more often now, I've noticed. Sounding just a bit more American every day. "A pivot depends on the woman and how she places her leg forward and into floor." He steps back and I stand solid, unwavering, in a pose that looks a bit like a fencer's lunge.

"And when we turn, we keep our bodies very connected" — and here he illustrates by pulling me closer, until our hips are almost fused — "and the spin is much faster." He releases me, stands back. "Spinning is about pulling in lower body, being very tight to partner because this reduces mass. It helps your —"

And here he looks at me. He knows the word but has trouble pronouncing it. He doesn't want to risk saying "Moo-mentum" in front of the class.

"Momentum," I say. "The closer you are to your partner in the spin, the more you create momentum."

"Yes," Nik says, with a professorial little nod. "Very good."

And in that exact second I'm aware that something has changed. Nik now treats me as an equal — more like a partner than a student. At some point something clicked in my head and I guess he must have heard it too.

We all clomp down to the restaurant after class and of course I end up again in the seat beside Steve. He was especially tough to dance with tonight. I'd had to practically muscle him through the steps. He smiles and moves over a bit as I sit down. He's been leaning across the table to talk to Valentina. Sometimes he treats the studio like his own little international buffet, making his way down the line of girls with an empty plate, having a little of this and a little of that. Valentina pulls back with a giggle, happy I'm there and she isn't stuck all alone listening to Steve. She has been trained to be polite — being nice to older men is pretty much her livelihood — and besides she's sweet by nature. But Steve's weird combination of arrogance and neediness can wear anyone out. He's like the male equivalent of Pamela.

"There's something I've been meaning to ask you ever since that night with Mary Tyler Moore," I say, when he finally settles back in his seat with his drink.

He gives me a look out of the corner of his eye. "What?"

"Exactly why does your ex-wife have it in for you so bad?" I ask. "What did you do to her?"

"She's a dancer," he says.

"You're kidding."

"No, she's as good as . . . what's her name, Pamela? That woman whose picture they keep in the window? Lucy was like that and she always wanted me to dance with her but she was a star. How was I going to catch up?"

"She didn't want you to go to competitions with her," I say, exasperated on behalf of this long-ago wife. "She was just trying

325

to get you to do the social stuff."

"Maybe so," he says, "but what was in it for me? I was just going to be one of those guys stumbling along behind his more talented, better coordinated wife. She gave me lessons for birthdays and anniversaries on more than one occasion, but I never found the time to go. Okay, save your breath. I know I was passive-aggressive or whatever you women call it. I told her I was too busy with my medical practice."

"God," I say, "you were such a husband."

Isabel's voice suddenly rises. She's having an argument with her end of the table. "Why can't a woman pay for it?" she's asking. "If a woman gets to a certain age and is of a certain means, why can't she put her money on the table and buy it just as good as a man?" Harry is laughing but Valentina has gone silent. I'm not sure if Isabel has noticed.

Steve nods, drains his drink. "I admit it. I was acting like a husband. So we split up — it wasn't just that, it was lots of things — and you'll never guess what I did the day the divorce papers were signed."

"You signed up for dance lessons."

He grins guiltily. "I've taken two hundred eighty-nine lessons in the past three hundred sixty-five days."

"Damn. You really are a male whale. We need to start calling you Moby Dick."

"Call me every kind of dick you can," he said. "I know it's insane. But the minute she stopped nagging me to dance, that was all I wanted to do."

# CHAPTER TWENTY

I've always thought that the saddest thing on earth is taking down Christmas decorations. Hospice House has stalled until Epiphany, January 6, technically the last of the twelve days of Christmas and thus the absolute dead end by all accounts of the holiday season. But it still gives me a little pang when I pull up in the parking lot and see the maintenance guys pulling the wreaths off the front door. The tree has already been dragged out and is lying by the curb, waiting for recycling like some sort of wounded soldier. I walk over to it, swap off a twig, and smell the pine. Stronger now, the sap higher in it. That final surge of life that trees often get when they're dying.

I dread going in. Carolina has been sinking all week. The cold has dragged on and her lungs have gotten worse. It's obvious to everyone that her immune system has given up. Now she's unpacked for the last time and put the family pictures back on the bed stand. She's been sleeping a lot lately, requesting higher doses of medication. I don't think it's as much about masking the pain as about masking the disappointment, but I don't know that for sure and it's wrong of me to guess.

Carolina had said many times she wanted to see my red dress, so yesterday I came straight from the studio to hospice with it, but when I got to her room she was asleep. Months ago, she'd asked me to promise her consciousness without pain, a gift no one can give, and when I'd seen her there in that deep, hopeless sleep, I knew that I'd failed her. I said her name but she didn't stir. Right now she can't stand to feel anything, I know that. She can't stand to open her eyes and find herself back in this place where Christmas is being carted away in boxes, where angels are being taped into bubble wrap and trees are leaning against the curb. I touched her but there still was no reaction, and I wondered for a second if she was choosing the slow suicide so many hospice patients opt for, if she was so eager to blot out the sadness that she was willing to blot out everything else too. But I looked at her kids on the bedside table and figured that I was just being melodramatic. I hung the dress on the hook of her door and unzipped the bag. It sprang out in all directions and I left it there, a message for when she woke up.

Some days this place just sucks you down. Each bed holds a different story and each story ends the same. Now I stand in the hall, looking one way and then the other, and finally decide not to go straight to Carolina's room. One of the other volunteers is spending a couple of weeks with her daughter in California over the holidays and she has asked me to keep an eye on her client, a ninety-four-year-old woman named Miss Eula who is confused, sweet, docile, and apparently utterly alone in the world. No one came to see her over Christmas and New Year's except a choir from a nearby church that makes an annual trek of coming on Christmas Eve, walking the halls by candlelight and singing "Silent Night." It's beautiful, I guess, but also a little creepy. The nurse on duty said Miss Eula had opened her eyes when the choir walked by. She hasn't spoken in weeks, so it's impossible to tell how much of it registered, but according to her file she had once played the organ in a Baptist church.

"She was employed by a church?" I said to the nurse. "Where the hell are those people? Why don't her former choir mates come to see her?"

"I don't know," she said. "I guess she outlived them all." And a little chill had run across me, light and quick like a mouse. When I look at someone like Miss Eula who has come to the end without a spouse or children, I see myself in that lonely bed. I've always assumed that Elyse will be the one to truly grow old with me. We joke about it in a not totally joking way — how we'll move in together, take care of each other. Make big pots of stew with nourishing root vegetables, move to Scotland, watch our movies all day long. But the joking hides a truth that neither of us wants to face — that unless we pull a Thelma and Louise, we're highly unlikely to die on the same day. One of us will outlive the other and become Miss Eula.

In most ways Miss Eula is easier than Carolina because she doesn't seem to understand what's happening. She is motionless when I come into the room, except for the gentle rise and fall of her chest, and I sit down beside her bed. I wonder if she can hear. They have said she's down to the final days, but I have always suspected that hearing is the last sense to go. I don't know why I believe this, but I talk to people as long as I can, until my tongue goes numb and rubbery and the stories I'm telling no longer make sense. I read to them from library books — children's stories seem the most appropriate and best — but I have no book today and I don't really know enough about this woman to guess at what sort of story she might want me to tell.

"Silent night," I say. "Holy night."

She doesn't move.

"All is calm," I say. "All is bright." It's not my favorite Christmas carol, but I do like that line. It's nice to picture heaven — or whatever word people assign to whatever comes next — as calm and bright. I could sing, I suppose, but I have a terrible voice and I don't want this poor woman, assuming she can indeed still hear, to go out on a wave of my discordant notes. "Round yon virgin," I say. "Holy and mild?"

It's surprisingly hard to remember the lyrics of songs without singing them, so finally I do begin to sing softly, just to get myself back in the groove of remembering. I mumble my way through "Silent Night" and "Joy to the World" and "God Rest Ye Merry, Gentlemen" and Miss Eula does not move. It's not the first time I have half sung to a patient, although it always feels a bit awkward at first. I finish up my little recital with

"It Came Upon a Midnight Clear" and stand up. Ease my way from her bedside as if she were a sleeping child, even though I know I could probably upend every piece of furniture in the room without disturbing this woman.

Carolina's door is open but she's still asleep. I could take the dress off the hook and go home but I'm not sure if she's been conscious during the last twenty-four hours, if she's even opened her eyes long enough to see it. I stand again in the hall, turning, indecisive. A young man leaves the room across from Carolina's. His T-shirt says "Love Your Enemy," but he is one of those angry boys, charging from some relative's bedside as if it were a bar where he'd been insulted. Maybe the phrase is meant ironically, a punk message. Maybe Love Your Enemy is the name of a band. I wander down to the lounge area. Some of the clients are sitting there, watching the disintegration of Christmas, and I wander back.

This time, her eyes are open. She presses a button and raises her bed a little. "Were you just here?"

"Yeah. Did I wake you?"

She looks at me vaguely. "You brought your dress."

"That was yesterday. I left it here last

night so you could see it."

She nods, slowly. "I've been thinking about what your friend Elyse said."

"You're going to have to be more specific. Elyse says lots of things."

She grins and for a minute there's a flash of the old Carolina. "She asked me if I'd ever been in love. But I didn't really answer her."

I sit down. "You want to talk about it?"

"Not all of it. I'm tired. But he . . . a long time ago, he made me mad." She swallows. I pick up the glass of water off the table but she shakes her head. "He made me mad and I stayed mad and then after a while he wanted to come back and see me and I said no."

"It's okay to say no."

"So you think I was right?"

Do I think she was right? She hasn't given me much to go on.

"I guess," I say, "it depends on what he did to make you mad in the first place." But the minute it's out of my mouth I think that I'm not at all sure that's what it depends on. "Did he want you to get back with him or just talk to him?"

"I didn't ask," she says, swallowing again. "But maybe if he had something he wanted to say to me, I should have at least sat there and listened. Heard him out, even if I didn't like it."

We sit for a moment, both motionless. I can't think of a single helpful response, unless maybe she wants me to sing "Silent Night" to her.

"Maybe I can find him on Facebook," I finally say. Carolina shifts her head and looks at me like I'm crazy.

"You don't need to find him on Facebook," she says. "I know where he is."

We sit for a moment, both of us thinking, neither of us talking.

"There's always one," I finally say. "That we can't quite get out of our heads."

"He turned my life," she says, a simple and beautiful phrase.

"Some of them do." This morning, just after breakfast, I'd clicked on my computer and there it was. His response to my picture came back, in the form of a single question: "Are you still you?"

I didn't reply. Instead I opened a Facebook page and studied it. Not Daniel's, but once again that of his wife. Because even though I never met the lady, I trust her version of events more than his. Her status read "Separated." No longer "It's complicated" but now "Separated." So I guess Christmas defeated them, as it so often seems to do.

"You can't undo what's done," Carolina says. "It would be like starting one of your sad movies over and being dumb enough to think it really is going to end different this time."

And then there's a shift in the air. The rapid patter of footsteps down the hall, the sound of a door slamming, some words I can't understand. They don't resuscitate or prolong at hospice, but death nonetheless does carry with it the sense of an emergency. It's a constant surprise, even here. I move to shut the door, glancing out into the hall as I do so, and yeah, the nurse is going toward the room I would have guessed. Miss Eula is leaving, maybe already gone.

I come back to the seat but Carolina is lying with her arms rigidly at her side, staring straight up at the clouds on the ceiling. It's impossible to pretend we didn't hear it, or that it could be anything other than what it was. My red dress undulates gently on the back of the door where I've hurried to shut it and the crystals shimmer with the movement, even in this faint light.

"I shouldn't have bought it," I say, or do I mean "I shouldn't have brought it"? It's obscene, swaying back and forth in this solemn room. Too bright against the white door, like a blot of blood on the snow.

Carolina turns her head again and we consider the red dress, all of its beads and spangles and floats. A thing of the ego, of the transient world, so out of place there in the threshold. There is another soft thud from the hall and Carolina raises herself on one elbow.

"Help me up," she says. "I want to try it on."

# CHAPTER TWENTY-ONE

Nik has taken his new whale to Miami, a woman who has just transferred over from another studio and who is prepared to compete every month, no matter where they have to fly. The word gets out that something truly amazing is happening. Anatoly is going to teach the group class. When I get there the place is full, with more of the feeling of a party than is typical on a Wednesday night. Anatoly never teaches group and in honor of the occasion, some students have shown up that would never ordinarily take a group class. A handful of the Gold and Silver dancers.

"God knows what he's going to put you guys through," Quinn says as I pause at the desk to sign the roster. "He's been running around with those nutty posters all afternoon. But Nik is flying back in tonight and he'll be able to calm him down. He's the only one who can even begin to cope with

Anatoly."

"What's going on?" I whisper.

She whispers back, "We found out today just how much the rent is going up. And it's a lot." And then she turns back to the door, where another group of women I hardly know are coming in, and I walk over to the couch where the usual gang is sitting, putting on their shoes.

"We've been overrun with newbies," Steve observes, as I wedge myself in beside him. Behind his head, three posters are clumsily taped on the mirror:

I would only believe in a God that knows how to dance

— Friedrich Nietzsche

Never give a sword to a man who can't dance

— Confucius

Wives are people who feel they don't dance enough

— Groucho Marx

"That's three weird people to quote," I say, although I'm actually amused, especially by the Groucho one. "I guess Anatoly's trying to inspire us."

"You want to practice our tango routine?"

"What? Okay, sure." Steve and I walk to the only halfway-empty corner of the crowded room. We go through the sequence a couple of times and I gradually become aware that I'm a little uneasy. I don't know why. The room is bright and full of people and he and I have partnered many times over the last few months. But tonight it seems he's taking the routine seriously. We're on the verge of actually dancing. Over his shoulder I can see the ladies' room door open and Jane come out in a white ball gown. She's shopping early for the Star Ball, but maybe she has to. Jane is so tall that I don't imagine many gowns fit her. This one is lovely — an off-the-shoulder drape with layers of chiffon. She seems embarrassed to step out in it with so many people around, but there's not a full-length mirror in the ladies' room. She turns toward her lover, Margaret, who's sitting on one of the bar stools, and Margaret picks up a camera and quickly snaps a picture. Smart, I think. Jane is a pro at renting dresses. She has them sent to the studio where she can try on several and she has Margaret take pictures so she can study them later, at her leisure. I try to catch her eye, to signal that I think it's a beautiful dress, but Steve has taken me into a series of swivels.

When I'd heard Nik wouldn't be back from Miami in time to teach, I almost hadn't come. The last week at hospice has been especially bad, but now I feel myself moving with Steve in an easy, open way and I'm glad I'm here, among the crowd and music and bright colors. It's often like this, that your best days of dancing come on the worst days of everything else. Sometimes the very act of overcoming your resistance, of opening the car door and putting one foot after the other across the pavement, the simple act of willing yourself to walk into the studio is enough to cure whatever's ailing you. Jane is standing in front of the mirror, staring at her reflection. She holds up the diaphanous overskirt of the ball gown and pulls it to her face as if it might be possible to inhale whatever it is she's feeling.

Anatoly steps into the middle of the room and claps for our attention. Group is beginning and there are probably thirty of us, maybe more. He tells us that we are going to have a special treat tonight. We're going to do an exercise that will break all the rules. That will help us come out of ourselves and travel new emotional ground as dancers.

Reaction to this announcement is, at best,

mixed. The Gold and Silver dancers exchange uneasy glances. They have come to dominate, not to travel new emotional ground, and no one is quite sure what Anatoly is talking about. I catch Valentina's face in the mirror and we smile. We regulars, the people who take group every night and have learned how to float with anything, we may do okay.

Anatoly's big idea is that we're going to dance to the wrong music. When he says "wrong music" he makes quotation marks in the air. We're not to worry about steps; we are to try to interpret the spirit of the dance in a new way. He puts on "Wicked Game" — Isabel perks up — and says, "Let's jive."

You cannot jive to "Wicked Game." But we try, and later we tango to "Bring in the Clowns" and foxtrot to "Zoot Suit Riot." It's bedlam. Anatoly cuts off the lights to help us be less self-conscious, and then walks among us, waving his big albatross arms and saying "Release." Those of us I think of as the Performers — Harry, Isabel, Valentina, Lucas, and myself — are galvanized into action. We've suffered through enough of the technique lessons where we've spent forty-five minutes trying to perfect a single step and we're happy to be in a class where it is impossible to do anything right and ergo equally impossible to do anything wrong. The serious dancers, the Competitors, are having a harder time, hiding in corners, rocking back and forth.

Anatoly grabs me at one point and begins whirling me around. I go with it as long as I can until I get dizzy and he says, "Afraid to fall, aren't you? I can tell." I nod crazily at him and he moves on to Valentina. Everyone is afraid to fall, I think. What sort of observation is that? We gallop, we flop, we stomp, and we twirl — it's like one of those kindergarten classes at a progressive school where everyone tries to be an earthworm or a thunderstorm. When he cuts the lights back on at the end, we're all flushed and sweaty. People are either saying it's the best class they've ever been to or the worst. Anatoly finishes with a little speech. He says you need both elements in dance, both passion and technique, both abandon and control, but hardly any personality has room for both. And yet, he says, we must keep trying, working to find a balance. "Dance is," he announces, in his best James Earl Jones voice, "an art in which everyone will ultimately fail."

We applaud. He bows. And as the noise dies down I hear Quinn's voice from the corner saying, "You look beautiful."

Jane has apparently been trying on dresses for the entirety of the last forty-five minutes. She is standing now in a sunshine-yellow ball gown, a thousand shades of gold and orange in the skirt. The cut is old-fashioned — most of the newer gowns begin to flare when they reach the woman's hips, and the most fashionable of all do not widen until they are at her knees. This is a cotillion-style dress, almost a hoop skirt, but Quinn is right. Jane looks beautiful.

Maybe it's the word that throws her. "Beautiful" is a description we rarely allow ourselves. Or maybe she was just surprised to find all of us looking at her, the lights suddenly on and the dancers, who had been so preoccupied with the music, now turned and staring. She seems stunned, as if she's been hit on the head with a basketball. She says, "It's not the right color."

"Yes it is," Isabel says.

"Anybody up for a drink?" Harry asks loudly, and we all nod and begin to collect our things. We need one more than usual tonight. I stop by to use the bathroom before I go and just as I get to the door Jane is there too.

"Come on," she says. "We can share." It's like this a lot — one bathroom for all these dancers, and I have likely at some point or another peed in front of every woman who comes to the studio. We go in together and I help her get her zipper started down before I lift my own skirt and sit on the toilet.

"Isabel's right," I tell her. "That color works on you."

Jane lets the dress puddle around her feet and steps out of it. "Why did Quinn have to say 'beautiful'?"

"I know. It's a scary word to hear."

"I mean, I'm not."

I pull on the toilet paper. "I think that's the dress you should rent and I think you and Margaret should come with us to Esmerelda's. We've all had a hell of a night."

Jane has her jeans and T-shirt back on. "Where was Pamela?"

"I heard she has some kind of stomach problem."

"From making herself puke?"

"She makes herself puke?"

She shrugs. "That's the rumor."

"I've heard something too."

"That Builder Bob is trying to run Nik out of town?"

"Yeah. He's raised the rent on Anatoly."

"Damn," she says. "It sounds like the gang needs a plan."

At first we laugh like fools at Esmerelda's, making fun of all the Silver and Gold dancers, how they'd been so stiff and self-conscious with Anatoly's little game. We split big quesadillas like they were pizzas and then at some point the conversation turns more serious, falls to speculation. Someone says that Nik found a note on his car. He crumpled it before anyone could see what it said. He might have to leave the country for a while and wait a certain number of weeks, then apply for a new student visa and reenter. It's all some sort of complex diplomatic game. Where do they go while they wait? Canada mostly. Toronto has a big Russian community with boardinghouses and attorneys. Practically a whole cottage industry just to shuttle people back and forth across the border.

So he'll be gone . . . what? A month? Six?

No one seems to know. Long enough to lose your students and your studio, if you have one. Long enough that everything you've worked for falls apart like a sand castle and when you come back you must start from scratch. Apparently student visas work whether you are teaching or studying, and Anatoly has tried to get Nik a job with the local branch of the state university, leading workshops in modern dance. Nik would even do it for free, just to be able to renew his visa. But it hasn't worked out. Other Russians in town are offering the school the same deal, or better.

So what's left?

Leaving and reentering is pretty much his only option. We all sit for a minute in silence. There's no doubt that Bob is prepared to escalate. Part of me feels sorry for him. His world must seem to be unraveling. He owns great blocks of property at a time when land values are dropping. He rents storefronts in areas where storefronts stand empty. And now his younger wife has taken an even younger lover, a man who must seem to Bob as if he's been genetically engineered specifically to torment him, to mock him with his muscular thighs, regal bearing, and unlined skin.

But still . . . the latest word is that Bob braced a chair against a door and tried to trap Pamela in the bathroom while she was taking a shower. No one is exactly sure why a man would attempt to barricade his wife in a shower, and the story varies about what happened next. Over the last few months, bank accounts have been closed, credit cards have gone missing, and glass has been broken — the small workaday vandalisms of a marriage falling apart. She refuses to leave the house and so does he, so they are living on different levels, coming and going through separate doors. A court date has been set and there are those who believe a private investigator is watching the studio.

Does Pamela love Nik?

Ah, that's the real question, isn't it? We suck on our straws, stare into space, reach for another chip.

Her husband's rich, someone says, and I shut my eyes. No way does a woman walk out on all that, says someone else, and there is murmuring all around. Some voices agreeing, some demurring. I think of Elyse assuming that my first impulse would be to write a check and solve the problem, and what irks me most is that she was right. But I sit quietly now, taking it all in. I spent the first half of my life thinking that if anybody liked me, it was because I was pretty. I'll be damned if I spend the last half thinking that people only like me because I'm rich.

Nik needs to get away no matter what, someone says. It doesn't matter who said it because we're all saying the same things, over and over, like a tragic chorus.

That's right. Let it cool off for a while. He

can always come back.

But it's very complicated to talk to Nik. He's hard. Not hard in the heart or hard in the head, but hard like a puzzle.

True. Just the same, someone needs to tell him to be careful.

Danger might be part of the eroticism. Sometimes the yearning is all that keeps it going.

Yeah. Exactly. When people actually find a way to be together, half the time it turns out they don't even want each other. Sometimes you're chasing so hard you forget what you're chasing.

"Seriously, Kelly, you've got to get him alone and find out what he's thinking," Steve finally says, turning his whole chair to me with a clatter, and everyone else starts nodding. "If he'll talk to anyone, it will be you."

When it's time to leave, Steve insists on walking me back to my car. We get as far as the studio door before I remember that I left my dance shoes in the bathroom. I convince him I can make it to my car without an escort — what's up with him tonight, anyway? — and dash in. Lucas is in the corner and I know he does this sometimes, stays after class while the rest of us go drinking so that he can practice an hour more. The sight of him dancing with his own reflection, so serious about it, both ashamed and kind of proud, has always moved me. Anatoly and Quinn are both doing their last private lessons of the night and Nik's duffel bag is over by the bar. Good, I think, he's back from Miami. But I don't see him anywhere, so I go into the bathroom and grab my shoes, which are lying just where I left them, beside the toilet. Then I slip back out.

There'd been so many people at the group class that I hadn't been able to park in my usual spot near the door. I'd driven around for a while looking and ended up several rows back, near the grocery loading dock, almost beside the Dumpster. Another of Builder Bob's little punishments has been to cut the number of parking spaces designated for the ballroom, so the instructors park out here, among the bits of rotting produce and the crushed cardboard cartons. It's dark in this part of the parking lot and most of the stores have closed. For a moment I regret not letting Steve wait for me but I flick my autoentry and the car responds, lighting up and blinking, and I walk toward it fast.

There's another car right beside me, parked so tight that I have to turn sideways to squeeze through to my door. There's a movement inside the car and I do a dumb thing. I freeze just when I should hurry. But it's just a movement, a person sitting there. No, two people sitting there. I open my front door, slip inside, and start the car as fast as I can. Hit the door lock button and throw it into reverse.

I'm being silly, I think. Silly and jumpy. So there were two people sitting in a parked car. What of it? But as I wait at the first stoplight, I can't shake the feeling that the car behind me has some intent. Am I being followed? It makes no sense. I try to remember if I've seen it before, but I'm a typical girl, not particularly good at identifying cars by their make or model, and besides, it was dark. I'm pretty sure that the car behind me now, the car that continues to stay in the same lane as me, which seems to be following just a fraction too close to my bumper, is not the same car that was parked beside me back in the lot. That car had been big. One of those monster SUVs you see all over this part of town. An Escapade, or maybe a Suburban.

The kind of car Pamela drives.

Which . . . once again means nothing. Half the women on my street drive Suburbans.

Good, the second light is turning yellow

as I approach it. A chance to verify my suspicions. I slide through just as the yellow light turns red and the car behind me does too — a fact that, while still quite possibly incidental, makes my heart pound a little more. Don't overreact, I think. A car is driving through town and another car happens to be behind it. Nothing noteworthy in that. But it has been such a strange night and I try to sort through the seemingly unrelated facts. Nik's bag was in the studio but I didn't see him. So okay, he was in the back. Or he and Anatoly were going out for something to eat, a chance to discuss the rent situation. Lucas had been embarrassed that I had seen him, dancing by himself. When I waved, he had not waved back, but that means nothing either, does it? The preacher had been dancing as if he were in a trance, swaying back and forth in a way that was strangely private, and then, then there was the matter of those two people sitting in a parked car in the dark. But there was no reason to think that they might have been Nik and Pamela.

Yes, he's been gone for a couple of days and yes, she might have been tempted to slip away and meet him upon his return. But would she meet him in the parking lot of the studio? Unlikely. That's way too risky

— but, once again, very much like the things Daniel and I used to do. Toward the end this is how it gets, I think, my eyes darting back and forth between the road and the rearview mirror. You'll do all kinds of crazy shit — you meet in a men's room, or beside a Dumpster. And you don't even care if it's degrading because part of you believes you deserve the degradation. You're desperate for a conclusion, even a tragic one, so sometimes you force the issue. Make a move that, for better or worse, will knock you off dead center.

And if this car is truly following me, why? Even if Pamela had felt she had to see Nik, even if they had been mindless enough to meet in the dark parking lot outside the dance studio . . . that still doesn't produce any reason why a stranger would be tailing me now. It's my imagination, I think, the result of an unusual day. Death and desertion and dancing to the wrong songs — and Steve, the way he pulled me into hold when we tangoed. And then I think of that whole ugly wall of guns over Bob Hart's shoulder as he leaned in his doorframe with an empty glass in his hand and appraised me. Appraised me and found me wanting, just an older, doughier, grayer version of his wife.

I turn left. So does the car behind me.

There's only one more light before the entrance to my neighborhood.

Maybe I'm jumpy due to the simple fact that Steve put his hand on my back in that particular way. Not just that he was flirting, because everyone at the studio flirts with everyone else. The problem was that when he touched me, for just a minute, I felt something. I don't want to feel something. I don't want to open the door that leads back into the room of men.

The last light is red. I roll to a stop and watch the car behind me move into the right-hand lane and turn. I sit alone, the only car within sight, and wait for my heartbeat to slow. I'm losing it, I think. I've gotten so paranoid that I can no longer be trusted to interpret the events of my own life. I count my breaths until they slow.

It's natural to tell ourselves stories about the past, but the trouble is, they're simplified stories. We leave out the contradictions, the inconsistencies, the inconvenient emotions. When I told Tory about the time I met Daniel in the Exxon restroom, I chose the most dreadful story I could think of, one that shows him at his worst and guarantees I will not become nostalgic. But there are other stories I might have shared, such as that first time on the picnic table at the park, the sun so high and bright, the trees forming a low canopy above the table. He had undressed fully, which surprised me, and I had been struck mute by his beauty — the pale, marble-like quality of his shoulders and chest, his upper arms. My reaction was disturbing — here I had spent a lifetime resenting men who only approached me because of the way I looked, but perhaps I was no better. What if I only wanted him because he was so perfectly formed, his smile so slow and sleepy, his hair so wild and thick? I remembered a line from a Yeats poem, something some man had quoted to me once, thinking I would like it. Something about how only God could love you for yourself alone, and not your yellow hair.

And I had bristled when he said it, of course I had. I wanted to be loved for more than my yellow hair and yet . . . I was on a picnic table in a deserted park, on the verge of sinning more deeply than I ever had sinned. Because Daniel was married, taken, a father of two, and yet all I could think about were the divots on his shoulders, how much I wanted to slide my hands across them, how much I wanted to hold on and ride and see where this pretty animal would ultimately take me.

I was not naked. Mostly so, but I had tied

my shirt around my hips. He pulled at it.

"Please," he said. "I want to see."

"Don't look at me there. Anywhere but there," I said.

On the way home, after it seemed the sex was over, he had sat at another stoplight, just like this one, waiting to turn left. Daniel had taken my hand and turned it over, palm to the sky, and begun to flick his tongue down the length of my lifeline. That was all there was to it, that was all it took. Just his tongue on my palm was enough to set off a trip line of shudders and jolts and my back arched forward and my right foot shot out as if I were the one who was driving. As if I were trying to stop something, my foot pumping the air, looking for the brake on a runaway car. This is the thing that no one gets about women like me. We are ripe for obsession. For not only do we get aroused, we stay aroused. In us, the desire never ends.

"You're so easy," Daniel murmured, my palm pressed against his lips. He used to tell me that I was the easiest woman he'd ever met.

I know it will backfire if I just flat-out tell Nik what to do. So instead, I introduce the idea of an exit strategy.

"Exit strategy," like "hobby," turns out to be one of those terms that don't translate well into Russian. It's taken a lot of persuading for me to convince Nik even to leave the studio. He's acting like I'm kidnapping him as he follows me four storefronts down to the pizzeria, and once we get here he refuses to eat. He orders a Sprite.

"Lunch is on me," I say. "That means I'll pay for it."

But he shakes his head. It feels like the first day of spring, surprisingly warm and breezy, and they've seated us on the patio beside big half-barrel planters of impatiens and ferns. What does he think when he looks upon this world, I wonder, and I remember he told me that the only time his mother ever came to America she walked around shading her eyes and saying, "Too bright, too bright." Does he let Pamela pay for things when they go out? Assuming, that is, they ever go out. He's so young and she's so loaded that you'd think it was clear who would pick up the check. But Nik has his strange old-fashioned ideas about men and women. It's entirely possible that he does not let his lover even buy him a Sprite.

"Anatoly doesn't need this," Isabel had said last week at Esmerelda's. "Nik's going to have to face facts and go to Canada for a while. Wait it out and then reenter."

"Otherwise he'll take down the whole studio with him," Steve had agreed. "He's smart. Anatoly is like a brother to him, and Nik isn't going to let him ruin his business trying to protect him."

But, looking at the man-boy who sits before me now, staring down at the table and sullenly fiddling with a plastic straw, I'm not so sure. Love, or at least the idea of love, stupefies us all, and it's ironic, to say the least, that I'm the one they've elected to talk to him. Two things have happened in the last twenty-four hours. I've learned that I have slightly over nine million dollars in the bank and I've agreed to meet Daniel in Charleston. He asked me an impossible question — "Are you still you?" — and I had written back, "You're the only one who can tell me."

"Come to Charleston," he replied.

He pointed out that we always talked about going there and that now, at last, there are no impediments in our way. At least that's what I think he meant to say. He miswrote, used the word "implements" instead, as if twenty years ago we had been in constant danger of stepping on a rake. When Elyse found out I agreed to meet Daniel, she exploded. She used words like "self-destructive" and "masochistic," words I might use now too if I thought Nik would understand them.

So here I sit on the patio of a pizzeria, the supreme hypocrite of the planet Earth, come to tell this boy he needs to do all the things I can't seem to do myself. I've gathered every sort of document Nik might possibly need and put them in — what else? — a manila envelope. The number of a bank account in both our names, set up as tenants in common, as if we were business partners. Either of us can make deposits to this account and either of us can make withdrawals. It's not much. Not much in the face of what I own. A couple of months' worth of allowance for me can buy a whole new life for someone like Nik. And there's a one-way plane ticket that was expensive because the date was left open, and contact information for an attorney in Toronto. I slide the envelope across the table.

"I'm going to insist that you take this," I say.

He opens the envelope. Sees the contents. He knows what it all means at a glance and he pushes the papers back in, his face flushing, as if I've brought him to this pizzeria patio and shown him porn.

"No one has to know about this except

for the two of us," I say, which is true. All the Esmerelda's crowd expected me to give him was advice.

He shakes his head, slides the envelope across the table toward me.

"I'm going to insist that you take it," I repeat. "It's up to you what you do with it once you're out of my sight, but we're not leaving this table without that envelope in your hands. You're always telling me to trust you, and I do. But it works both ways."

"I am fine," he says. There is a slight tremor in his voice. I wonder how long it has been since he slept eight consecutive hours.

I love this boy, I think, and the realization comes to me with a shock. It is, needless to say, a different kind of love and yet I know I could make the same mistake with Nik that I made with Daniel. I could so easily convince myself that he has some special magic. Put him on the pedestal that has stood vacant for so long. I already half believe I can't dance without him, that the world of the ballroom is something he has given me, something I couldn't have found with anyone else. When they were all talking at Esmerelda's about how he had to go to Canada, I had known that they were right and yet one thought had snuck in, a splash of selfishness among all the altruism.

But if he goes to Canada, I'll never waltz again.

As he slumps here before me now, staring at the table, fiddling with the wrapper of his straw, he has never looked younger or more scared. Elyse accused me of making him the son I never had and women my age idolize their sons, this I know without question. I have heard them tell themselves a variation of this new fairy tale over and over. His father may have failed me, but my son never will. The world may be going to hell but my boy — my Joshua or Eli or Jordan or Andrew — he is perfect. He will be with me to the end.

It gives me an idea. "If your mother was here," I ask him, "what do you think she would tell you to do?"

It's unfair to play the mother card, but I'm desperate. I know how much he loves her, worries about her, the look that comes across his face when he tells me about leaving his village so long ago. If she were here, she'd tell him to get his butt to Canada and we both know it.

"This is my fate," he says. What he means is "Pamela is my fate."

"People can change their fates."

He shakes his head. "It is not your problem," he says, and his voice is devoid of an accent. It's just like when Isabel said Anatoly's voice changed when he told Builder Bob he could suck his cock. I guess anger makes people sound like Americans.

"Not all affairs end well," I say. "You know that just as well as I do."

He stands up and pulls out his wallet. Carefully counts out two ones and leaves them on the table for the Sprite.

"Yes," he says. "These things you say. I know them all."

But when he leaves he takes the envelope.

# CHAPTER TWENTY-TWO

I jerk awake. It wasn't a bad dream, just one of the vague ones, and it's slipping from me even as I open my eyes. I try to lie very still and think about the ocean. Maybe if one wave of sleep carried me into wakefulness, another one will carry me back.

But the clock says 4:00 a.m., that impossible point where you've been in bed too long to go back to sleep. This is all going to catch up to me this afternoon. Exhaustion will undoubtedly hit me at the worst possible time, twelve hours from now, when I'm due to meet Daniel in Charleston. After a few minutes of indecision, I rise and pull an afghan over my shoulders like a shawl, then wander down the stairs and out the French doors leading to the garden.

The night is still remarkably warm, and the moist soil promises an early spring. I feel among the bushes for buds, but they're not quite there, not yet. The night that Mark died had been very much like this one, another large low moon. I'd jerked awake then too, and had known at once that something was wrong. I'd put my head on his chest but there was no movement within, no heartbeat. And so I'd done what I always do when there's trouble. I called Elyse.

It was even more the middle of the night in Arizona and she had been, of course, disoriented by the ringing phone. It had taken her a while to understand what I was saying. She seemed to think that Mark and I had a fight, and when I said that he was cold and I couldn't get him to talk to me, she started giving me her usual bad advice about men, and when I kept saying no, not that, she finally said, "Are you telling me you're going to divorce him?" and I said, "Elyse, I'm telling you that I think he's dead." We've never discussed that night, never laughed about that ridiculous conversation, although I suspect there is something sickly funny in the story. But when I said the word "dead," she gave this little scream and her scream scared me, woke me out of my trance, and I finally started to cry. She asked me if I had called 911.

Of course I hadn't. I had called her. But then I remembered that I should've called 911 so Elyse and I hung up and I did. While

I was standing at the bedroom window waiting, looking down the driveway toward the road, I saw not the ambulance I expected but rather a whole line of golf carts, coming toward me one after another, in the growing daylight. Because within this self-contained community almost all of our neighbors had abandoned their cars for golf carts, and one of the women already had a jug of iced tea on her lap. It seems the 911 dispatcher had called the security guard at the gatehouse, who had, in turn, lit up the prayer chain, whose efficiency was so remarkable that my neighbors, experts in the rituals of southern death, had beaten the ambulance to my house.

The garden is beautiful by moonlight. The air is sweet and soft and the wind doesn't really blow as much as it breathes. The trees arch above me and for the hundredth time I feel guilty that I haven't mourned Mark more. He deserves to be mourned. In the dream I think we were on some beach. He was calling out to me from the dunes and his face seemed terribly sad, but I can't remember what he was saying.

I sigh. Look up at the moon. I should climb back into bed and catch a couple of more hours of sleep. Maybe I would even remember whatever it was Mark was trying so hard to tell me. Some people claim they can do this. Elyse keeps a notebook on her bedside table to record her nocturnal impressions, as if the gods of Arizona are talking to her by day and by night.

But I've never been particularly good at recapturing dreams.

"So you're really going?"

"Yeah," I say to Carolina. "I'm already on the interstate."

"Are you excited?"

"Mostly scared."

"Of what?"

"He might not be like I remember."

Across the phone line I can hear the creak of Carolina shifting in her hospital bed, and a cough. She's getting another cold. I wore a surgical mask the last time I was in to see her and she made fun of me. But we can't be too careful. "I've never been to Charleston," she says.

"Someday we'll go."

A hollow promise, and she makes no comment. "What's it like?"

"Old. Pretty. Kinda touristy. One time Elyse and I took Tory when she was a little girl and we all went on one of those candlelight cemetery tours where the guides dress up like southern belle ghosts. They painted

366

their skin real white and had cobwebs hanging off their straw hats and our guide called herself Scarlett O'Scara. I don't know why we thought that was a good idea. Tory was only about seven and I think we scared the crap out of her."

Carolina laughs. Talking about tombstones and cemeteries never seems to bother her. In fact, on our last movie night she requested the theme be "ghosts" and we'd watched *Portrait of Jennie* and *Blithe Spirit*. I believe she's studying up on how to haunt someone but I'm not sure whom.

"Does Elyse know you're meeting Daniel?"

"Oh yeah, and she's thrilled about it. Thinks it's a swell idea. But I've spent my whole life letting Elyse talk me in and out of things and that's got to stop. And besides, she started coming around a little when I got into the details of the trip and I was asking her about what makes a hotel a good place to meet a lover. She loves trysts."

"Twists?"

"Trysts." I spell it for her. "That's Elyse's word for meeting a man in some fabulous place." I've come dangerously close to letting it slip that it was I and not Daniel who planned this meeting. That I was the one who called the hotel and read out the sixteen digits of my credit card number. A credit card still in the name of Kelly Madison and maybe that's why I dreamed about Mark last night. He's paying for all this from beyond the grave, which is terribly wrong when you stop to think of it. No wonder he was yelling at me to get out of the water, because it's coming back to me now, that I was in the water and Mark was in the dunes and he was waving like he saw some sort of danger coming up behind me, a shark or a powerboat or a tsunami. But this is something that I have to do, whether anyone else understands it or not. It's like I'm taking the grand tour of my old life and I've got to see Daniel the way Elyse had to see *David* in the Accademia. I need to see him just so I can say I have.

"My sister Virginia got back with an old boyfriend one time," Carolina says. Her voice is a little breathless, and I realize she's on her cell and walking.

"How'd that play out for her?"

"She's living with me, ain't she? Okay, here we go. Tryst. I got the dictionary off the nurse's desk." Carolina's breathing is really quite ragged. She must have walked the entire length of the hall. "It means 'a secret meeting between lovers.' Well, shoot, we already knew that. Can be a noun or a verb. Here's an example in a sentence: 'Both lovers had to hurry to keep their noontime tryst in the park.' Rhymes with cyst, fist, grist, mist, twist, and wrist."

"I had to twist his wrist to make him tryst," I say.

Carolina ignores me. "Okay, listen to this: It might come from the Middle English word for 'trust' or it might come from the Old French for 'to lie in wait,' like where hunters used to hide in the bushes until the deer came by. Well that's two weird things to get confused, isn't it? I mean are you supposed to trust them, or are they gonna shoot you? It seems like they would have to know what words mean better than that before they put them in the dictionary."

"That's all very interesting," I say, although the truth is that part about lying in wait creeps me out a little. "What are you going to do today?"

"Nothing as exciting as what you're fixing to do. I guess I'll watch a movie, since you left me about a million of them. Maybe that Elizabeth Taylor one your friend Elyse thinks is so great."

"*Suddenly, Last Summer?* You need to wait until I'm back for that one. Trust me, it's intense."

"Wait a minute," she says sharply. "It's

Friday. If you're already in the car you must have canceled your lesson with Nik. I didn't think anything would make you cancel a lesson with Nik. Does he know where you're going?"

"Of course not," I say. "Nobody knows but you and Elyse."

I pull my car around the circular cobblestone driveway and park it beside a moss-covered fountain. The lobby is very small and quiet. A young man looks up from behind the counter and greets me by name. I'm expected, he tells me. My room is ready.

The spell of the place grips me at once. I leave my car keys on the countertop along with my sunglasses and the young man has to pick them up for me. He seems used to it. Used to picking up after people who are drunk or weeping or high on the fumes of romance. I follow him down the hall to my room, which has a name and not a number. Like hospice, I think fleetingly. Elyse has told me each room is a tribute to a different impressionist, that this is the theme of the inn, but it's subtle, not overdone at all, and I should ask for the Manet. "Manet, not Monet," she'd said. "They're two different painters." I told her I knew they were two different painters. Despite what everyone thinks, I am not an idiot.

As the young man opens the door the first thing I see is a large white bed, high and placed in the dead center of the room. It's covered with pillows in the faintest tints of pink and blue, so subtle that you think at first you've imagined the colors, that it's some sort of trick of the sunlight.

"I hope this meets with your approval," he says.

I murmur something noncommittal and walk past him into the room.

"Do you need help with your bags?" he says.

I shake my head. There's no need to dissemble or pretend I have any luggage beyond this one small satchel. This young man knows what I'm about. After all, this inn is painfully expensive, on a back street, close to nothing, on the way to nowhere. People only came here for one reason.

He opens the French doors leading out to a balcony that overlooks the garden, then places my car keys and sunglasses on an antique desk. "Here you are," he tells me.

Here I am.

I'm grateful to have an hour before Daniel is due to arrive. A time of transition, a chance to settle in. There is, per my request, a bottle of champagne cooling in a tall pewter bucket. I pull it out, shake off the slivers of ice, and look at the label. Another of Elyse's ideas, a château and a vintage that she claims are something special. I'm pretty sure they drank champagne in *Love in the Afternoon* or maybe even *The Apartment.* In the old movies, corks were popping all over the place, and I must have mentioned this to Elyse because she had said "Absolutely, champagne" and that we should get this certain kind. "It's like you've stepped into a painting by Monet," she had told me. "Monet, not Manet. It feels like you're drinking flowers."

I look at the bottle. I know that it costs $140 and that the wine inside will be very pale, with flavors as subtle as the colors of these pillows. That it will have an elegant sort of restraint, because I'm already beginning to understand that when you come to a place like this, what you're paying for is the absence of something. I look around the room. Pull off my clothes, fold them, and put them in a drawer. I run a tub of water and pour in bubbles but then I change my mind and pull the plug. I climb up the step stool and dive into the rapturous duvet on the tall white bed. It is so high and so fluffy that it invites — perhaps demands — comparisons to clouds. This is what I wanted all those years ago, I think. This is how a man treats his true mistress. He sits her on clouds. There are cheeses and fruits on a tray but I ignore them. It seems that a real mistress would not eat, that she would be like those ferns called maidenhair, the kind they claim are capable of existing solely on air. I pull the bottle from the bucket again and walk out to the balcony. Consider the roses below and the dignified drone of the fountains. Lift the champagne to the light and try to find the oceans of foam that Elyse had promised were tumbling inside it.

I am moving slowly, being careful. I have remembered to wipe the bottle off with the white linen towel. So on this early-spring afternoon in an expensive inn four hours from Charlotte I have no explanation for why the champagne slips from my hands. No explanation for why it falls like a unit, perfectly, descending toward the balcony floor so slowly that for a minute I imagine I might actually be able to pluck it from midair. No explanation for why the wine explodes in all directions, dampening my feet and sending a thousand shards of glass skidding across the flat gray stones. A minute later Daniel finds me just like this. On the balcony, splashed to the knees, afraid to move.

Why, he asks, why am I weeping in such a beautiful place? It is the first thing he has said to me in over twenty years. He tells me he can always call down and order another bottle. Of course they will have another.

So I am not Audrey Hepburn, or Shirley MacLaine. I am not even Elyse and when I tell her this story tomorrow, she will claim that she never described the champagne as drinking flowers. She'll say that's tacky and that she could not imagine ever saying such a thing. But it had to be her. Who else knew I was going to meet Daniel, who else would have ever thought to compare a wine to a painting? And then she will say "But you got another bottle, right?" because Elyse has a talent for infidelity. She has that recessive mistress gene, the one that allows her to stand back and tilt her head critically, to wait for the man to prove himself worthy, to wait for the man to come to her. Elyse can lift a bottle to the sunlight and see a whole world inside of it, so she would remember the name of a wine that pleased her, and she would not hesitate to ask for it again. Some women exist to cause men trouble just as some women exist to make life easier, and men like the first kind better. There's no justice in it, but it's true. All my life I have made the same mistake with men over and over: I have been convenient.

When he finds me there on the balcony, wet and weeping, Daniel walks across the patio, the glass crunching beneath his shoes with every step. He picks me up. He carries me through the double French doors and stretches me across the fluffy pastel bed. Of course they have another bottle, he says, amused at my tears, and my excessive guilt. He will call down to the desk. They will bring it right up.

And when the champagne comes, it is lovely.

But, for the record, it does not remind me of flowers.

# CHAPTER TWENTY-THREE

I don't know why they use the phrase "bed of roses" to mean a good thing. Even if you get rid of all the thorns, even if you strip the flowers down and make a cushion of petals, as some poor maid must have done last night while Daniel and I were out at dinner, the scent becomes overwhelming after a while. In fact, the next morning, it's the smell of the roses that wakes me. I open my eyes and my first thought isn't that Daniel is beside me or that this is, in our long and complicated history, the first time we've slept together. Slept together in the most literal sense of the words, as in "lay down in the same bed and went to sleep." My first thought is that I have a headache. Petals are in my hair and sticking to my skin. They trail behind me as I slip carefully from under the sheets and walk to the bathroom, little dots of red and pink dropping to the hardwood floor.

The clock says 8:55 and Daniel lies motionless in what my grandmother used to call the sleep of the dead. He doesn't stir as I fumble for pants and a sweater, and when I whisper "I'm going for a walk," he makes no response. I pull the door closed, then slip down the staircase and past the dining room, where a few people have drifted in for breakfast. Out through the lobby and into the street.

The city feels empty, like a bowl. I start down toward the bay and when I am almost there, I turn for no reason and double back. Charleston does this to me. Makes me weave and meander. I walk without pattern through the sun-splashed streets, nodding at the runners, the people walking their prancy little city dogs, at the elderly lady who shuffles out onto her porch to pick up her paper. "Mornin', ma'am," I call, aware that my voice is absurdly southern, that the moment I drove over the bridge and into the city my accent began to thicken. She lifts one arm in an arthritic salute.

A horse-drawn carriage plops by. The driver is a young black man dressed in a bright blue shirt and khakis. He probably goes to the College of Charleston. Probably is a history major. I wonder what he thinks about as he drives these streets, pointing out churches and cemeteries with a whip he rarely otherwise uses. Because they make this same loop and tell the same stories every day, this horse and this young man and their cartload of Yankee tourists who stare out from the carriage in a kind of stupor, listening to his singsong voice.

I could go back, I think. Daniel is probably waking up now.

Instead I buy a latte from a Starbucks and sit down on a bench.

When Elyse and I brought her here, all these years ago, Tory was scared of the ghost belles. At first, when we had begun the tour in broad daylight, on the sidewalk, she'd thought it was a grand adventure. She'd wanted to have her pictures taken with all of them, even Scarlett O'Scara. But later, when darkness had begun to fall and we were deep among the gravestones, her nerve had faltered. She had said "mommymom-mymommy" in that fretful droning way she had. She still has it. She still calls for her mother exactly like that whenever she's sad or frightened. And Elyse had stooped and carried her, even though she was seven. Tory's legs had locked around her mother's waist and Elyse must have become exhausted almost immediately. I volunteered several times to take her, but Tory wouldn't have anyone but her mother that night. She didn't want to leave the tour, even though we suggested it, but neither would she release Elyse and thus we had stumbled along behind the group in the darkness, always on the verge of getting left. I knew Elyse was moving as fast as she could but even so, I was a little frightened too. We'd wandered so long that I was no longer entirely sure where we were or which direction would lead us back to the street. Each time I would reach for Tory she would shake her head and clutch her mother even tighter.

This is just one more thing I've lost, the right to be clutched by a child with such fierce certainty. As many times as I've heard Elyse and Tory snap at each other through the years, I have just as often heard that anger fade into laughter and I know that no amount of distance or disappointments can ever truly dissolve the bond between a mother and her child. I don't have this and never will. I'm the end of a line.

A church bell rings ten and there's more life in the streets now. People at café tables eating pancakes, families, a young man alone on a park bench singing along with his iPhone, slapping his hands on his knees. I pause before the window of an art gallery and stare at my reflection in the glass, flicking a final rose petal from the side of my hair. The galleries are all full of pictures of Charleston — watercolors of the bay, pastels of the houses, oils of the gardens. It's a little self-congratulatory, like a beautiful woman who keeps portraits of herself all through her house, but in this particular shop window my eye falls on a collection of pottery that seems out of place among the landscapes. There's a small, squat bowl in the middle, and inside the bowl there's a kachina, with a picture of the artist propped above it all. Elyse, looking startled, as if she has just turned, or more likely the photographer had told her not to blink, because I know Elyse. I know how often she has ruined photographs by shutting her eyes at the last minute. So he said "Don't blink," and here she is, looking surprised to find herself in Charleston, in this window. The prices on the card shock me. I keep forgetting that Elyse is a real artist, that people pay money for her strange little gods.

I stretch my arms over my head and turn back toward the inn. Why am I out wandering the streets when Daniel is just blocks from here, probably stretching too right now and rolling over, facing my side of the bed? He won't know where I am or when I'll be back. He won't know if he should go down to breakfast. I have waited for him so many times. This may be the first time he has ever waited for me.

He refuses to understand why I went walking. Why I left him, even for an hour.

"I've failed you," he says. "What happened to me last night has never happened before, I swear it. I just drank too much."

And when I say that none of that matters, which it doesn't, he asks, "Did you think everything was going to be the same?"

That I can't answer.

"I did," he says. "I thought everything was going to be exactly like it used to be. But I failed you."

"I kept your letters," I tell him.

He is promptly distracted. Daniel was always easy to distract. When I knew him at twenty, at thirty — and now at fifty-three — he could be coaxed into changing his mood in an instant and I wonder fleetingly if he has that adult sort of ADD. "You really kept them?" he asks, rolling over and reaching for one of the white cotton robes. "I'm glad."

"Yeah. For years I carried them around in the glove compartment of my car. I'd see them every time I looked for a map. Of course I didn't see them often because you

381

know me, I hardly ever go anywhere new. But then I had to get rid of them."

"Because you got married."

I nod. He picks up the champagne bottle and shakes it, but I could have told him that everything inside was long gone. "I know your husband died last year," he says. "I hope it doesn't freak you out or make you think I was stalking you, but through the years I got curious from time to time so I'd search you on Google. And then Facebook, yeah." He laughs. "The old boyfriend's weapon of choice. I found a magazine article about a rose garden. Was that really your house?"

"It still is."

"It's freaking huge." He pauses, just long enough for a brief spasm of grief to grip his face. The first real emotion he's shown. "Were you happy with him? Or did you . . . you know . . . ."

"Did I what?"

"Look for something else."

I shake my head. "I never cheated on Mark."

"Good for you," he says, and by the tone of his voice I'm not sure if he believes me. I don't ask if he's had affairs through the years — other than the one with me, that is — because I already know the answer. Men

382

either cheat or they don't, just as Mark tried to explain to me before we married. It has nothing to do with the women. The wives, the girlfriends, the attractiveness of strangers. How much they love them, how much they don't. It's simply a decision a man makes at a certain point, and he makes it alone, in the privacy of his own mind.

"But I did find something else," I say. "Completely by accident." I rummage in my small overnight bag and find my dance shoes. I hand him one and Daniel stares down at it, mystified.

"Why did you bring this?" he finally asked. "Did you think we were going to go dancing?"

"No, I just wanted you to see what my life is now."

"So . . . why don't you dance for me?" he says, lying back down on the bed and smiling that syrupy smile that used to melt me. That smile that always seemed so innocent, even when whatever we happened to be doing was so dirty, that smile that always reminded me of farm boys come to the big city. "Show me what you've learned."

"It's not like that. I dance ballroom. Waltz, tango, foxtrot. The slow, elegant stuff." I pause, looking at him stretched over the pile of pillows. "One of the women at the studio says it's better than sex."

"That's a sad thing to say."

"No it isn't. You'd know if you danced."

"And is she right? Is it better than sex?" His face is wary. He's still thinking about last night and he fears the answer.

I start to tell him that all those times we lay down together — on picnic tables and in cars and boats and now on this beautiful bed — my desire for him had been genuine. That I had felt true excitement in his arms, certainly more than I had ever felt with any other man. And that if somewhere in that process something clicked off in my head . . . if I started to become Elizabeth Taylor or Marilyn Monroe or Elyse or anyone else who I thought I should be, that the fault was fully mine. I was the one who gasped, who shuddered, who rushed to make it easy and quick for the man, who was willing to almost leave her own body in the moment of pretending. It's not that I just don't come, I think. The real problem is that . . . I go.

"Why are you smiling?" he asks, smiling too.

I could tell him the truth, all of it — that for me, saying that dancing is better than sex really isn't setting the bar very high. But I don't. Such a statement would only make him determined to try again, to pull off everybody's clothes and go through the whole rigmarole one more time. To do everything longer, and harder, or maybe just at a slightly different angle, until we're both just tired and sore and somehow even farther apart.

His hand is on the knot of his white cotton bathrobe, ready to undo it at the slightest provocation, ready to pull me back into the bed cloud once again. This is why he thinks we've come here, for sex, and I guess I thought that too on the drive down . . . that maybe in some belated, last-gasp way, I was going to figure out how to truly tryst. He is still handsome. The things that drew me to him once are all still there — the dark hair, mixed with silver now, but relentlessly full and soft and mussable. The crinkles at the edges of the eyes, the lopsided smile. Even his body, lean but lightly muscled, retains a buzz of erotic energy and I think that Daniel has held up well. Middle age becomes him. But now that we are finally here in this dreamy room, looking at each other face to face, with no impediments or implements between us, I can see that sex isn't why I drove to Charleston at all.

I've come to forgive him.

And I've come to say good-bye.

He stands up from the bed and goes to the window. Yanks the curtains open and lifts the glass. The sun hits us like a wave. We jerk, both of us older in the sudden light.

"Are you hungry?" he asks. "I think they throw in breakfast as part of the deal."

"I said I kept your letters," I tell him. "But that's not completely accurate. The truth is, I gave them to Elyse."

"How is Elyse?"

"She never liked you."

"Ah," he says, looking out the window, pondering the garden below. "Well, I'm glad someone has them. Because I worked really hard on those letters. I copied them with a genuine fountain pen, did you ever notice? That it wasn't plain old ballpoint but a real pen? And good paper. Linen."

There is a moment of utter silence.

"You copied them?" I ask.

"Yeah. Very carefully, word by word. My college roommate Davis . . . he was traveling with me in Europe that first summer. Do you remember him?" I shake my head. "Well, he was the English major, he was the poet of the group, and he gave me some ideas."

"Somebody named Davis wrote those letters. He wrote them for another girl." My voice is flat. I can hear it myself. Daniel

386

turns from the window and looks at me.

"Oh no, they were for you," he says quickly. "I gave him all the ideas, he just helped me spiff up the wording." He grins. "If anything, some other girl probably got your letters. I think Davis messed around with them after I was finished, changed the hair color and place names and stuff like that, and then sent them to whatever girl he was currently trying to seduce."

And then I gave them to Elyse and she used to pretend they came from Gerry, I thought. I imagine the letters, spinning around in the air, catching the breeze like butterflies, floating from one woman to another. It seems futile and ridiculous and a little sweet, like something in a foreign film.

"I was in love with the guy in those letters," I say.

"I'm sorry that I hurt you," he says, the words suddenly tumbling out. "And I know I did. Especially when I left without saying good-bye. If I could take the whole thing back, I would."

"Truly? I wouldn't. Not the whole thing. You mattered tremendously to me."

"You never answered my question," he says, his hand still on the knot of his robe.

"Which one?" I ask, dropping my dance

shoe into my suitcase. I am suddenly raven-
ous. Hungry in a way I haven't been in
weeks, months, years. I can smell bacon
wafting up from the kitchen below, and
beneath it, the fainter aroma of cinnamon
and burnt sugar.

"Are you still you?"

"No," I say. "And I never was."

# Chapter Twenty-Four

"So you just ate breakfast, and packed, and walked out?" Elyse says. I called her the minute I was back on the interstate. "What on earth did he think?"

"I'm sure he thinks it was because we didn't have sex."

"But I mean, does he think you're going to meet him somewhere again? That the affair is back on?"

"Maybe. I was vague. It's easier to leave when the other person doesn't know that you're leaving. He taught me that much, at least."

She pauses for a moment, considering this. "Are you disappointed?"

"Not really. He was pretty much exactly who he always was. I'm the one who's changed."

"No, I mean, are you sorry because it wasn't the . . . you know, the big love affair. All that stuff we build up in our heads."

"I'm not sure. I feel funny today. But really alive, you know? Like I'm noticing everything. I saw one of your bowls in an art gallery window, by the way."

"The shop on East Bay? What did they have it priced at?"

"Three hundred and eighty dollars."

"Good." There's a moment of silence and then Elyse says, "So . . . I'm trying to ask you something and it's something big, but I'm not sure exactly how to phrase it. I guess what I'm saying is . . . Do you feel like you've lost something?"

"Not anything that I ever really had."

"Yeah, but you always knew he was out there. That you might suddenly see him in a Whole Foods, standing there holding an artichoke. Standing like *David,* just waiting for you to find him. It sort of sustained you."

"He wasn't worth it."

"I know. They hardly ever are. I guess what I'm saying is that maybe losing the dream of the man hurts more than losing the actual man."

I laugh. "These things you say. I know them all."

"What?"

"Nothing," I say. "You're afraid I've given up on love, and I know I probably sound a little weird today. But don't worry. Whether it looks that way or not, for the first time in a long time, my life is full of romance."

She goes silent. This is one of the flukes of our friendship, that we do not talk the entire time we're on the phone. At some point we stopped saying the alphabet back and forth and both became willing to sit, just like this, connected but not speaking, holding a certain open space between us. My eyes flick from one side of the highway to the other. Interstate 26 between Charleston and Columbia is not the most scenic drive in the world, but today it is interesting to me . . . the bumper stickers on the cars, those little flares of anger or sarcasm or humor, the billboards urging me to give my heart to Jesus or stop for gas. Is the dream really gone? I'm not sure, only that the world seems somehow different. The sunlight has a greenish cast and each thing I pass, from the trees to the shredded tires in the median to the mileage markers, seems sharp-edged and clear. As if my whole life is starting to come into focus.

"Elyse?"

"I'm still here."

"There's something that I've been meaning to tell you for the last thirty years."

"Oh. Okay."

"I don't really like sex. At least not the

way that you do."

"Well, sure, as you get older it definitely —"

"No, what I mean is that I don't have orgasms. Not just now. I don't think I ever have."

Another moment of silence and then her voice, tentative and slow. "You've never exactly mentioned this."

"I know. I've been faking with you longer than anybody."

"But I don't understand. Why would you —"

"I guess I was embarrassed. And once you start with a lie, it's hard to stop. Wait a minute, I've got another call coming through."

"Don't pick up. It's Daniel. Trust me, they call you like, three or four times on the day after they're impotent."

"No, it's Carolina's number. Hold on, this won't take a minute."

But it's not her. It's a nurse.

"Mrs. Madison?"

I know at once. My heart freezes.

"I'm on I-26. About ninety minutes out. I'll get there as soon as I can."

It's the young nurse who's calling. The freckled one with the high, thin voice. "That's all right, ma'am," she says. "There's no need to rush."

The road swims before me. My ears begin to buzz and coffee rises in my throat, bitter and warm. No matter how ready you say you are, you're never ready. My eyes jump from mirror to mirror, looking for a way to ease over and get out of the traffic, but of course that's impossible. This is the interstate, the road for people who are going somewhere fast and hard. I have slowed down, instinctively taken my foot off the accelerator, and trucks are whizzing around me. The sound they make as they pass is like a scream.

"Mrs. Madison?" says the young nurse. "Have I lost you?"

She's asking if she's lost the connection, that's all. Around hospice, I'm considered a seasoned volunteer and I've had . . . what? A dozen clients die? More? Twenty? There's no need to break it to me gently anymore. I'm a pro at death, well versed in the protocol of what it takes to transition from one world to another, someone who knows a thousand ways to say good-bye. And yet the road still trembles and the edges of my vision have burned away, so that it seems that I am looking through a spyglass. A car behind me honks and I realize I am drifting into their lane.

"They say she went real easy," the young nurse is chirping along. "She was watching a movie and somebody went in with her lunch and saw she'd just slipped away. No pain or panic or anything."

"Did she get to the end of it?"

"Ma'am?"

"The movie she was watching? Did she make it all the way to the end before she died?"

The nurse hesitates. She must think it is a strange thing to ask, and I guess in the overall scheme of things it is. "I don't know," she says.

"Because *Suddenly, Last Summer* is a very dark movie," I say. "It has cannibalism and lobotomies and all sorts of awful things and I'd hate to think she died before Montgomery Clift saves Elizabeth Taylor. I'd hate to think she never knew it was okay, because some of the most unlikely stories end happily, you know, some of the ones that seem the most hopeless turn out just fine, and I'm not sure she ever knew that. I'm not sure I told her."

"I don't know when she passed," the nurse says cautiously. "But I think I heard someone say they cut the movie off."

Out of the corner of my eye I see . . . not a rest area, but one of those places where they weigh trucks. I pull off and roll to a stop, the car bumping as the wheels struggle through the unmown grass. I manage to say the right things to the girl on the phone. The things she expects me to say, the things that will reassure her I haven't lost my mind and get her to hang up and leave me in peace. Then I roll down the windows and cut off my car and lean back, popping the seat belt loose with one hand and turning the visor against the sun with the other. And I begin to cry.

Sobbing is a relief after the last forty-eight hours and I give into it, until I am not sure anymore exactly why I am crying, for what or for whom. My little car, so vulnerable and so badly parked, trembles anew at each semi that rumbles by it, and each tremor sets off another small hiccup of grief. And then, when the weeping fit finally subsides, I just sit for a moment, smelling the diesel fuel fumes from the trucks out the open window, my eyes fixed on one tiny daffodil standing alone in the clumps of grass. Premature and probably destined to freeze, but focusing on it calms me and I take a sequence of deep breaths until I'm sure I'm not going to faint or throw up or anything.

I start the car again. Roll up the window and turn on the radio and fasten my seat belt and ease back onto the exit ramp, and then the truck lane, and then the general highway. I point the car toward Charlotte and let it drive me home. There's nothing else to do.

The hospice chapel sees a lot of use. People who die alone have their services here, like Miss Eula, whose memorial was only attended by the staff. And people like Carolina, who, despite the plaque I saw that day on her wall, apparently had no particular religious affiliation.

So she gets the boilerplate service, but at least she does have a crowd. Her sisters are in the front row, flanking her sons. The boys appear to have new suits for the funeral. They don't cry, but then again, maybe boys that age can't cry. There's at least a dozen middle-aged ladies sitting behind them, who I guess came from the hair salon where Carolina used to work, and they're grieving hard enough to make up for everybody.

In this sea of wailing women, the thin, bushy-haired man stands out. I suppose he is the ex-husband, or at least the father of her sons. They look just like him. I noticed that he greeted the boys when he came in but then stood back obligingly while Virginia put a hand on each nephew's shoulder, pulling them away from their father, as if he were the edge of a canyon.

Is this the man Carolina loved but did not forgive?

The hospice chaplain claims that he can do any kind of religious ceremony, but it's closer to the truth to say he does the same service for every client, be they Catholic, atheist, Baptist, or Jew. He has a gentle, abstracted quality. He certainly knows his Bible verses and prayers by heart, but he checks his notes as he rises to greet the congregation, presumably to confirm the name and a few particulars of the deceased. When I came in, I noticed that someone else was already moving into Carolina's room. Boxes and a scruffy recliner waited in the hall while they rearranged the furniture, along with the man himself, who sat in a wheelchair and stared down at the floor in front of him.

One slides out and another slides in, I think, as I watch the bushy-haired man take a seat in the last guilty row of the chapel. We are all replaceable.

Carolina requested cremation. Most of the ashes go to her boys, and the rest come to me, in a smaller urn along with a note in Carolina's handwriting, instructing me to take her to places she hadn't yet visited. "Which should not be hard," she had written, "considering I never went anywhere."

So I leave the memorial service with her last shy joke and a small, surprisingly heavy urn. It's in the trunk of my car as I drive to the dance studio. There's less than a week before the Star Ball, and I've booked a double lesson. I don't know how much Nik may have heard about Carolina, or where I've been for the last five days, but he greets me with a hug and says I should come and talk to him while he puts on his shoes. I follow him over to his desk where he sits down and rather ostentatiously leaves the top drawer open while he bends to tie his laces, giving me plenty of time to see that the manila envelope is there. I suppose it's his way of showing me that my words did not fall on utterly deaf ears.

"What song do you want to dance to?" he asks.

"Norwegian Wood," I say. It's my favorite for Viennese waltz. I sing out loud as we walk to the center of the floor. "I once had a girl . . . or should I say, she once had me." He looks at me with the sweet, patient, serious expression that I will always associate with him, and I start trying to explain what it all means. How sometimes the people we think are under our control actually have us under theirs and that sex, even when seemingly casual, has the power to change our whole life. And how some people think it's about drugs, or how others think that there's no meaning at all beyond the surface and people will always read things into things, won't we? It's what people do.

He listens to me for a few seconds and then he pulls me into hold.

"Darling," he says. "Shut up and dance."

# CHAPTER TWENTY-FIVE

The Star Ball is on a Saturday in the middle of March. We agree to meet at the studio early, around three in the afternoon. I drive in my bathrobe, with my armor-suit of underwear on beneath, and my ball gown strapped into the passenger seat like some sort of headless queen. My fancy Italian competition shoes arrived via UPS last week and, remembering the girl who was bleeding through hers at the Holiday Classic, I've worn them around the house every day in an attempt to break them in. But now they are in their silk drawstring bag, waiting, along with the jeweled headband I will wear in my hair, my long drop earrings, and a sparkling butterfly-shaped ring I ordered from the same Italian catalog. Nik helped me pick these things out, both of us peering through the pages and debating the advisability of one accessory over another. He especially liked the ring, which he said would catch a judge's eye even in motion, even from across the room. I protested it was ridiculously big, the jewelry equivalent of a Cadbury egg, but he said the size would accentuate the fact that I have very nice hand position, that I rest my fingertips on his shoulder at just the right angle, with my ring finger and pinky well lifted. Nice to know, after all this time, that he thinks at least one thing about me is graceful.

So for the first time in twenty years I am in public without my wedding ring. And, even stranger to contemplate, I have taken it off because it's too small.

Anatoly has hired a stretch limo to drive us all to the competition — a huge white monstrosity that's already parked in the back when I arrive, with a scary-looking driver leaning against the hood. I struggle through the door with my dress and see that Quinn has begun lining people up for hair and makeup. I want a simple chignon, and she decides to take me first, saying this is a style that will stay up for hours while the more elaborate ones, like the high stiff waves that Isabel has requested, need to be done at the last minute. Considering how much hair spray Quinn uses, it doesn't seem like it would really matter what order she takes us in. Jane told me that, after the Holiday

Classic, she'd gotten into the shower and the water had literally planed off the side of her head, splashing the wall like rain coming off a tin roof. She'd had to put an entire bottle of conditioner in her hair and then sit on the bed for an hour, watching TV, and try it again. Even then the texture of her hair felt odd for a week. "Don't let Quinn fool you," she said, "once that shit goes up, it takes an act of God to get it back down."

I find a place at Quinn's makeshift table. Valentina, Jane, and Isabel are already in their dresses, taking turns warming up with Anatoly and Nik, who are both still in practicewear. Harry and Steve are sitting over by the bar. Quinn is making my hair so tight that my eyes are watering, but I don't complain. Or maybe my eyes are watering because I remember the last three times a person has touched my head: Carolina's gentle hands anchoring that single rose at Christmas, the quick palms of Tory blonding me a few days later, and finally Daniel, stroking my hair as we fell asleep on the tall white bed. Stop it, I tell myself. Don't think of any of that. If you let yourself start crying, you'll never stop, and this isn't the time or place. Quinn sticks a hairpin into my scalp with special emphasis and I jump.

"She's not dancing, you know," she says

through gritted teeth. "We just found out."

"Who's not dancing?"

"Pamela."

"You're kidding."

Quinn turns me toward her, as if to check the symmetry of my part, but really so that I can read her lips.

"Anatoly is about to go crazy," she whispers. "She was signed up for eighty heats so there goes our shot at Studio of the Year. And we found out today that on top of everything else . . ." and here she whips me back around as Nik foxtrots by with Isabel and we stare at each other in the mirror.

"She's disappeared," she continues when the coast is clear.

"Disappeared?"

Quinn nods and reaches for my hair band. "There was some big blowup at the lawyer's office between her and Builder Bob. He's got documentation of her various, you know, activities, and he's threatening to tell her boys everything, and show them the pictures. Yeah. He's got pictures. He says she's not going to get a damn cent of his money and she stands up and runs out and nobody knows where she's gone. Well, I guess maybe Nik does."

"Wherever she is, he'll go there too. Oh God, he's getting ready to blow everything."

Nik and Isabel weave by us again and Quinn finishes anchoring my head band.

"That okay?"

"Great," I say without looking, and then I am engulfed in a cloud of hair spray. I watch Nik in the mirror. He is pale, but no paler than usual, and his hair is already slicked back in a thin, low ponytail, a style that makes him look a bit like a Revolutionary War soldier.

"Looks good," Quinn says, and she puts her hands around my throat to unhook the towel. "Don't worry," she adds as she bends over, "Nik won't go to her unless they have a plan."

"Yes he will. He thinks it's his fate," I say miserably. "Is he even going to be able to dance tonight?"

"Of course. He's Russian and they can dance through anything. Nik has this great ability to . . . compartmentalize. When the two of you step on the floor, you'll have his full attention and you would even if Pamela was dangling from a noose in the center of the ballroom."

Somehow I doubt that. Quinn slides me in my roller chair right down to the desk where they've spread out all the makeup. I tell her I can do my own, and she nods, clearly overwhelmed by the task at hand.

All the teenagers are there, reaching over each other for blush and eyeliner, and she has Valentina half-finished and Jane waiting behind her and I keep staring at Nik while I'm dabbing on the foundation. If Quinn had not told me about Pamela, I wouldn't have noticed any change in his behavior. Anatoly is the one who looks like a wreck. He keeps going over to the computer at Quinn's desk by the front door and staring at the screen.

I try to send Nik a message in my mind. Don't do it, I think as hard as I can. You're just in love with the idea of each other. Within a year she'll be bored sick with you and start wondering what on earth she's done, sacrificing her home and her family to watch you sit on the couch and play video games. Don't go. But he doesn't look at me. He has not acknowledged I'm even in the room.

Valentina's done and standing near the bar, talking to Harry. I ask her to help me into my dress, along with a couple of the teenagers. We move into the back room, where clever Quinn has set up the dress racks like the walls of little dressing rooms. I pull off my robe and put on my shoes, while Valentina holds the dress. "This was Pamela's, wasn't it?" one of the teenage girls says, and Valentina adds, "She's going to be sorry she sold it when she sees how good you look in it." Apparently not everyone has noticed that Pamela isn't here yet, or maybe they didn't expect her to come to the studio at all. She's never been one to hang out with the gang, and I can't imagine her piling into a long, white limo driven by a thug. It's not her style. So everyone seems quite unconcerned that she isn't here, and besides, they're all too busy to dwell on anything for long.

The teenagers get the dress over my head, both commenting on how heavy it is, and begin to fasten the hooks. With the exception of the family dinner after Carolina's service and too much champagne back in Charleston, I've had practically nothing but protein shakes for the last two weeks. The scale today went below 140 for the first time in months, but I'm still anxious as Valentina begins pulling up the zipper, stuffing in rolls of flesh as she goes. I've tried the red dress on before, but this is the first time I've seen it with the floats, and the hair, and the jewels. I'm suddenly shy and I wish there was some way I could slip back into the ballroom without a fuss.

But no, of course not. Valentina even claps her hands and makes an announcement as I enter and there are all these oohs and aahs. Nik can't avoid looking at me now. I'm blushing as I come in, still fastening the left earring, but probably no one can see it underneath the mask of my makeup and Nik says to hurry, we need to warm up next. Everyone in the studio goes back to their business within ten seconds of my grand entrance and I'm not terribly nervous as we begin to waltz. I make a couple of stumbles, nothing major, and I often do this at first. It takes me a while to get into the rhythm of the dance. So I'm surprised when Nik speaks to me sternly, telling me not to fight him, and to relax.

You can't order someone to relax. Besides, he's the one who's off. I don't say anything and we start again. But then there is another slight miscue and he snaps, "Do we need to get the blindfold?" and it hits me why he's so upset. In the red dress with my hair lightened and slicked back, I look far too much like Pamela. We are the same size now, at least almost, and my emergence from the back room has been a shock to him. Forced him to remember that she's out there somewhere, scared and angry and alone.

"Yes," I say. "You should blindfold me." If he doesn't see my face, perhaps he can pretend I am Pamela. I don't know if that will make things better or worse, but the present situation isn't working, that's for sure. He goes to the desk when Anatoly is still staring gloomily at the computer, perhaps trying to figure if we have a chance of ranking at all now that he's lost his ultimate whale. Nik pulls out the Hermès and brings it to me. I tie it lightly. I don't want to mess up my hair and makeup — hard to say if that even would be possible — and I don't really need to obscure my vision. Because for once, I'm not fighting him. He's fighting me.

Once the scarf is in place I stand still, listening. I can hear the clink of glasses at the bar, Jane saying something and Steve laughing. Quinn telling Isabel to hold still, she's almost done, and the young girls fussing with their jars and the clatter of tubes of makeup against the desk. I don't think anyone else is on the dance floor. Nik chooses "Fly Me to the Moon." At least he remembers that I'm the one who likes it.

The music starts and, just beneath the melody, I hear something crack. Nik must have stumbled against a chair. He's more nervous than I've ever seen him. It's my first competition, I think, in a wave of petulance. It's unfair that I have to be worried about him and how like Pamela it is, to trump tonight, just as she has trumped all the others, to somehow manage to be the most important thing going on even when she's isn't here. There's another thud, the dull drag of a chair.

Come on, Nik, I think. Get it together.

I hold up my right hand and wait. The song is already to the part about what spring is like on Jupiter and Mars and I wonder what's keeping him. He should be here, taking my hand, pulling me forward and beginning the dance. Instead I feel him moving behind me, slipping his hand around my waist and inviting me to step backward, into shadow hold. We do not begin our foxtrot in shadow hold. He's even got our routine mixed up with someone else's, I think irritably, but then it occurs to me he's just testing me. He's always saying that no dancer should get too dependent upon her routine. That in competition there are so many couples on the floor that you rarely get through anything the way you rehearsed it, and that I should be ready, at any moment, for him to do an unexpected step.

I laugh and say, "Are you trying to trick me?"

And then I feel the cold circular imprint of something pressed against my temple.

The arm around my waist tightens. And someone screams.

Another scream, another thud, and out of nowhere my grandfather's voice comes to me, something he used to say, what was the phrase? The business end of a gun. The business end, the barrel, and there are noises coming from all around me. "Fly Me to the Moon" and a door opening and slamming, something else crashing to the floor. The arm around my waist is trembling, vibrating so fiercely that it makes both of us shake, hard enough that I can feel my earrings flick against my cheeks.

"You're not going to leave me," a voice says. "I won't let you go."

It is not until much later that I will understand exactly what happened. That Pamela's husband had been as upset as she by the meeting with their lawyer. That after she ran out, he ran out too and had spent the last twenty-four hours searching for her, driving in one wide furious loop between their lake house, their mountain house, their beach house, and their Charlotte house, ripping open each door and finding each room empty. How his fury and panic had risen with each passing mile. How he'd gotten speeding tickets in three different counties within hours of each other and some computer had finally triggered in Raleigh. Telling the authorities that there's a dangerous person out there, a man driving wildly from one end of the state to another, a man who'd been doing ninety in a sixty outside of Asheville at eleven in the morning and was stopped again just four hours later, almost to Wilmington, for failure to yield. Despite the fact that they had put out an APB on his license plate, he'd somehow made it back to Charlotte undetected and to this studio. Did he really think she'd be here? He'd sat outside watching the door for some time, a witness would later confirm, and then at some point he had grabbed the gun and gone in. A pistol, not one of his rifles, a smaller gun that he kept hidden in his bedside table, a gun he claimed to have bought for his wife's protection. He'd seen a red dress through the window and the slender shape of a blond woman and in that split second he'd made the same mistake as Nik. The woman was getting ready to dance. She lifted her right hand as if she were waiting for a man to come and claim her and that had been too much. He'd grabbed the gun with no idea of how he was going to use it. That's the strangest part of all. That during all that driving, all those hours alone in the car, he had not formulated a plan.

Of course I didn't know any of this when I was standing there with the pistol pressed against the side of my face. I didn't know that a few seconds earlier Bob had brought the butt of this same gun down on Anatoly's head as he came through the door or that Anatoly had been so intent on his computer screen that he had never seen it coming. But Nik had looked up from the stereo at the sound of the first thud and had known what was happening at once. He must have started for the back door, and it's hard to say with all the noise, with all the confusion, with the music so damn loud, what happened next or in what exact order the other people in the room became aware of the gunman's presence. I was standing there like a ninny, blindfolded with my right arm up, probably looking like Justice without her scales, and when the gunman grabbed me I had even tried to dance. At what point did he realize he had the wrong woman? When I asked him if he was trying to trick me, did he know at once that was not Pamela's voice? Or was it not until his arm went around my waist? Maybe I moved differently, smelled differently, or maybe there was something in the shape of my shoulders or my hips that told him his wife had eluded him yet again. That he was holding a gun to the head of a stranger. That he was as much a hostage to the situation as I was.

"I'm not your wife," I say, but by now I'm only telling him what he already knows. The barrel pulls away from my cheek and there's the sound of a shot, impossibly loud, so much so that the room echoes with it, reverberating, turning it into a thousand shots at once. I roll away from him, using all my strength, and he releases me so abruptly that I lose my balance. I feel myself tumbling through the blackness, hitting the wooden floor hard enough that one of my earrings flies off, and when I pull the blindfold away I'm lying on my side, half under Quinn's desk. From this angle the ballroom looks strange, as if the whole world has tilted and slid. Anatoly is stirring in the chair above me, mumbling like someone coming out of a deep sleep. He tries to stand and falls back, saying one word in Russian. *Izvinite.*

From my vantage point beneath the table, I can see it all. See the women moving as one to engulf Nik. Surrounding him, shielding him, pulling him toward the back door. They move as if they've choreographed it, as if this were all some sort of dance they'd

413

been secretly rehearsing for months. Isabel has a cell phone pressed to her face as she walks. Calling the police probably, and her expression shows more irritation than fear. She yells back toward the gunman, "You can't come in here," as if he were nothing more than a badly trained dog, and then she holds the door open for the other women. Nik's eyes are searching the room for something, but it's like he's being carried away on a great wave. He understands that the gun meant for him has been turned on me. The man who is so proud that he refuses to let anyone buy him a Sprite knows full well that he has run up tremendous charges and is leaving a woman to pay his bill.

Later the story will improve, become nearly epic in the retelling, and will require them to use words like "overpowering" and "wresting," but the truth is that by the time Steve and Harry are across the floor, Pamela's husband has already dropped his hand to his side. The mirror behind him is shattered, a spiderweb of broken glass with a dark hole in the center, and he stands helplessly, turning in a slow circle, his face as thoughtless as a child's. Steve got the gun from him easily, and it took only the slightest nudge from Harry before he toppled to the floor, a gunman no more. Just a jilted husband, a man who panicked and shot at his own reflection, a man named Bob. The music has stopped and his sobs are the loudest thing in the room. Steve kneels and puts one hand on my shoulder, saying, "Are you all right?" When I say yes, he stands and turns to Anatoly, pressing something against his head. He has taken my blindfold, I realize. Pamela's scarf. The Hermès is now covered with blood, and it takes me another second to remember that, beneath all the jokes, Steve really is a doctor. He's speaking calmly to Anatoly and saying, "You'll be fine. Just sit back."

The police come thundering through the back door. When Isabel had called, they were already on their way. The witness in the parking lot, who we would later learn was a busboy from Esmerelda's, had reported a man leaping from a parked car with a gun. He read them the car's license plate number and they've come with their full SWAT team, only to be met by a group of women, running across the parking lot toward them in sequined dresses, shrieking words like "hostage," "gunshot," and "blood." But in the ballroom all they find are four men and a woman. One of the men is on his knees, sobbing. Another man is holding a gun on him while the third is pressing a cloth to the head of the fourth man, who appears to be wounded. The woman is crawling out from beneath a desk and swatting at the long strings of cobwebs clinging to her red dress.

Bob is taken away. They handcuff him and put him in a car and then they insist on escorting me and Anatoly out to the ambulance. When I step into the parking lot — as surprised by the bright sunlight as if I were exiting a movie theater — it sets off a fresh spasm of weeping among the women and the sight of Anatoly behind me on a stretcher only makes it worse. Now that it is over, we're collapsing. Of course we are. Jane's knees buckle and the medics look her over too. I can't stop shaking, so they wrap me in heated blankets and have me lie down in the back of the ambulance. They check Anatoly's head, thinking perhaps he has a concussion. Through the ambulance door I can see the men making gestures in the air and the women all on their cell phones calling God knows whom.

Quinn and one of the cops are also standing at the door of the ambulance and she tells him the name of everyone who was in the studio when the gunman entered. She enunciates the names slowly and methodically, helping with the Russian spellings, talking loudly enough that I can hear her. There is one name she leaves out. I raise my head, dizzy and trapped by the heat of the blankets, and our eyes meet. I nod, to let her know I understand.

Nik was never there. That's our story and we have all silently agreed to it, with negotiations composed of raised eyebrows, meaningful glances, and texts sent to the person standing right beside you. I remember Isabella's words back in the food court and if "some sort of trouble" can get a man permanently deported then it is simpler, cleaner, smarter, to pretend that Nik was nowhere near this particular trouble. Anatoly is telling the medic that he doesn't want to go to the hospital and he tries to prove that he's fine by counting backward from one hundred. "You must let me stay," he says to the doctors as they bandage his head. "This is my studio. I am responsible for these people."

The cops take statements from everyone, including me, although since I was blindfolded for most of the crisis, I am not exactly the world's best witness. The blindfolding seems to confound the young officer interviewing me. I have trouble making him understand that it was not the gunman who

417

blindfolded me, that it was already on when he came through the door. Struggling to explain, I almost slip. I almost mention Nik's name but then I tell the young officer that we often dance blindfolded at the studio, that this is a way for ballroom dancers to check their balance. He seems to believe me. He looks around, then expels a big long sigh. We look crazy to them, I realize, standing in the bright sunlight in our false eyelashes and Swarovski crystals.

The police had known they were dealing with a domestic incident the minute they confirmed Bob's license plate and I gradually see, with growing relief, that they are inclined to leave it at that. Divorce makes people unhinged — this is the general consensus of the crowd in the parking lot. The man just snapped. They've been looking for Pamela too, ever since Bob got the second speeding ticket and had just found her minutes before the busboy's call, at a friend's house, drinking chocolate martinis. A domestic incident, says the police captain. That's about all they deal with these days, now that the world's gone crazy, and nobody keeps their business to themselves. It's just a shame all of us had to get caught up in it.

"Can you remember anything else?" the young officer asks me.

I shake my head and realize I'm only wearing one earring. Quinn has come up beside me. The ambulance and the cops have gradually begun to leave. Quinn smiles at this young man, who's trying so hard to be thorough, and asks if he can continue with me at another time. She says, "It's almost six. We should be leaving soon."

And that's how I learn that apparently they all still intend to dance. Amid the confusion of the past hour, Quinn has been quietly going around, finding new combinations of partners to accommodate Nik's absence. They'd had a vote. They are in agreement. If Anatoly can do it, if he can get on his feet and cover his routines, they want to go to the hotel as planned and compete.

Anatoly seems as confused as I am. "We can't compete," he says. "Not without . . ." He looks around at the scene and exasperation flits across his face. This probably isn't the first time he's lost someone in a squeal of tires, and it's no wonder he thinks Americans are naive. We're always so shocked when bad things dare to happen. So angry when we can't fix them. I suspect he sees us all as golden retrievers — big, dumb, and strong, bounding across open fields, drooling from our permanent smiles, blissfully unaware of the wider world around us. We stick our snouts down the hole and are surprised by the snake every time.

"Come on," Quinn says firmly. "The limo's back. We've missed the banquet but if we hurry, we can be there for the first heat."

What does she mean, the limo's back? Where had it gone? I scan the parking lot. When I'd first arrived at the studio, it had been over by the grocery loading dock, and now it's pulled facing the opposite direction, ready to go. The women must have thrown Nik into the limo, I realize dully. He's at the airport now, or perhaps he has already taken flight. Quinn is pushing a legal pad into Anatoly's hands, explaining to him that he can cover most of the extra heats. By extra heats, I guess she means the heats Nik would have danced, but she doesn't say this. And for the heats where there is a conflict — by this I gather she means heats where Nik would have been dancing at the same time as Anatoly — the civilian boys have agreed to step up. We can just do the routines we learned in group class. It will be fine. Steve was dressed to dance anyway and they'll come up with something for Harry. And she has called Lucas. He saw the whole thing on the news and was already putting on his best preacher suit when the phone rang. He's going to meet us at the hotel.

"We can work out the details in the limo," she says. "That is, if the two of you are up to it."

"Why bother?" Anatoly says. "Group routines and half of us dancing with the wrong partner? We won't place."

"Oh, honey," Quinn says, laughing. "That's small potatoes considering what we've just been through. We need to do this. Every damn one of us. Even you."

"Well," Anatoly says, looking skeptically at the list Quinn has made on the legal pad. "I see that I am supposed to tango with you, Kelly. Are you able?" Kind Quinn. I'm beginning to think of her as superhuman Quinn, the way she has orchestrated all this, and she's even remembered that the tango is my favorite dance, the only one I have a prayer of placing in, and that's the dance in which she's paired me with Anatoly.

"I just need to get my earring," I say. "I lost it in the studio."

"Don't go back in there," says Quinn. "Tell me where you think it is and I'll get it."

"I'm fine," I say. "It won't take me but a minute."

Anatoly pushes himself slowly to his feet and starts toward the others. Valentina is holding his tux on a hanger. She motions for him to hurry. Quinn starts to say something, then stops. I start to ask her something, and then stop. We stand for a second, looking at each other.

"Things are okay," she says. "As okay as they can be."

"How do we know?"

"We'll hear from him eventually, I'm sure of it." And then she adds, "The good news is, your hair's still perfect."

I walk into the studio. I don't know what I was expecting — crime scene tape? A CSI team taking pictures? But everyone has gone, writing this off to just another marriage gone sour, just another rich man who'll buy his way into a psych ward instead of a prison. I find my earring, taking care not to step in the shards of glass. The crumpled scarf is still lying where Steve left it after he had pressed it to Anatoly's head to stop the bleeding.

I walk to Nik's desk and pull open the top drawer. It's empty.

In the limo, the mood has changed to a spirit of euphoria. There are no cops and ambulances now, just high fives and loud declarations of how it would take more than this to bring us down. We're so crowded that we're piled half on top of each other. Harry, who had not been expecting to dance, is struggling into Nik's slim tuxedo, which Quinn found hanging on the back of the bathroom door. He strips down to his underwear, doing a little shimmy on the limo floor, and all the women take turns slapping his butt. Isabel is acting as a sort of emcee, calling out the new order of who will be dancing with whom. Quinn is on the phone explaining to the organizers that there will be some changes in our lineup, that we are running late but on our way. Steve opens the champagne and for once Anatoly does not protest that we should wait until after the competition to drink. Steve pours it, warm and bubbly, into small paper cups. No more than an inch for anyone, no more wine than you would get at communion.

At some point someone notices that Steve has blood on his shirt. His tux doesn't have a vest, but Harry's does. Harry makes a great show of sacrificing it for the greater good, and the vest covers most of the stain. It takes me a surprisingly long time to re-alize that the blood on Steve is Anatoly's, that Steve must have gotten smeared when he'd bent over him to examine the cut on his head. Quinn pulls a little marker of Tide to Go out of her purse, dabs at the stain, and then leans back and announces, "You can hardly see it."

Of course you can see it. It all but glows in the dark. I can't seem to look at anything else.

Anatoly clumsily moves over beside me. We review which steps I know in tango and he tells me what sequence he'll try to work them in. He reminds me that when we get out on the floor with other dancers all around us, I shouldn't be surprised if he mixes it up a bit. There isn't always enough room to move along the clear line of dance. People step in front of you, sometimes by accident, but there are even dancers who will deliberately try to cut you off. I have to trust him, he says. He knows how to find the open floor.

"But even if you do not always know where you are going," he says, "you must take big steps."

I nod, staring straight ahead and holding the champagne in my hand. Don't worry, I tell Anatoly. Nik has explained all this to me many times.

# CHAPTER TWENTY-SIX

By the time the limo arrives at the hotel, we are celebrities. Aerial shots of the studio have apparently run all over the six o'clock news with the banner HOSTAGE BALLROOM. I have twenty-two calls on my iPhone and I send quick e-mails to my mother and Elyse, asking them to get the word out that I'm okay.

Perhaps because the story has beaten us to the competition, Quinn has no trouble getting our heats switched up. She comes back to the table with three tags reading 384 — this was the flight that took Nik out of Moscow, years ago. He'd always considered it his lucky number and requested it for comps, and now Quinn pins the tags on Harry, Lucas, and Steve. An organizer brings us plates of left-over food from the buffet and says, "Bless your hearts." Jane takes the heat sheets and gets us lined up and from there it all becomes a blur. I'm having so much trouble following events in a linear fashion that I wonder if I hit the floor harder than I realized and if maybe I'm the one who's concussed.

I suspect we're quite bad in the early dances. The routines from group class weren't designed to show well in competition. One of the other studio owners stops by our table and says "Bad break, man," but Anatoly barely responds. Which bad break is the man referring to — the crack across his head, the loss of Nik, our dismal showing in the early rounds? Or perhaps the fact that Anatoly is the proprietor of a studio that, thanks to the news stories, the citizens of Charlotte will ever after refer to as Hostage Ballroom?

"We should have had twenty firsts by now," Anatoly says to Quinn, "and we would have, if only —"

She puts her hand to his lips. It's a small competition, not even a regional, and we've been through a hell of a day by anyone's standards. Yet all he can think about is that he looks foolish in front of the other studio owners? He should be ashamed, she says, so hush up.

He does loosen up a little through the night, after the first and the worst of the embarrassment is over. He is dancing almost every heat, and he begins to enter the same zone the rest of us are in, the zone of just coping, moving mindlessly through one song and then the next. Steve and I have danced well together lately and we might even have placed in our foxtrot heat if we'd remembered to keep our heads to the left. But for some reason as the music begins he looks me right in the eye and I look back. We do not break this gaze throughout the entire dance and when we finish, he kisses my hand. We place fifth out of six couples, beating only an eighty-two-year-old woman whose instructor had to drag her through her routine.

But overall Steve has a good night. He wins all the heats he dances with Quinn — although, of course, in many cases he's the only person of his gender and age group entered, so the vast majority of his wins are uncontested. Valentina reminds me that there's another small drama playing out tonight — that Steve's ex-wife is here and this is the first time he has danced in her presence.

At the break they give out the second set of awards, and I sit back in my chair and listen to Steve's name being called time after time. Quinn had wanted him to leave the dance floor with handfuls of ribbons, and so he shall. Some people might say that being the best dancer because you were the only dancer is a hollow victory; just a few weeks ago, I would have been one of those people. But now, upon reflection, I've decided it is not. Quinn has always known just what Steve needs, and she knows he needs her to walk with him across the dance floor after the break is over: to walk straight up to the table where his ex-wife is sitting with her own instructor and her own hand-fuls of medals and her dress, which looks even heavier than mine. Where he tells her, "You dance beautifully. And it is to my eternal discredit that I never told you this."

So that's it, I think. He's done. You can blame or explain, or try to demand answers and hope all that will bring you what the shrinks call closure. Or you can just forgive and that's the spiritual fast track. A road like one of those beltways that circle cities, which take you smoothly around all the snarls and tangles of memory, and onto the open road beyond.

As Steve and Quinn start back across the floor, someone takes their picture. If you know just where to look, you can see a few drops of blood on Steve's crisp white shirt. This was not a hollow victory, not hollow at all. Steve has defeated all the men who didn't dance tonight. He is first among the millions who are home watching TV, all those men angry at their ex-wives, angry at their present wives, the men masturbating into a towel in front of their computers, the men who stay silent, who stay sullen, who stay scared, who stay small — tonight Steve has bested them all. And when he gets back to our table he announces — to the mixed horror and amusement of everyone except his loyal Quinn — that his real strength may be Latin and he wants to start competing in the cha-cha.

But Jane is the one who breaks through. She wins her scholarship. Her first dance is the waltz, and as she walks onto the floor with Anatoly, she's trembling so violently that I wonder if she'll be able to perform at all. She takes a deep breath and steadies herself and then she's granted a privilege given to very few athletes. She gives the performance of her life when it counts — in competition, in the spotlight, in front of the judges. She dances with a kind of bewildered femininity, a confused and gentle grace, and in a sea of women who are trying too hard and smiling too grimly, she stands out. She is fierce in the tango, playful in the foxtrot, dynamic in the quickstep, light in the Viennese. When she comes back to the table and hands her trophy to the beaming Margaret, we're all hit with a new whiff of hope.

"How are we doing in the rankings?" Harry asks, and Quinn, snickering, says, "Horrible."

"Horrible?" we all say at once.

She nods, still laughing.

"This calls for more champagne," Harry says, and goes to get it.

"You'd think they'd cut us some slack," Steve says. "Considering we're 'Hostage Ballroom.' " This sets off more giggles, which last until Harry is back with a bottle of champagne.

"Don't drop it," I say, and he says no one in his right mind would drop a twelve-dollar bottle of champagne. But he is careful as he pours it and then suggests a toast. Even Lucas takes one of the plastic cups. We hold up our glasses and the table falls silent.

"To Canterbury Ballroom," Steve says. "They might say we can't dance, but goddamn it, they'll never be able to say we didn't dance."

"How many heats are left?" Valentina asks.

Quinn consults her list. "Twenty-two, so we're almost done. Kelly, you tango in three. And Harry and Valentina are up after that."

Harry, Valentina, and I move to the waiting area just off the stage. Anatoly comes by, mops his brow with the edge of the nearest tablecloth, and tells me that he's going to grab some water.

"Valentina," I say when he's gone. "What does the word *Izvinite* mean?"

"Who taught you this?"

I shrug. "It doesn't matter. I'm just curious."

"It is a funny word for you to ask about," Valentina says. "It means 'Forgive me.' "

As Anatoly and I find our place on the floor, the light is blinding. It falls straight down upon us so that we leave no shadow. I have forgotten the steps we discussed in the limo and so I have no choice but to follow Anatoly. He does the simplest and gentlest of tangos, leads me almost like a father would do with a child. He lifts his arm, and I move under it. He steps back as I step forward, and for some reason I think of what Quinn said the first day I came into the studio, something about how you have to lose your balance in order to find it. I had no idea what she meant at the time and I still don't understand it fully, but I know that somehow, somewhere, a spell is being broken. So many things have been taken from me lately — some of them ripped away with more cruelty than I would have thought possible — and yet I am dancing. I stretch my rib cage and inhale. Let myself become big. The floor beneath my feet feels broad and solid and my story, I believe, will end differently this time. The prince has come and gone but Cinderella is still at the ball.

# CHAPTER TWENTY-SEVEN

Yes, it had been a strange night. We had pulled it together and performed, but Anatoly must have known we were all on some sort of unnatural, adrenaline-fueled high. I imagine him the next morning, going to the empty studio and walking around, reenacting events in his head. Wincing at the sight of the shattered mirror, stopping at the spot where Pamela's husband had first seized me, wondering if he would ever see any of us again — for we could easily scatter. Stop dancing entirely or find another studio. We would be justified. People take up ballroom dancing for fun or exercise or to meet members of the opposite sex. They do not take up ballroom dancing with the expectation they will be shot at. Who could blame us if we hesitated to return to the literal scene of the crime, if we had found ourselves unwilling to remember that night?

So when we had all walked in at our usual

time . . . shrugged off our jackets and buckled our shoes . . . when Isabel had looked Anatoly straight in the eye and coolly asked, "So who's teaching group today?" for a strange moment I had thought he was going to salute us.

Perhaps because he has no home of his own, Anatoly works very hard to give us one. He tries to step into the void that Nik left. He observes the way Quinn jokes around with people, and I know he wishes he could emulate her easy gift for friendship. He makes notes on his calendar so that he can remember birthdays and anniversaries of the day a student first came into the studio. He tilts his head sometimes and watches us, as if you can tell just by looking what each person hopes or fears.

I bought the strip center from Bob. Everyone always said he was unreasonable, but as it turns out, a man who owns so much property that he can't pay the taxes on it can prove to be reasonable indeed. And if he is making his business deals from a pay phone in a psychiatric hospital, his thirst for negotiation is even further slaked. The rumor is that Bob and Pamela have reconciled. She visits him each day in the lockdown ward, so maybe this is what she wanted all along — a declaration of love so violent and bizarre that it would make the evening news.

So I get a good deal on the property, and Anatoly is happy to take me on as a silent partner in the studio. He swears no one knows, which probably means everyone does. I set up a trust for Carolina's boys — nothing extravagant, but enough to make sure Virginia can see them through college — and I take Isabel with me to the pound to get a dog.

"Just go in and grab one," I tell her. "I can't face it. I'll see those sad eyes and those cages and end up with twenty dogs."

She's back in ten minutes with a whole file full of paperwork and instructions and a scrawny brown puppy that crawls in my lap and immediately pees. I call her Apple — it was after all an apple that brought me to ballroom dancing in the first place.

The last thing I do is put the house on the market. I decide to pack up a few of my things and move to an apartment during the time it's listed. Because it really was my home in the end, my home as well as Mark's, and I don't want to hear people complaining about the colors as they walk through it with their Realtor, making plans to knock out walls and change the rugs. Ultimately I suppose I will buy a condo, but for now I like the simplicity of the apartment. It has hardwood floors for practice and a balcony where I have placed a single rosebush, in a pot. I pulled it from the garden the morning I left and as I drove out of the community that final time, I sat in the car and watched the gates close, ever so slowly, in my rearview mirror. I could see the potted rosebush in the rearview mirror too, its pink petals barely visible from the backseat where I had wedged it between my books and dishes. You always take something with you. That's just how it is.

And each morning I check the total in the Bank of America account. For weeks there is no activity. But then, near the end of the second month, there is a withdrawal. He must be settled in Canada.

In the weeks and months that follow, I will forget exactly what his face looks like. I'll begin to dance with Anatoly and learn to love him too, but I'll continue to have arguments in my head with Nik for the rest of my dancing life. And at some point — there is no doubt of this — the money I loaned him will come back into the joint account. Nikoli Demidov is a man who pays his debts.

The light is so different here. Clean and

bright. I can see for miles. I've come to Arizona, as I often do, in the late spring, and Elyse and Apple and I have taken a hike to scatter some of Carolina's ashes. We follow the trail for over an hour, then sit for a minute, drinking water and resting. Elyse says they'll give me some time alone. I unzip my backpack and take out the baggie.

As I was walking through the canyon on the way in, I kept thinking about Mark, that dream in which he told me something I still haven't been able to remember. I came to him heartbroken, scared of everything, devoid of hope, and lately I've started to see just how much I cheated him out of while we were married. I always told myself that he liked our neat little existence in our neat little community, but now I see that I never gave him the chance to have a whole life. A whole wife. *"Izvinite,"* I whisper. I may have woken up beside a dead man once, but he woke up beside a dead woman every day.

I say *"Izvinite"* again, not just to Mark and Nik and Daniel and Carolina, but for every moment I have wasted. For the moments I will waste in the future because I'm not some sort of saint, and odds are I'll barely be out of these hills before I start making all the same mistakes over again, in very slightly different ways. Who knows — I may even find another man to hurt and be hurt by, and in that instant a sudden breeze whips the piñon trees around themselves. The leaves show their soft silver underbellies, and a whooshing sound comes up from the canyon, something holy and solemn in the air of everyday life.

I open the plastic bag and release Carolina over the hills. The air takes her, lifts her, then drops most of the ashes among the cacti and the pebbles and the snakes. But a bit more is pulled higher and blows all the way down into the valley where Elyse and Apple are descending, scrambling and sliding their way through the piles of pale rocks. Spring is almost over. Soon the full heat of summer will be upon us and even from this distance, I know that Elyse is talking to the dog. They are planning what we'll have for dinner, the chicken and artichokes we will roast on the grill, the wine we will drink on the deck. All the birds we will bark at as they swoop and dive their way across the endless unformed possibility of the western sky.

Wait for me, I call, pushing to my feet. I'm right behind you. I'm right here.

# ACKNOWLEDGMENTS

Thanks first of all go out to my dance family, the students and teachers at Piper Glen Ballroom, as well as the staff at Metropolitan Ballroom. Without this dedicated group, I never would have been introduced to the life-changing world of dance.

I'd like to thank my warm and unfailingly sensible agent, Stephanie Cabot, and the team at the Gernert Company, especially Anna Worrall. Words can't express how grateful I am to Kim Hubbard for introducing me to Stephanie, who in turn helped *The Unexpected Waltz* find a perfect home.

Which leads me to the wonderful people at Gallery Books. I am thrilled to be working with Karen Kosztolnyik once again and couldn't ask for a more supportive editor. Special thanks to Gallery Books president Louise Burke, publisher Jen Bernstrom, and publicist Jen Robinson. I'm grateful to Lisa Litwack for her beautiful cover art, John

Paul Jones for his production edits, and Davina Mock for the interior design. Kudos to executive assistant Alex Lewis for her nonstop good ideas. And, of course, none of this would mean anything without the marketing team of Liz Psaltis, Ellen Chan, and Melanie Mitzman.

On a personal note, writers are so very dependent upon other writers. All my love goes out to Dawn Clifton Tripp and Alison Smith, who were with me from the very start of this journey, when our books were no more than half-formed ideas. I'm also grateful to the Brinkers Writers Group for their critiques on everything from overarching themes to the placement of commas. And I'd be lost without the savvy advice of Marybeth Whalen, Erika Marks, and Kim Boykin, aka "The Panera Bread Literary Society."